Wicked Abandoned

a·ban·doned

Adjective - having been deserted or cast off

Wicked Abandoned

The Tenth Anthology of the
New England Horror Writers

Edited by
Rob Smales
Scott T. Goudsward

Foreword by
Steve Van Samson

Cover Art © 2024 by Mikio Murakami
Interior Layout and Design by Dan Keohane
Published in September 2024 by Wicked Creative
ISBN 978-0-9981854-7-7
Printed in the United States of America

Other Anthologies of the
New England Horror Writers

Wicked Sick
Edited by Scott T. Goudsward,
and Kristi Petersen Schoonover

Wicked Creatures
Edited by Scott T. Goudsward,
Daniel G. Keohane and David Price

Wicked Women
Edited by Trisha J. Wooldridge
and Scott T. Goudsward

Wicked Weird
Edited by Amber Fallon,
Scott T. Goudsward and David Price

Wicked Haunted
Edited by Scott T. Goudsward,
Daniel G. Keohane and David Price

Wicked Witches
Edited by Scott T. Goudsward,
Daniel G. Keohane and David Price

Wicked Tales
Edited by Scott T. Goudsward,
Daniel G. Keohane and David Price

Wicked Seasons
Edited by Stacey Longo

Epitaphs
Edited by Tracy L. Carbone

Content Warning

Like with most things in life, even Wicked Abandoned has a content warning. The editors and owners of Wicked Creative LLC take it very seriously. Everything in this book is a work of fiction; in other words, it is all made up, not real, and should not be conflated with the actual beliefs/opinions of the authors.

Horror is, almost by definition, meant to be uncomfortable. Thus, some of the subject matter leans toward the darker side of human (and sometimes not-so-human) nature. In this volume of the New England Horror Writers, some of the potential triggers include: mental illness, animal neglect, sexual assault, and opinions regarding religion(s).

If that should sway your decision against this book, please check out one of the other nine volumes from the New England Horror Writers.

Dedication

*Several blows were struck to the horror community
in 2023 & 2024.*

We lost iconic director
Roger Corman *(4/5/1926 – 5/9/2024),*
Legendary authors
Brian Lumley *(12/2/1937 – 1/2/2024)*
and the amazing
Ray Garton.

We also lost two of our own.

Richard A. Scott.
If you're ever in Michigan do stop by coordinates:
Latitude: 44.68387985
Longitude: -84.61034393
and look for Richard's memorial tree.

And the great
James A. Moore
A mentor, a motivator, a brother and hell of a nice guy.

Table of Contents

Introduction
Steve Van Samson

What does it mean to be *abandoned*? To be discarded, disavowed, or willfully forgotten? For that matter, how does it feel? This latest entry in the New England Horror Writers' Wicked series sets out to explore these somber questions. Here, the cold concept of abandonment is a framework for eighteen tales and poems which speak of lost things and of the shadows that sometimes find such cast-off husks—claiming the unwanted for themselves.

Certain stories within this collection feature characters who have been abandoned in some way; others tie the anthology's theme to a place, describing settings many decades past their heyday, where cobwebs have long since replaced things like laughter and light. A ramshackle farmhouse, a hospital out of time, a defunct New England theme park . . . these are but a few.

Picture the epitomal cabin in the woods. It was someone's dream once, someone's private retreat away from the hustle and the bustle. Of course, that was before. Kristin Dearborn kicks things off with her take on this classic horror setting. As it unfolds, "Ghosted" aims to keep the reader guessing, forcing them to change their mind again and again as they try to discern what, exactly, is going on. It's a perfect way to begin, especially since the anthology's theme is hard coded into the story's DNA. "Ghosted" is the type of yarn that could only be told in this modern age of cell phones and online dating, a time where endless electronic distractions do little to soften the sting of true loneliness.

Now let's shift to another place and time: a possible future when humanity is trying to find its legs in the wake of a strange event known only as *the Wave*. Every now and again you come across a work of short fiction that simply begs to be turned into something longer, a novel or perhaps an entire series of novels. Without a doubt, "The Space Between" is one of those. Daniel G. Keohane has made a career of working his faith and spirituality into horror. His early novel, *Solomon's Grave*, is a perfect example, skillfully blending strange bedfellows in a way that never feels like he's selling something. "The Space Between" employs a unique use of the anthology's theme: What if you were abandoned, not by family or friends . . . but by your own immortal soul?

Speaking of short works that beg to be longer, consider "The Sparrow and The Shredded Heart." Here, Morgan Sylvia employs her trademark mastery of poetic prose to weave something wholly unique. The world she has crafted here is dense, and the genres and themes employed are often surprising: horror and mystery with a dash of mad science, echoing the cross-genre work of Guillermo Del Toro, Barker, or even Shelley. We follow the tale's heroine as she tries to reconcile the one unexplained event that has cursed her adult life, shaping it into one of solitude, regret, and, ultimately, revenge. Unfortunately for her, the old McGrady house is not quite so abandoned as she imagines.

Of course, these particular stories take a reactionary stance on the theme. They all deal with the fallout—how being discarded can sour and taint a person or a place. But what if the act was ongoing? If, instead of a sword through the chest, abandonment was a series of small cuts dispensed over time? In Christopher Kelly's "Rigby," we meet the titular dog and quickly learn that Rigby is a very good boy—too good, perhaps, for his master. But then, Curtis is Rigby's whole world, especially since the other members of the family have all gone away. Sometimes, Curtis gets mad and hurts Rigby . . . but the love of a loyal dog is a blinding, illogical, wholly unwavering thing. Eventually, Curtis understands Rigby will be with him to the bitter end—and that is something he cannot allow. Even in his diminished state, the man knows Rigby deserves better.

Likewise, in Trisha Wooldridge's Miyazaki-styled fable, "Shisa Hachiko," the main character is experiencing a form of abandonment in real time. Rachel has moved to Japan to support her girlfriend, who's just landed her dream job working for a video game company. Unfortunately, she finds that as time goes on, there is less and less time for Rachel, forcing her to explore her new home on her own. And, being American, Rachel knows little of the places that have not been so much abandoned as set aside: places that belong to the spirits now. Though not really horror, the tale certainly deals with the supernatural and with various aspects of Japanese mythology. Also referenced is the true story of Hachiko, the Akita dog who continued to wait for his master at Shibuya Station for nine years after the man passed away.

For me the standout of this fantastic collection is the tale that hit the hardest. You'd be forgiven if you thought Elaine Labbee's "The Ballad of Johnny and Carmen" sounded like the title of a harmless 1950s-style love song. The reality, however, is a very different thing indeed. To describe what happens in this story would be doing both it and the reader a disservice. Suffice it to say the events are horrifically brutal, sexually explicit, and will leave you needing a shower.

What does it mean to be abandoned? These are but a few of the eighteen darkly twisted pieces presented in this collection. *Wicked Abandoned* is a fantastic addition to the long running Wicked series. Though once you've finished it, you'll probably require a hug.

—Steve Van Samson
Lancaster, Massachusetts
August 2, 2024

Ghosted?
Kristin Dearborn

Shauna checked and rechecked her directions on Google maps. The phone icon for *no signal* blinked at her, but Google Maps led her onward. She'd left the pavement some time ago, and the dirt roads had grown more and more narrow.

"I can't wait to finally meet you," John had texted. He'd told her about how the cabin would be cute, romantic, the perfect place for them to finally meet after six months of texting and phone calls.

Shauna knew the drill: for first dates, one should always meet in a well-lit, public place. But this wasn't that. She'd known him for six months. Six months of talking every day, FaceTime, sharing their most intimate dreams and desires. Two months ago, she'd told him she loved him. He'd reciprocated immediately, and they'd never looked back.

The cabin sat in the Green Mountains of southern Vermont, equidistant from her home in Albany and his in Portsmouth. They hadn't figured out where they would live, if she'd go to him and be by the ocean, or if they'd both pack up and meet somewhere new. He'd made it pretty clear he didn't want to come to Albany, and she supposed she couldn't blame him; it wasn't a romantic city, though it certainly had everything she'd ever needed.

John said he'd gotten a great deal on the cabin because it was the offseason, and it was *kinda far away* from a lot of the touristy things to do in Vermont. They'd met in a chat room for horror enthusiasts, and meeting in a remote cabin had seemed so funny when they'd talked about it. It would make a great story to tell everyone back on Discord.

Fall foliage had come and gone, and in early November the skiers hadn't descended yet. Outside her car, everything was brown and wet, and cold rain drizzled down on her. She'd dressed to meet her honey, not to deal with a winter monsoon. It wouldn't be a big deal; she'd only be outside for as long as it took to dash from the car to the cabin. She'd gotten some looks when she stopped for gas. Drink it in, suckers. She looked hot. Hot for her man. Finally.

Some friends had asked, *Aren't you worried? Like, what if there are no fireworks? What if he's not as good in person?*

She wasn't worried. Not at all.

The GPS told her to take a right onto a narrow track she wasn't actually sure was a road, but she eased her aging Accord down the even more rutted path, wincing as something scraped underneath. She'd asked if she needed four-wheel drive, but John had told her she should be fine with the Accord. Branches scraped the sides of her car . . . this would be something they laughed about. Maybe he'd buy her a new car someday. Maybe they'd be the kind of couple who bought each other cars and put giant red bows on them for Christmas surprises. John had a job in finance and made good money. Better than good. In private moments, she wondered what he saw in her, a chubby bank teller from Albany. But they'd just clicked in the Discord chat, talking about the merits of the new generation of *Piranha* films against the purists who actually had the gall to advocate that *Piranha II,* with its crazy flying fish, was a better movie than *Piranha 3-D.* Just because a movie was old didn't automatically mean it was good.

She turned a narrow corner, the Accord protesting another scrape to its undercarriage. Through the barren branches, she saw a structure: their cabin. He'd sent screen shots from Airbnb, and it had looked cute but rustic—maybe *too* rustic—but John was excited, and she would be, too.

In person, the place looked like it hadn't been touched in years. It was definitely the same structure as in the pics he'd sent, but now green moss coated the low, flat roof, which seemed to sag under an invisible weight. A porch spanned the face of the cabin with the front door in the center. The railings leaned like snaggled teeth, and the windows looked like dark eyes.

John wasn't here yet. She frowned. She was a little late herself, actually; it was three fifteen instead of three like they'd planned.

He'd texted her when he'd left Portsmouth, given her updates about stopping for gas, including a selfie from the New Hampshire liquor store where he'd showed her the expensive bottle of champagne he'd picked up.

Shauna sat in her car, engine off and making little ticking sounds after the long drive. She stared at her phone.

No service.

They'd known that, expected it. It was part of the charm. Part of the horror joke. Off-grid, where no one could bother or interrupt them. This weekend was all about getting to know the parts of each other you can't know through the phone and the internet. She'd seen every inch of him, but yearned to know what he felt like. Excitement coursed through her. Soon. Maybe the cabin was nicer inside. The pictures looked it for sure.

She sat a few minutes, listening to the rain thrum on the roof of the car. She hadn't made the reservation and wasn't sure if there was a hidden key or a code.

Surely John would be along any minute now.

Irritation crept in, threatening her fantasy. The place looked like it kind of sucked—taking the creepy cabin-in-the-woods thing too far—and John was late. She realized he'd never responded after she'd told him her revised ETA was three fifteen.

She looked back at his last message, closer to one o'clock: "Can't wait to smell, see, touch, and taste you."

How could she be irritated at that?

Her back hurt from sitting in the car. She decided to chance it, make a run for the porch and see if she could get in. Maybe she could get inside and get things ready for John. She slid out, wobbling on her heels, covered her head from the rain as best she could (she'd had her hair styled in anticipation of meeting him), and tried to run for the porch. Each stride had to be a cautious one: the leaves were both slippery and crunchy, the three porch steps were slick, rotting wood, and these were not the shoes for questionable terrain. The right side of the stairs was a gaping hole, and she tried to place her weight carefully on what was left, not wanting to crash through. The porch itself was a little better, sheltered from the rain, but off to the far side, it looked like one corner had caved in. What *was* this place? Not cute at all.

She refused to feel the disappointment threatening her. Not yet. The inside could be nice. In a futile gesture, she tried the door and… it swung open.

Oh. Well, okay.

Instinctively, she reached for a light switch and found one to the right of the door. It didn't do anything. Gray rainy light lit the room to some degree. She gave herself a moment to let her eyes adjust. It didn't look like anyone had been in here for quite some time. It was clearly the same room John had sent Airbnb images of, but those pictures had to be years old. A green couch sat against one wall; a braided rug lay on the dusty floor. In the back of the room was a kitchen, and to her left would be a hallway to the bathroom and two bedrooms. She went to the kitchen (optimistically trying each light switch she passed) and turned the faucet on the sink. It coughed, spat some rust-colored water, then nothing.

She remembered John saying there was a generator, and they'd have to turn that on before they could use power. He'd assured her he'd take care of all of that, and she wouldn't even notice. She looked at her phone again. He was almost forty-five minutes late. She'd bring her bag in—as long as she didn't crash right through the steps with it—and wait for him a little while longer. She didn't know where one might find a generator—outside, she presumed—and if she did find it, how to turn it on. It couldn't be that hard, though, right? First step: bring her bag in.

She paused. Bringing her bag in meant she planned to stay when he showed up.

There was a fireplace, which would be cute once they got it up and running, but once the electricity was on, she guessed they'd have to run into the nearest town (which would take a very long time) to get something to eat. Unless John had thought to bring a meal, which *could* be why he was taking so long. She probably had texts on her phone saying he was running late.

Unless something had happened to him.

Another thought, one she *really* didn't want, entered her mind, but she shoved it off.

A car accident, maybe. Stopping for gas and getting shot by a tweaker who'd just robbed the cashier.

Or.

What if he just isn't coming?

He was coming. Of *course* he was coming. How could she write him off so quickly? *Jesus, Shauna, way to be a bitch.* She'd go out to the car, bring in her bag, see about getting the generator running, and would have everything nice for him when he got here.

Stepping outside, she saw the rain had turned into stinging sleet. The drops weren't snow, but were icy, and hurt against her skin. Her winter coat, her overnight bag, a pair of boots, were all in the car. She ran as fast as her heels allowed, ankles screaming in protest. These shoes were a better fit for a dinner out or a movie. The straps bit into her skin. She honestly hadn't expected to be wearing any of this for very long once she got to the cabin.

She broke a nail trying and failing to open the car door. Fuck.

Locked.

Keys fully visible, dangling from the ignition.

The icy sleet internalized, shards sluicing down her spine. *No.* She tried the back driver's side door. The trunk. The back passenger's door. The passenger's door. *No!* It'd been years since she'd done this.

Her car. Locked snugly with everything practical she would need inside.

The stinging rain soaked her red dress, turning it a shade closer to black. She stuck her broken nail in her mouth while her mind spun. She needed a winter coat. Her boots. Dry clothes. The temperature hovered around freezing, and the cabin was cold. What she really needed was to get the fuck out of there and regroup in a place with heat, electricity, and cell service. She'd left her phone in the cabin, but it was a useless brick.

Whatever she was going to do, or needed to do, she couldn't do it standing outside the car in the sleet. She trudged back to the cabin, arms wrapped around herself but still shivering. Inside, she took off the shoes; better tetanus than four-inch spike heels. There was nothing to be done until she felt a little warmer, until her teeth stopped clacking as she shivered.

She needed to smash a window in her own car.

She *needed* John to show up, full of apologies for being late. He'd take her in his arms. He'd have a pair of sweats, just a little too big for her but warm and dry. The pair could go down into town and she could use AAA to get her car open without smashing it. They'd get something to eat—drive-through, she'd look ridiculous with the heels and the sweats—then get a motel room somewhere and laugh about this.

A moth-eaten wool blanket draped the back of the couch, and

Shauna reluctantly pulled it off and wrapped it around herself. It itched and carried a smell she couldn't put her finger on, but it was warm. She curled on the couch. Four thirty. Already dark. The sleet not letting up.

Where was John? To be this late, something serious had to have happened. Right? Like a car accident?

Driving up to the cabin in daylight and rain had been harrowing enough, she tried to imagine doing it in the dark with ice falling from the sky. She didn't like driving at night to begin with. Her vision wasn't the best. Living in Albany, she could handle driving in winter weather, but those were plowed roads, and less than three miles between her home and office, not this rutted road with a stream off to one side. She thought of *Misery*, and Paul Sheldon; they hadn't found his car 'til spring, long after Annie Wilkes had taken him away. The idea made her laugh, because to be in Paul Sheldon's predicament, someone had to give a shit about you, and Shauna clearly didn't have that problem. She'd told her roommate she'd be out of town for the weekend and completely unreachable. Her best friend was a woman from a chat room who lived in Iowa. She'd get concerned, but again, only after Shauna didn't get home on Sunday night.

Maybe she could get the generator working and at least have some light. Staying a night here would suck, but in the morning, she could smash out one of her back windows, get in the car, and drive away. Outside, the sleet seemed to be shifting to snow and back again, a slick of ice forming on the already treacherous porch and railing. In daylight, this would all be easier to deal with (though daylight was a long way away). They'd known to expect winter weather tonight, but had expected to be here and settled before it hit. Shauna'd fully expected to barely leave the bedroom this weekend. Imagined him bringing her coffee in bed. Imagined spending an entire day doing nothing but loving John, and learning him, and being loved in kind.

He did love her. He was just . . . what? Dead?

Would she rather he be dead in a ditch, or sitting behind his computer in Portsmouth, yucking it up that he'd sent some chick to the cabin from *Evil Dead* in southern Vermont?

She shoved that thought away. The answer didn't make her feel like a very good person.

Generator. Maybe the cabin would be cuter with the lights

running. A door off the kitchen led out to a back porch and, lo and behold, there sat a generator, and next to it a red gas can. Shauna didn't know if this was too close to the house, or how generators were supposed to work, but she was happy to see it in the dim glow of her iPhone flashlight. The cold of the porch floor reached into her bare feet and sapped the warmth from her. What little warmth was left. Okay, pull-cord thingie? That seemed right. Was there another button she had to push first? She'd never actually touched a generator before and, until today, hadn't imagined a situation where she wouldn't be able to give it a quick Google if she needed to. She ran the flashlight over the thing, a faded red. A thick cord ran from it to a hole someone had drilled into the cabin, so that was good.

She picked up the gas can and something sloshed inside. That was good, too.

Unless it's not even gas

She told herself to shut up. Of course it was gas. Someone was clearly prepared to power the cabin, so all this was nicely set up. She just needed to figure out what to do next. Pop culture taught her it wasn't just an on/off switch, but she did see one with options being *ON, OFF, START.*

If it blew up in her face, it would solve a lot of problems all at once.

She switched it to *START* and held it there. It didn't do anything, but that didn't seem super weird. Pulling a cord for a choke? One summer she'd worked bumper boats at an amusement park. *Something something choke, oxygen in the mix.* She ran the light over the machine looking for a handle to pull. There, on the left. Her manicure (blood red, shaped into stilettos to match her stupid shoes) looked comically out of place as she reached for the handle and pulled. Nothing. She still wasn't discouraged. Thinking about the bumper boats, there was probably another switch somewhere that needed to be in the right position . . .

A fuel switch! Set to off! She flipped it to *ON* and tried the cord again. This time, the machine sputtered a bit. She was pretty sure there had to be still another switch. She remembered it had to be open in the beginning, but once the bumper boats had been started you had to turn it down. Something about the fuel mix being too rich.

It would be the greatest success of her life to get this generator running.

She ran the iPhone light around where she'd found the fuel switch—and there it was, kind of hiding, black on black. She switched it as far as it would go in the other direction, and gave another pull. The generator sputtered with more confidence this time. She squealed, yanking the cord again. Couldn't do too much, she recalled, or it would flood. She'd been excellent at flooding the bumper boat engines, and it had usually fallen to Matt, a deeply tanned college freshman, to fire up all the boats.

The generator caught.

Oh my fucking God! Shauna froze. Took a deep breath. Let the machine find its rhythm. Slid the choke back to the left as slowly as she could, listening to the motor's tenor change as she did so.

Holy fucking shit, she'd done it.

Holy fucking shit.

She hadn't realized how cold she'd gotten out here. Once the euphoria passed, her teeth started knocking together again. She stared dubiously at the machine. Would it stay on if she walked away? But she didn't have a choice. She cast her phone light out into the darkness of the night, a *Star Wars* hyper drive galaxy of falling snow. She had light, she could make a fire, and in the morning, she'd make a plan. At least here there wouldn't be noisy neighbors. And her friend at work who was always talking about intermittent fasting? Well, Shauna would give it a whirl tonight.

She giggled, stepping back into the cabin. Trying the light in the kitchen. A sick glow flooded the place, dim, but *light*. It showed her just how gross the cabin was, but whatever; it was hers tonight, and she'd made the lights come on. She noticed a second kitchen door, tucked almost behind the fridge, and opened it, expecting a pantry closet.

Stairs.

Down.

Into darkness.

Oh hell no. She closed it, making sure the little hook was latched on her side.

A stink of musty root cellar rot had wafted up with the opening and closing of the door. It tickled her gag reflex. She'd been too anxious to eat this afternoon, just a venti crème brûlée latte from Starbucks, and the coffee's sweet remnants lingered, making her breath feel foul. Intermittent fasting.

She couldn't help but look back at the basement door. The little hairs on the back of her neck rose. So many bad basements drifted through her memory: *Barbarian*, obviously, which she and John had watched together on a video call. *Silence of the Lambs, Get Out, Don't Breathe, The Conjuring, Psycho* . . . Her brain flitted to *Cabin in the Woods*, though that basement hadn't been really scary. She refused to let herself think of *Evil Dead*.

She had to make a fire.

Shutting her cell phone off to conserve the precious battery, she used a lamp in the living room to evaluate the fireplace. There'd be a flue that needed to be opened; she remembered a cousin making that mistake once at a rental property and filling the house with smoke. A basket of kindling sat by the fireplace, and she dumped it all in. She wished she smoked. Wished her vape pen wasn't in the car, but for different reasons. There had to be matches or a lighter here somewhere.

Back in the kitchen, she pulled out the first drawer. It was like someone had halfheartedly tried to move out, and only taken some of their things. Or, maybe, no one had ever lived here at all, and the items left behind had just accumulated. There was a sporadic collection of unmatched silverware and a healthy collection of mouse shit. No matches. No lighter. Fine, there were many other drawers to go through. The drawer closest to the stove, a gas stove, contained a mostly-disintegrated oven mitt and a box of long matches.

Shauna didn't know where John was or what had happened to him, but she was going to be okay here. She lit the kindling, reveling in the warmth. She fed the baby fire slowly, got a good blaze going, then curled up on the couch under the wool blanket.

The dress and the push-up bra she'd worn were not the most comfortable attire for sleeping. The first thing she'd do after breaking her car window would be to change into normal clothes. At first light, she'd evaluate. For now, she'd ignore the pinching clothes and fall into the hypnotic dancing of the flames. She watched the fire. When was the last time she'd had nothing to do? No internet to distract her? No books, computer games, work, or chores? People didn't live like this anymore. She didn't want to do it again, maybe ever again, but maybe she'd remember this night as a peaceful meditation. Her eyelids sunk closed. Shauna dozed.

Thump!

A house-shaking thud woke her. There was a fleeting moment of panic, of *where the* fuck *am I*, then the memory flooded back.

Her fire burned low.

The lights were off, the generator gone silent. How much gas had been in it when she'd started it? Didn't matter. She'd work on the fire.

But what was the thump? Heavy snow falling off trees? A tree falling outside? A tree falling onto the cabin? It didn't matter. She needed to get her fire built, get back under her blankets, and go back to sleep. She had a long drive ahead of her.

Where was John? Was he laughing at her? She hated to think like that. The twin victories of generator and fire had pushed these thoughts away, but now, crouched and poking at reluctant embers, she wondered. What if there'd never *been* a John? He had a LinkedIn and an Instagram where people had commented. He had a TikTok account . . . But anyone could do those things and say they were anyone.

More likely, he was stuck somewhere, frantic that he couldn't get ahold of her, probably wondering why she hadn't left the cabin to come back to cell service. She didn't know any of his friends or family to leave a message with, even if she *could* call someone. Maybe he'd used her IG to reach out to someone, and maybe someone would come?

Her phone told her it was just after midnight. She doubted anyone would come tonight.

She peered out the window at her car, now a hump under the snow.

All of these were tomorrow problems. The fire had perked back up, so she curled up under her blanket, ready to doze off again.

In the absence of the generator noise, other sounds filtered in: creaks of the house settling, wind howling, the ting of snow against the windows. She realized she'd never even checked the bedrooms or the bathroom . . . which she needed to do now, 'cause she had to pee. She flicked on the phone's flashlight, glancing at the battery. Forty-five percent. Yeesh. Okay. Well, it'd get charged as soon as she broke the car window in the morning.

Opening the first door, she found a bedroom, and quickly closed it. Then, a tiny room with a mildew-crusted shower stall and vile black toilet. No paper; that'd been too much to ask for. She tried to hover over the seat, spattering the dry toilet bowl, not caring that it was rude to take a piss in someone else's house and just leave it. It was rude that she was stuck here alone to begin with.

Back in her little nest, her mind whirled. She kept checking her phone. The battery percentage seemed to tick down faster than the minutes. She needed to stop looking. Just try and relax and be calm in this deserted house in the middle of the woods when no one knew where she was except for some douchebag who'd been trolling her on the internet for months. Why had he sent her out here? Just because he could? Fucking asshole. John. Probably wasn't even his real name. John Anderson. An unGoogleable name. Should have been a red flag. The complete and utter lack of red flags should have been a red flag.

Thump!

Shauna drew into herself. Pulled the stinking, scratchy blanket to her face.

It was the woods. The woods make noises. Old houses make noises. She just needed to suck it up for—she checked her phone—five or six more hours, until it was light enough outside to evaluate things further. Shorter than a shift at the bank. She could do this. She closed her eyes.

Thump.

Softer this time. Less like a branch falling and more *intentional* sounding.

What if he'd led her here specifically to make sure she was isolated and out of touch? That was stupid. Trolling was one thing, setting her up was . . . criminal. She was so not worth the bother of hunting. She was boring, bland, not even all that clever.

Thump.

From below her this time.

The basement?

Shauna struggled to swallow, but all the saliva had dried from her mouth. Probably some animal was down there, hibernating, and her clomping around up here in heels had disturbed it. Maybe the warmth from the fire had confused it and now it thought it was spring?

Thump.

Why did a cabin like this have a basement, anyway?

Thump.

She drew the covers up to her chin. Fear and curiosity battled in her. She ran through every horror movie protagonist's bad decisions. This wasn't a horror movie, though, this was just a shitty November night, the devastation of her fantasy that she was worthy of someone's love. That she deserved something better than her small, online, lonely life.

Thump.

She wouldn't go down to the basement, she'd just take her flashlight (her phone battery said thirty-five percent) and take a quick look. If it was empty, there'd be nothing to be afraid of anymore. She wasn't interesting enough to be in a horror movie. Seeing whatever was in the basement would be easy enough. Something mundane would let her go back to sleep and be ready for her stupid drive in the morning.

Right?

Thump.

There had to be a reason for the sounds. She sure as hell wasn't falling asleep while they went on. The car had a half tank of gas; if she went out and broke a window, turned it on, and slept in it running in the driveway . . . no, that didn't make sense. She'd be less protected there than she was here.

One quick peek into the basement, see for herself that it was something dumb making the noise, and then she'd be able to fall asleep.

Shauna stood, dirty floor icy against her bare feet. When she got home, she'd scrub them clean in the shower. She held her phone out like a weapon, but deep inside didn't think it was going to be something *scary*. She was just too boring.

She crossed the kitchen, flipped open the little latch on the door, and turned the knob. Shauna opened the door. The dark below her pooled infinite, and she eased down onto the first step.

*   *   *

John Anderson rubbed at his bleary eyes, willing himself to wake up. The cold helped, but he didn't dare stop for a coffee. Shauna was going to be so pissed. He'd been running late, then hit a patch of ice and gone off the road. He'd called a tow truck. The driver had made sure he was all right, then said there were a bunch of more serious accidents, and he'd get there when he could. If John got too cold, the driver had said, he could call the cops to come get him. John's mom had gotten him one of those silver space blankets, so he'd wrapped up in that and run the car when he'd needed to, always running around to the back to dig out the exhaust. The tow truck had gotten to him, with the driver's many apologies, around seven, as the sun was coming up.

He'd tried calling Shauna until her mailbox was full. She either had her phone off or, more likely, was sending him straight to voicemail. He'd told her he was running late, told her as soon as the car had gone off the road, but she'd never answered.

A bouquet of roses sat on the seat beside him, looking the worse for wear from their night in the cold car.

Why hadn't she called? The cabin didn't have service, which had seemed funny when he'd booked it, but she must have known something was wrong last night when she hadn't heard from him. She couldn't have spent the night in the cabin, just waiting for him, could she? Had she driven away, seen his messages, and kept going? Had she been there at all?

GPS led him off the secondary road onto a plowed side road, and he ascended into the mountains. Maybe all-seasons hadn't been a great idea. The tires struggled on the road, but he followed the blue line on the GPS down an even worse driveway. At least it was plowed out.

John gaped at the cabin. It was the same as in the picture from the Airbnb site, but neglected looking, the roof droopy and sad. Yet they'd plowed it out after a snowstorm. Because they'd rented it out? Her car wasn't here, and all he saw for tracks in the snow were big beefy truck tires. She'd left last night when he didn't show up? It didn't make sense. Her last text had been cute and flirty. Seriously, had she heard all his messages and just decided . . . what? He was making up the excuse of being stuck in a ditch? She could have come to get him; he hadn't been *that* far away. His back and neck screamed from the uncomfortable night.

Had she ever even come at all, or had the whole thing been a joke to her? He imagined her turning her phone off last night and laughing with girlfriends—or Jesus, what if she were laughing with her real boyfriend?

He thought back to the hours they'd spent on Zoom. On the phone. The time she'd made her sister Cara talk to him to tell him her recipe for risotto, which he'd immediately made and texted Cara to say how great it was. All the hours talking about horror movies. About life. Plans. What if she'd been in an accident, too? None of it made sense!

He raised his phone to snap a picture of the cabin. When he got home (oh man, he dreaded explaining this to his housemates, who didn't expect him back until Tuesday) he'd go after these jerks on Airbnb, renting out a dump that didn't match the pictures at all. Shame welled up in him, threatening to spill as tears.

You want a sensitive guy, Shauna? Well, here he is.

He could see her being frustrated that he was late, but when she'd left, she had to have seen and heard the messages where he told her he was stuck. His housemate Glen had been right, it had been stupid to set this all up for a first date. *Just go get pizza*, he'd said, *and then get a motel if you still want one.*

They'd made a perfect, romantic plan. He'd imagined a life with her. And now what?

The tears came. There wasn't anyone here to see anyway. He threw the bouquet out of the car, the roses blackish red on the snow.

He had to piss, and might as well do it in the dump he'd paid for for two nights. He wiped his tears away, stomped up onto the porch, and opened the door.

It was warmer than he'd expected inside. It should have been the same temperature as outside; for some reason that now seemed unspeakably stupid, they'd been fine with a generator and fireplace. She'd been so excited to wait until they were done and share the story of their first meet up on the Discord channel. *I know if I tell anyone before*, she'd said, *they'll try and talk us out of it!*

He knelt by the fireplace. Took the poker and jabbed around in the ashes. Embers flared and glowed. Jesus, she'd been here. Or someone had. Long enough to make a fire. He took in the room from the kneeling vantage point. Everything dusty, abandoned, but . . . under the couch. A red, pleather shoe, a high stiletto heel. John's throat tightened. She'd shown him the shoes, modeled them for him, she said she'd wear them but with the snow he'd assumed . . .

Thump.

John froze. "Shauna?"

THUMP!

From beneath him. A basement? "Shauna! Hey!" *Where was her car, though? Where was the rest of her stuff? Why had she let the fire die out?*

John threw open doors: bedroom, bedroom, vile bathroom. Finally, there in the kitchen, so close to where he'd started, the gaping maw of a basement. Surely, she wouldn't have . . .

THUMP!

John descended the stairs.

To Find Mother
Patricia Gomes

When he wakened
under a dark porch,
litter-filled with paper plates,
crunchy leaves, and crushed plastic bottles,
he was uncertain
if he was newly born
or recently dead.

He was cold, terrified,
and missed his mother's voice
beyond measure.
He wanted
an eight-note lullaby
and a good night caress.

Above him was blinding light,
clamorous noise,
and nauseating smells
of boiled root vegetables
and humans.
　　Was he here? Was he there?
Why were his wings cracked,
his scales burnt?
Was he too big to be devoured?
Too small to be seen through the eyes of gods?

Too fast to catch?
Too ugly to love?

Mewling soundlessly, he willed himself to stand,
then move,
and finally run
as far and as fast
as his six hairless and insectile legs could move.

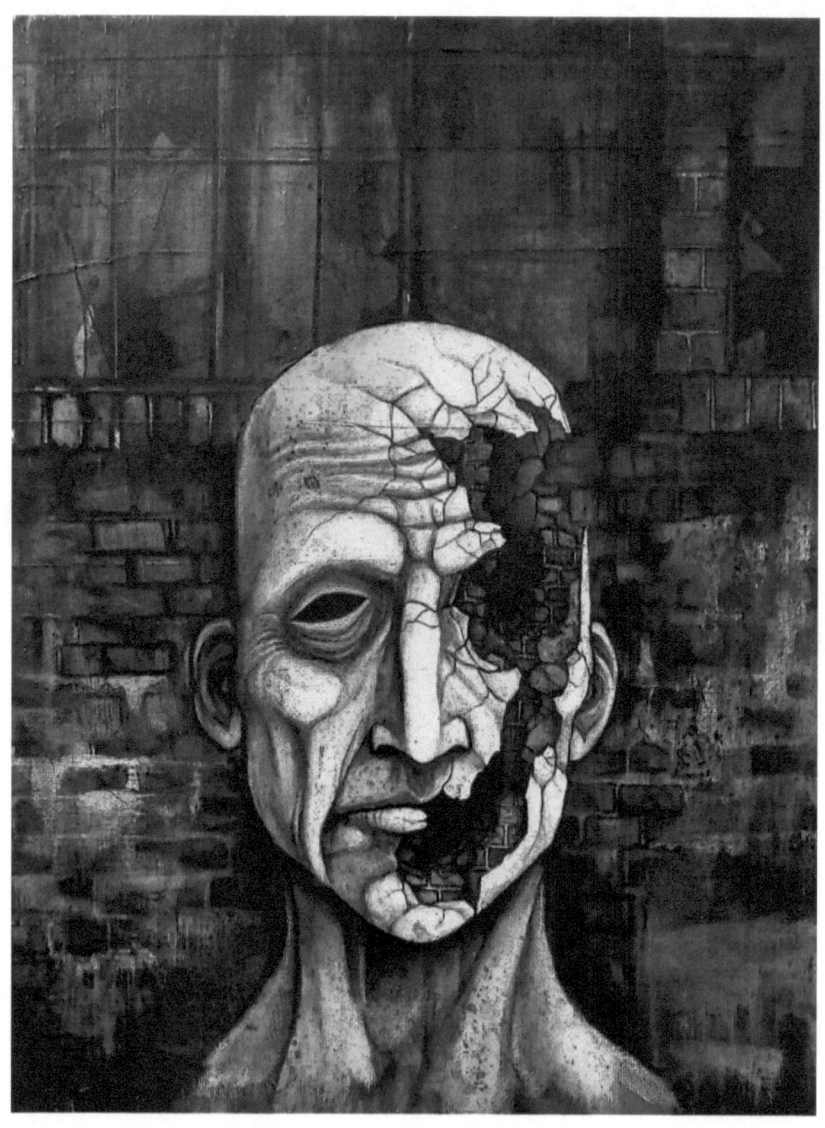

Illustration for "The Space Between" © 2024 Aaron White

The Space Between
Daniel G. Keohane

Day 0

Something was coming. A thunderstorm, or maybe just a drop in pressure. Whatever it might be, Brent felt it vibrating through his bones.

He gave the woman beside him a sideways hug and stepped aside to open the door of their place of worship. The woman wasn't his wife. Sheila never joined him here.

Something was coming.

He shivered through a sudden wash of heat. In that final moment of his true existence on this earth, Brent wondered if his childhood fear of a faraway enemy nuking his insignificant little town had come true. Even now, the heat and flames might be just a moment away from—

Day 32

Sheila rested the back of her head against the kitchen counter and let the cigarette smoke drift toward the ceiling. Lung cancer or an oxygen tank didn't seem like much of a concern for her future. Nothing really mattered since the Wave.

"Grow up," she muttered, then tilted herself forward in the chair, falling away from the counter. When the front legs hit linoleum, Sheila used momentum to get to her feet. She imagined she must look every bit like the wobbling Russian doll she felt like . . . or was it a Weeble? Words from her long-ago childhood.

The look was accentuated by the quilted robe she wore; a *housecoat* people had called it once upon a time (not her mother . . . *she'd* had a much more amusing name). The stiff robe reached the tops of her feet. It had been her mother's, one of the few items Sheila'd kept when they'd cleaned out her house three years ago. She'd found it yesterday as she'd quietly gone through her and Brent's stuff, pruning the closet. Sheila hated the dress but loved her mother so much. Her absence was still a physical ache.

Dalek, she thought suddenly. *That's what Mom used to call this dress.* A warm memory hit of the woman walking about in this frumpy, stiff coat as she vacuumed, shouting, *Exterminate! Exterminate!*

Would Mom have become vacant if she'd lived long enough to be caught in the Wave? She had baked enough pies for *her people*, visited enough helpless bedridden in her time, that Sheila was certain the woman would have been taken. Or hollowed out.

There it was again: the panic, that itch deep in her chest shuddering like a frightened pup. None of any of this could possibly be real but—

"I'm home." Brent stepped through the door. As always, his voice teetered on the edge of either sadness or rage. They *all* sounded like that now. Emotionless.

Soulless.

Sheila took a deep drag. "I didn't make anything for you. I fed Emmet and Doyle an hour ago."

Brent paused, car keys dangling from his fingers, not *quite* falling into the ceramic dish Doyle had mushed together in preschool two years ago for Father's Day. Every aspect of Brent these days was *not quite*. Not quite sad. Not quite angry. Not quite sociopathic.

Brent is gone. You're married to the body he abandoned. Words spoken by Ricky three nights ago, in bed, one of his many attempts to keep her with him after one of their nights out. Each time trying his best to convince her never to go home. Not that he ever offered to pay for whatever insane amount the babysitter might charge if that happened. What he'd suggested about her husband was sick, and of course she'd obsessed over it during the drive home that night. An eleven-thirty return from what she'd claimed was a movie that had begun at six.

Brent hadn't cared. He'd been sitting on the edge of the couch, staring at the TV and probably seeing nothing. Justina Rollings had been sitting at one of the kitchen bar stools, keeping as much distance from the man as possible. At least the girl wasn't so worried about him she'd gone home before Sheila'd gotten back. No one in their right mind would trust what Brent had become to watch the kids.

Now, watching the smoke dissipate lazily above her head, Sheila decided Ricky's words might be the truest thing she'd heard since the world had gone mad.

The keys finally dropped. "Okay," Brent said, then walked to the fridge. These past couple of days, Sheila had given up trying to elicit any emotion from him, good or bad. There was nothing there. And all she felt was pity for the form bent at the open refrigerator door: if Ricky was right, they'd both been abandoned by the same man.

Day 67

"In the aftermath of the Wave, as most of you refer to the anomaly that ran across the globe this summer, we must . . . take . . . specific . . . steps,"—these last four words were emphasized by a raised voice and the President's left hand pantomiming a series of awkward karate chops—"to ensure that this great country remains stable and secure." He paused, staring into the camera for some sort of effect. "Since the phenomenon has affected every corner of the planet, for the foreseeable future we are closing our borders to any but the most necessary immigrants."

All but the most white-looking immigrants, you mean, Nabib thought. Maybe he was being hard on the guy. The president wasn't the fastest rabbit in the hutch to begin with, but having to face such a new and unprecedented pandemic, where a third of the human population had suddenly . . . changed . . . well, who knew what the right choices were?

Nabib absently touched the edge of the red sweatshirt's hood to make sure it was in place. He kept it pulled over his head most of the time now and had no illusions about it; the act was akin to a child clutching a security blanket.

The president droned on, never once mentioning what had happened in Benoni. Maybe it was a replay from an earlier press conference. If this was live, and any of the reports crashing the internet with their latest hysteria were true, this narcissist would gleefully point out it could never happen here. No sir, no giant, broken chains, too big for even the biggest kaiju monkey, would dare appear in 'Merica. The most ludicrous of the stories insisted the tarnished gold links, spread two thousand feet across a South African farm pasture and its neighboring township, were either radioactive or releasing some sort of hallucinogenic gas. People reportedly went mad if they got too near the area.

Since the Wave, the news had become unreliable, to say the least.

Nabib watched for a while, hoping to hear something helpful, something pointing to an answer—specifically, why he was still, well, *him*, and not like these other people moving through the world with nary an emotion or glimmer of recognition. These people had become zombies, in the original, Robert Southey sense of the word: emotionless husks devoid of any essence of who they'd been. *Soulless* was becoming the accepted moniker throughout social media.

Had his people's fabled *Yawm al-Qiyamah* really come, or perhaps some unexpected version of the Christian rapture? Houses of prayer and worship were emptying since so many of those who had attended now lived their lives on autopilot. There were others who'd raised their arms during worship or knelt toward Mecca or donned their Tallit, but had done so only for the benefit of the person beside them. These people were finally dropping their charades. Places once called holy, Nabib assumed, would soon run dry of spirit. If they hadn't already.

Which brought him back to his one question: What of his own life had been so false he'd been passed over? Had his own faith been a lie? He hugged his arms tighter around himself, turning off the television and sliding lower into the chair. The sweatshirt hood fell over his eyes, a veil protecting him from whatever answer might be out there.

Nabib's phone buzzed. When he finally picked it up, his voice sounded small even to himself. "Hello?"

"Dude, you up?" Boney Wan was the only person besides his *didi* who still made voice calls.

"'Course, I'm up. It's only . . ." He glanced at the top of the phone. Seven minutes to midnight! "Oh. I guess I fell asleep."

Wan laughed through the speaker. "No worries, not looking to

play. Still have work tomorrow. Keep the city lit another day."
They were both electricians with Volty the Power People ("*We keep
you in the light with more than our smiles!*" the cartoon mascot sang) and
both had to be at *Angry Lady*'s house at seven tomorrow. If anyone
in this post-Wave world was the epitome of its growing sense of
rage, that half-bald woman was it.

Nabib sat up straighter to keep his voice sounding more awake
than he felt. "I know why you're calling, Boney. The world's not
ending. Please talk about other things or I'm going to block you."

"You can't block me. You love me. And you know I'm right.
You saw it. You *told* me you saw it."

"I've seen pictures of people screaming and ripping their
clothes interspersed with a barely passible piece of CGI, showing
something in a field that makes *zero* sense."

"The hole, though. You saw what came out of that hole."

"Well, they had to hide the chains somewhere."

"Dude, not the chains! That's old news. I'm talking about the
giant naked steamy thing stomping up the continent . . ."

Nabib disconnected the line. Enough. He slouched back down
then stared under the edge of his hood toward an electrical outlet
across the room.

Regulators. Every electronic had something inside to maintain
voltage. Every horse had a bridle and bit. Whatever had been
regulating the human tendency for irrationality had washed away in
the Wave.

Or left the planet.

Everything was going to shit.

The urge came back. So many times, for so many weeks, he'd
fought the siren call from the roof. How many more times will
Boney call to point out the newest insanity from either down the
road or across the world?

How many more times could he handle the news?

He should pray. Now, though, the consideration felt hollow.
He'd missed something important along the road of his life. It was
too late.

He pulled the hood completely over his face, causing the
sweatshirt to ride up his back. This did nothing to hide the
nightmare the world had become, or himself from it.

Nabib was alone, and because of this, he finally, desperately,
pushed himself off the couch. There were no more options. He

pressed the hood off of his head and walked toward the apartment door as the time on his phone changed to midnight.

Day 68

Sheila pressed herself against Ricky's shoulder. They were sitting on the couch watching the news on her phone, footage of something monstrous and naked sauntering across the African continent. Commentators' buzzing voices speculated on what it was, where it was heading. Of the three voices, one had become too worked up with sobs and prayers to participate much in the conversation.

The other two droned their questions into Sheila's living room, pressing her harder against her boyfriend. One of them guessed the being in question was heading toward the Holy Land. The other reluctantly agreed. Neither was specific as to *which* Holy Land: Mecca or Jerusalem or Riyadh or some other no one paid attention to anymore. Just the Holy Land. The conversation veered off at that point into a debate on the meaning of *holy* in these dark times. They spoke over each other in competition and fear, trying to pin blame, at some point wondering if the being that had risen from its hole in that indistinct South African township was a monster or the savior they were all looking for.

How come it's so blurry, asked the newest comment posted under the live feed's discussion. A moment later someone commented, *People are guessing it can't be photographed. That anyone who actually sees it for real goes bonkers.*

Rick gently turned the phone his way and read the comments. With his other hand he aimed the TV's remote, as if at any moment he would decide to shut down the news and put on some mindless comedy show. Ten minutes later, when he'd finished scrolling through the phone's conversation, the other hand had not moved. The TV remained dark.

He finally mumbled, "People are just making stuff up at this point."

Sheila closed her eyes and pressed her face into his arm. "Probably."

Behind them, Brent farted from his chair at the kitchen table. The boys laughed. They were playing a board game, sitting across from each other and pretending the husk of their father, sitting in his customary end seat, was participating. Brent only stared down at the board while Emmett and Doyle took turns moving his piece for him.

Ricky nudged his shoulder enough to get her attention. Sheila sighed and sat straighter on the couch.

He nodded behind them. "What are we going to do with him?"

She glanced back to the boys playing and laughing and pretending Brent was listening. She shook her head, wanting to say, *Let's kill him, shove his head into the toilet and see if he snaps back*, but knew that could never be her suggestion. Not in front of the boys. Instead, she went with the easier option. The one Ricky wanted, and the only real one left to them.

"I'll pack the boys up tomorrow and we'll move in with you. I guess."

"He'll be fine here, by himself."

"No, he won't. Or *it* won't. Brent's gone."

Ricky looked about to say something, then showed surprising wisdom by staying silent.

*   *   *

Over the past month, the desire to come to this place had been like a rash just under the skin that worsened with every strange twist in reality since the day people better than he, apparently, had been taken from the world. Each wave of desire to come up here was a little stronger, made a little more sense. Nabib had practically run out of the apartment, hesitating at the door to the inner staircase. In Case of Fire Use Stairs, the sign read. Well, the world was on fire in so many ways, wasn't it? He pushed through and took the steps two at a time for the first two floors, then slowed and caught his breath for the final flight to the roof.

The roof door had been locked once upon a time, but at some point been broken open. The cold night air swirled around him as he cleared the narrow kiosk surrounding the doorway. The steady beat of aluminum vents buckling under the constant wind around him became a chorus accompanying his walk to the edge. Only there did the sounds of the city reach him. He wasn't that far from the street: three floors up from his own, four more to the pavement. How far was that, he wondered? Seven times nine feet?

Far enough. If he did it right.

Nabib wondered if he should face Mecca when he jumped.

29

Was that blasphemy? Did it matter? Tradition dictated *Qibla* to be southeast toward the Ka'ba. He stepped from the edge, considered a moment before walking across the roof in some semblance of that direction. The corner of Ames and Jacoby. One of those streets will need to be cleaned soon . . .

Stop. Don't.

Nabib knelt atop the short, raised edge at the corner of the roof. Should he pray? No, that would only be stalling. He took in a deep, cold breath and stepped up onto the raised ledge. Far off across the lower rooftops, the occasional figure moved. Headlights swam slowly between buildings, moving deeper through the city until they reached the ocean. He was pretty sure the water was in that direction. Farther still, along the horizon, a red glow spread. What time was it? Had he become so distracted the sun was already rising? Nothing else that far away would be so easy to see from here.

If he checked the time, Nabib knew it wouldn't yet be one o'clock in the morning. So, he did not check. *Last chance to turn away*, he thought, then moaned out loud, as if answering the thought.

The future was before him, but there was no hope in it. Anything he'd considered to be true *hope* in his life, even since boyhood, was behind him. Lost in the past.

Gone.

Whatever that amber light rising in the southeast might be, he would not wait for it to reveal itself. *You could stay*, the light said, *but in truth I do not care. I never will.*

Nabib's left foot hovered beyond the edge of this final corner of his world.

He hesitated. What if death was not escape? If the world had truly descended as far as he feared, what was waiting after? He imagined himself dragged through some hellish sewer then shat back through Boney's South African hole, or spat from the mouth of that latest bit of news wandering across the dark continent.

If he just stayed under his hood and stopped talking to anyone, maybe the world would begin to make sense someday. Of anything, *that* thought made him take the final step. Nabib fell into the space between future and past. One he discarded as undesirable; the other apparently had discarded him for the same reason.

For the first time in his life, facing the onrushing pavement,

Nabib prayed there was nothing waiting for him beyond.

Day 93

Brent opened his eyes. Upright again. Back on the couch. Couch? He'd been in the kitchen a moment ago. A week ago. What day was today? Since the work people told him he should go home and not return, this house had become the only world left to him. He slowly scanned the living room, wondering if the woman had returned . . . her name was gone to him now, like his old job. Everything in the house was empty: the shelves beside the television screen, which flashed confusing images, the cabinets where he used to find food. Those had been empty a long time now. His gaze finally settled on a ceramic frog filled with dead flowers. The frog stared back.

Brent sighed, and the weightless feeling filled him with pain again. *Close your eyes*, he told himself. *It must be time to sleep, because you are tired.* He did not. Instead, he took one final breath.

Eventually, the air escaped of its own accord, drifting into the room unseen and unheard. The empty body remained upright even after death, eyes open, drying, staring at the images flashing across its face and making no more sense of them than when it had been alive. It looked content, as if waiting for the moment its loving family returned.

House of Horrors
Chad Anctil

Dylan and Eric slipped through the rusted chain-link fence and overgrown weeds, keeping an eye out for security or anyone else who might object to their evening excursion into the abandoned amusement park.

For Rhode Islanders of a certain age, summer was synonymous with the trinity of school vacation activities: Del's Lemonade; hot, crowded beaches; and the Rocky Point Amusement Park. For following generations, however—like Dylan and Eric's—Rocky Point had become either a tale of wistful nostalgia or one of lost innocence and temptation.

The teens crept along the perimeter of the once bustling park, weeds and vines already reclaiming the once well-maintained outskirts of the midway.

"You're sure we can get in?" Eric peered into the growing gloom. Strange structures cast long, sinister shadows as the August sun dropped below the horizon.

"Derek and Angela were there two weeks ago." Dylan led Eric between empty concession stands. "They said there's a door with a broken lock. Nobody's doing maintenance anymore, so it should still be open."

They paused underneath the steel tracks of a broken roller coaster, surveying the skeletal frames of long-forgotten rides silhouetted against the dusk-hued sky. Faded and peeling paint distorted the names of the dismantled rides and attractions not yet sold or scrapped: Skydiver, Musik Express, and the Rock 'n' Roll.

"You're sure nobody's around?" Eric scanned the area, shifting nervously at every shadowy movement. "I feel like we're not alone."

"There's no full-time security anymore," Dylan said, "but a car comes through every few hours. If there's anyone else here, they're like us—they shouldn't be here. We're almost there; it's across the midway from that Ferris wheel-looking thing."

They checked for movement one more time before making their way across the cracked pavement to their final goal. The ride they'd come looking for was a monument to a glorious bygone era. The mismatched castle facade and pulp horror font emblazoned across the front of the building—*House of Horrors*—would not have looked out of place on the set of an Ed Wood film, but in the thickening twilight of the abandoned midway, the sight gave both boys a chill despite the warm summer air.

Neither had ever been to the park when it was open, only heard tales from parents and older friends who'd experienced the place before it had finally closed its towering gates. Shadows grew darker as the pair took in the sight.

"It doesn't look that scary." Eric didn't sound convinced.

"That was the point. It's not supposed to," Dylan said, near a whisper. Having finally reached their hallowed goal, they hesitated. "It was like, campy horror, not real scares. But everyone said it was the best ride in the place. I've always wanted to see it."

"Well, we've seen it. Do we really have to—" Eric started, but Dylan pushed forward, heading through the broken teeth and into the grinning skull marking the entrance to the ride.

*   *   *

The greasy metal tracks for guiding ride carts through the attraction were still bolted to the grimy concrete floor, though the carts had long since been stored or sold off. Eric started to follow the path the ride would have taken, but his progress was barred at the heavily-boarded cart entrance.

"People lined up halfway across the midway to ride this thing," Dylan said, admiring the faded facade and spook show aesthetic. "I've seen the pictures from when Rocky Point was, like, the most popular spot in Rhode Island. It was packed."

"Must have been a loooong time ago," Eric said, looking dubiously at the decrepit ride: the small piles of dead leaves and garbage trapped in the corners and crevices, the paint peeling off of every surface.

"The door is this way." Dylan led Eric around a corner, under a rusted railing, and along an age-stained wall until they found the service entrance. As they'd hoped, the door was not locked, and Dylan and Eric slipped from the rapidly fading light of summer into the damp darkness of the abandoned amusement ride.

Dylan pulled a red, plastic Ray-O-Vac flashlight out of his back pocket. Its sickly yellow glow barely illuminated anything around them, but was enough to navigate the debris-strewn floor as they moved deeper into the House of Horrors proper.

"Whoa," Eric said in an awed whisper. The flashlight beam illuminated one of the old ride cars, all chipped and weathered blue paint, a werewolf in a bull's-eye emblazoned across the front like it adorned some kind of World War II bomber. Dylan's hand slipped across the time-worn lap bar that had closed upon countless gleeful riders.

They examined the cart like archaeologists exploring a tomb of Egyptian antiquity. Eventually, Dylan said, "I see the track up ahead," and they continued on. They moved through mounds of garbage and park refuse that had fallen when the ride was active or been tossed down below the tracks after it had closed. Dylan saw a popcorn box, broken boards, soda cans, and other, undefinable objects flash beneath the weak beam of his light, his heart pounding in his chest with excitement and just a hint of fear.

They made it to the narrow wooden walkway following the tracks and began moving along it. The wood was stained with age, worn smooth with decades of use, and everything smelled of the grease and rust that seemed to hold the place together. The building settled, creaking and moaning as they made their way through the black light-painted tunnels, carefully exploring the claustrophobic rooms that had entertained so many people over the decades.

"What was that?" Eric asked as they moved up a ramp following a heavy chain embedded in the track, where the ride pulled cars up to the second floor.

"What was what?" Dylan shone the light on the far wall, where there was a crude painting of what looked like a mountain surrounded by Halloween-style bats—a grade-school interpretation of Transylvania.

"I heard something below us," Eric whispered, peering down over the shaky wooden railing.

"We're just knocking debris off the walkway and it's making noise down there," Dylan said, shining the light down into the darkness. He thought he saw something dart out of the way of the light, and started.

"Did you see that?" Eric hissed.

"It was just shadows." Dylan shone the light at Eric. "Or maybe rats—the place has been abandoned for years. It could be rats, but rats can't hurt us. Let's keep going."

They continued up to the second floor, following the steel track around Halloween-mask monsters and garishly-painted, papier-mâché ghouls mounted on pneumatic rods to titillate and frighten those brave enough to make the trek. They passed a steel cage holding the remains of some kind of display: mannequin parts and what looked like a hard hat still sitting inside the four-foot by four-foot box. Dylan couldn't see a way to get in to grab a souvenir without damaging the place and—more importantly—making a lot of unwanted noise. They headed farther along the track.

"Did it get darker?" Eric asked nervously.

Dylan pointed the light toward him. The bulb seemed to be losing its glow. "The sun's gone down. There's no more light coming in from outside, so yeah it's pretty dark. I think I've seen enough. You want to get out of here?"

"Yeah, that's a great idea. Do we turn around? Or—"

"No. If we keep following this track, it should bring us back to where we started, by the service exit. It's just a big figure-eight kind of loop, from what I've heard. The ramp back down to the first floor should be right around this bend."

As they'd hoped, the track took a downward slope, and they followed along on the service ramp. No chain on this side; Eric figured the cars sped down using only heavy plastic wheels and gravity. *It must have been quite a ride*, he mused.

"This ramp seems to go down farther." Dylan sounded anxious. "We only walked up a few feet on the other side, but it feels like we've dropped more than double that, and it's still going down."

"It's probably just your mind playing tricks?" Eric said, more a question than a solution. "We're still following the track, and that has to bring us back to the start, right?"

They continued down in silence, the only sounds their footsteps on the old wooden walkway and the creaks and sighs of the decrepit building.

A loud click sounded, below and to the left. They froze.

"What the hell was that?" Eric whispered, near panic.

"I have no idea." Dylan's voice shook as he pointed the flashlight toward the sound. The sallow beam barely punctured the darkness now, and Dylan feared the batteries were nearly expended.

Eyes glinted in the dim light, then disappeared into the darkness.

"We've got to get the hell out of here," Eric hissed.

"It's just rats," Dylan said, weak flashlight beam still aimed below. "Big carnival midway rats."

"That's not helping *at all*. How do we get out of here?"

"We're nearly at the bottom of the ramp." Dylan started walking quickly. "We just need to get to that maintenance door and we're out."

They got to the bottom, followed the track to the left, around a dark corner—and stopped.

"Fuck!" Dylan shined the flashlight at the floor, where the old steel track ended abruptly. The concrete floor was scarred and scratched, as if the track had been torn up by massive hands.

"Oh, what the hell?" Eric squeaked. "Where did it go?"

"It's okay, we can just—"

More clicking sounds shattered the silence, closer this time, echoing strangely in the oddly-shaped space.

"Let's go back up." They retreated toward the ramp they'd just descended—then a sound like a glass bottle rattling across the old concrete floor caused both teens to jump.

"You still think it's rats?" Eric said angrily, voice rising.

"Whoever's down here, it's not funny!" Dylan shouted. "We'll kick your ass if you don't knock it off!"

"Really, Dylan?" Eric snarled, turning on his friend. "You really think that's going to help? Let's just get the hell out of here! Now!"

In the darkness behind them, something skittered across the concrete. It sounded bigger than a rat.

They spun, the light momentarily catching something moving, low and awkwardly, away from them. There was the impression of limbs both too long and strangely jointed, but hard to make out in the gloom.

The fading flashlight finally went out. The sudden darkness was absolute.

"Fuck, fuck . . ." Dylan slapped the cheap plastic flashlight a half dozen times. Weak glints of light appeared and disappeared with the first few strikes, then nothing. The flashlight was dead, and the two teens were frozen in the pitch darkness.

"Oh God, oh God," Eric whispered, huddling close to Dylan, who still shook the dead flashlight, hoping for a miracle. "What do we do now? What the hell is down here with us?"

"Just stay calm," Dylan said, but his trembling voice belied his words. "We just have to find the track on the floor and follow it out. We'll crawl if we have to, and once we get out of this level, we can find another way to get to the maintenance door."

"In the dark?" Eric said. "And what the hell is down here with us? You saw that thing before the flashlight went out. What was that?"

"We don't know what we saw. It might not have been anything—a trick of the light. Let's try to follow the track and get the hell out of here. I'm going to get down on the ground and feel around for it."

Dylan dropped to his knees and heard Eric do the same. He felt his way across the damp, grimy floor, searching blindly for the track or any indication of where it might have been. He found small rocks and pieces of undefinable debris, but no track. "Where is it?" he whispered to himself. "We weren't that far away from it." He hadn't been paying attention to where he was standing when the flashlight had died, and he wasn't sure what direction he'd been facing in relation to the ramp. "Eric, feel over to your left. It must be over there." He heard Eric shuffle off to his left, just behind him—then came a shout and a shriek.

"*What the hell was that?*"

"What? What happened?" Dylan turned, trying to follow Eric's shouts in the darkness.

"I touched something . . . *alive*. It moved!" In the blackness, Eric backed into him.

"What, like a rat?" Dylan jerked his head around, looking for anything to focus on in the pitch-black space.

"No, like a hand! Like some kind of fucked-up hand!" Dylan could feel him shaking. "I touched it and it jerked away."

"We have to find that track. I'm all turned around in the dark, but I think it's this way. Just stay close to me."

Dylan crawled in the direction he believed the rail was in, hands scrabbling across the cold floor, pushing aside trash, bits of glass, and what felt like animal bones. He moved in what he hoped was a straight line, but wasn't feeling anything but dirty concrete. Panicked breathing followed as Eric shuffled along.

"I've got something!" Dylan exclaimed. Then: "Shit. It's the wall, not the rail. We can make this work though. The wall has to lead us somewhere, right?"

Eric crawled up beside him. "This is concrete, Dylan. When we entered, the service door was set in a structural wall."

"So?"

"So," Eric said, "that means we must be in some kind of basement level, below the actual ride. We're at least one level below the service entrance we entered through."

"So there must be a way—"

"If this *is* some kind of storage level, there's probably no way out from down here. We're below ground level. I think that ramp may be the only way up."

More chittering echoed around the space.

"Oh, I really hate that sound," Dylan admitted.

They stood in the darkness listening to strange noises come from every direction. The things in the dark—whatever they were—seemed to be getting closer, but because of the acoustics, they couldn't be sure.

"If we can keep in a straight line perpendicular to the wall, we've got to hit the track, right?" Eric asked, working his brain around the current situation.

"If we can stay straight, maybe," Dylan said. "Make sure you're starting as close to square as you can, with the wall behind you, and walk heel-toe, heel-toe. That should keep us in a straight line."

They walked slowly from the wall, heel-to-toe as Dylan had suggested. After four steps, something scraped across the floor several feet from where they stood, making them both yell out and freeze in place. Fetid air brushed them, disturbed by something passing close by. Something big.

"It touched me!" Dylan shrieked, lashing out blindly in the darkness.

The chittering came again, closer this time.

"Something's breathing on me," Eric said in a terrified whisper.

"We need to run," Dylan said softly. "Just run straight ahead. We have to find the ramp out of here. On three."

"On three." Eric confirmed nervously.

"One . . . two . . . three!"

*   *   *

"The morning security team found them behind the House of Horrors, just after eight a.m.," the paramedic said, shining a flashlight into a pair of vacant eyes.

"Two males, apparently in their teens," the other paramedic said into the radio handset. "Both unconscious and unresponsive. Neither show any external injuries, aside from minor scrapes and abrasions."

"What do you think happened to these two?" the first paramedic asked as they loaded the boys into the back of the ambulance.

"Probably drugs," the other paramedic said, locking the stretcher down. "Let's get out of here. This place is giving me the creeps."

Sparrow and the
Shredded Heart
Morgan Sylvia

She returned, as I thought she would, in moonlight and dusty shadow. I feel her presence as soon as I step through the peeling door.

The house looks smaller than I remembered. As hard as I've tried to forget this place, I never quite managed to. I look around, finding a strange mix of familiar and unfamiliar. I walk through empty rooms, small, forgotten details jumping out at me. The pencil marks Mom left on the walls to gauge our growth. The broken handle on the back screen door, a reminder of the July Fourth water balloon fight, when I chased Dad out of the kitchen. The details on the crown molding.

Dead flies crunch beneath my heels as I cross the floor.

Every step I take draws me into the past, as though my footsteps move me back through time, reviving the faded kitchen to sunlight and color. A layer of dust covers everything, but my brain interposes a different era, recalling a time when the kitchen had been bright and sunny.

Once there was laughter here. Once there was life.

There is just thick fetid stillness now.

I trace my finger over the Formica table, following the lacy spiderweb pattern. We had pancakes there that morning, none of us knowing it was our last family meal. Mom chattered on the phone with her sister as she spooned thick batter onto the griddle, the cordless set cradled between ear and shoulder. Dad read the news and grumbled about sports and interest rates, tossing our dog,

Pippin, small pieces of sausage whenever Mom's back was turned. Sparrow shredded her toast and pancakes. She had a strange fascination for tearing her food apart before she ate it.

This silence isn't peaceful: it stifles and strangles and chokes.

There are still traces of us here and there. I open the cupboard, expecting it to be empty. Instead, I find canned goods from a decade ago. Dad's work gloves sit on the kitchen counter amidst a mass of dead flies. Sparrow's report card is still stuck to the fridge with magnets from our old dentist. Three *A*'s, two *B*'s, and two *C*'s. She always excelled where I failed; I was a word girl, while she was a math whiz. I found history intriguing; she scraped by with a *C-* that year, but aced her science and biology courses.

I still remember the day Dad brought her home. She'd been a preemie and had to stay in the hospital for nearly a month. "She's so tiny," he said, eyes brimming with emotion as she reached her teeny fingers around his thumb. "So fragile. I can feel her heart beating. So frail and weak. A little sparrow."

After that, we always called her Sparrow.

When we searched the woods that day, that's what we shouted.

I move on to the living room. My footsteps leave tread marks in a thick layer of dust. In the living room, a *TV Guide* lies on the floor, surrounded by yellowed coupon pages from the Sunday paper.

The silence upstairs is heavy, almost tangible. The stairs still creak. I pause at her room, then open the door. It's untouched, a shrine, everything just as it was. One of her dolls sits in the middle of her desk. I wonder what would happen if she came out of the woods and found the place empty, everything gone but her belongings.

Then again, I don't really have to wonder. I know exactly how that feels.

I move on to my old room. The note is still on my dresser. *You can have the house and the Jeep. We've unlocked your college fund and paid the insurance in full for the year.* And then, to punctuate the point, a receipt from the insurance agent.

That was it. Not even a goodbye. What they *hadn't* said screamed out from the empty spaces on the page. *We blame you. We can't forgive you. It should have been you.*

Even now, the sour empty feeling of grief hits hard. I wipe the tears away, crumple the note and toss it onto the floor, then take a breath, collect myself, and look around.

I'm not even sure why I've come. It's not like I'll get any kind of closure. Anything I left behind ten years ago and haven't missed by now isn't likely to be important. Mom and Dad took everything they cared about, even the dog. It's only my own things I have to sort through.

I work the whole afternoon, looking through the wreckage of our lives. I hold myself together until I come across one of Sparrow's old drawings in the den. She had drawn a bunch of birds and scrawled a caption in childishly large letters. *Sparrows represent hope, love, and community. They also announce the arrival of a loved one. They live in flocks because they're safer that way.*

And then, she'd drawn a heart and put the word *Family* in it.

*   *   *

I stay out of the dining room as long as I can. As soon as I step in, I'm back in that night.

I hear the echo of angry voices in the air: a cacophony of shouting, screaming, tears and sobs and grief. Memories rush back: the flashing red and blue lights outside. Flashlight beams crisscrossing the woods. We were all over the news by then. Most of our extended family had shown up, bringing casseroles and coffee, their faces pale and pinched, as ours were.

They kept giving me the side-eye.

Things fell apart as the cop questioned me again. "There's nothing in that ruined house," he said. "And there's no sign of disturbance, other than her footprints. And a dead bird on a bloody plate." He looked at me. "Why did you go into that place?"

"I wanted the dress for prom." I sniffed. "It was so beautiful . . . Very Wednesday Addams."

Mom frowned. "Who?"

The cop ignored this. "So you went back for the dress, and Sparrow went with you, and you got lost."

"We didn't get lost. The woods *changed* around us. There was no way out. We didn't walk into the void, or step into mist. We found ourselves on a path, and we kept trying different turns, but they all only led back to the house. And we saw this creature . . . it looked like a massive groundhog or something, but it was the size of a cow. Then I came around a bend in the path and we were somehow back at that house again, but there were lights inside. I put my arm out, like this, to tell Sparrow to stop . . . and she just wasn't there. I saw her looking at me from the door. There was someone with her. I saw her get pulled in, and the house went dark and the door slammed and I started screaming. That's when they found me."

The cop frowned. "Who was with her?"

Josephine, the wind whispered.

Josephine, the forest breathed.

"Josephine," I told him.

"Josephine McGrady has been dead for fifty years," the cop said coldly. "This will go better for you if you tell the truth now."

"I am telling the truth!"

Dad put his fist through the wall. "Stop with these lies!"

"I'm not lying." I was sobbing. "She's alive! I know she is!"

"Then tell us the truth!" Dad yelled, half-mad with rage, the vein popping in his neck. "Where is she? Just tell us. You were gone for three days. Where is she? Did she fall into a hole? You were supposed to be watching her!"

"The lady took her," I insisted.

They never believed me, no matter how many times I told them what had happened. I can't blame them. I barely believed myself.

The rest is a blur. Screaming and shouting, glasses breaking. Mom, crying and wailing, keening: a scream ripped from the bottom of her soul. Dad threw the glass against the wall. Mom sank into her sister's arms, sobbing.

I curled into the corner, crying into Pippin's fur.

*   *   *

By the time the light starts to fade, I've stuffed four boxes and two garbage bags. Random choices: my old coffee mug, a few tattered paperbacks, a couple of pairs of jeans, and shoes so outdated they're now back in style.

The slant of the sunbeams on the dusty linoleum floor tells me I'm running out of daylight. I had planned to be in and out in a few hours, just making a final sweep before I turned the place over to the cleaning crew and realtor, respectively. Instead, I just sit there, flipping through old photo albums and looking around at the debris of shattered lives while the sun sinks toward the trees.

As the last light bleeds from the sky, I feel the once-familiar sense of unease that always came with nightfall here. The sense of something out there, watching and waiting.

I haul a load to the car, then turn to the den. I didn't think there was much left, but I find the closets and shelves in there are full.

There's no way I'm getting this done tonight. I resign myself to staying over, turn the radio on, and get back to work.

Eventually I grow tired enough to stumble back to my old bed and slip into nightmares.

*   *   *

I'm not sure what wakes me. Some sixth sense, perhaps. The feeling that something is wrong. Something makes a faint rustle in the shadows. I freeze, every hair on my body standing on end. "Sparrow?"

I hear a tiny *click*: the crack of a stiff knuckle. Her elbow, which always popped. I open my eyes to a thick, swirling darkness.

I don't want to look in the corner, but I can't stop myself.

She's wearing her old clothes. The red hoodie. Her blue Chucks. The old, faded jeans. The shark tooth and crystal necklace she'd taken to wearing that year. She's changed in the intervening time. I suppose that was only to be expected. What I didn't expect to see was a faint, opaque visage of her old self. I see, behind it, the rotted flesh, exposing the bones beneath. Bits of hair still cling to her head. I can still see her face, though, superimposed over the shadows.

She hasn't grown as she was supposed to. She's trapped at eight forever.

Moonlight carries her whisper to me. "You left me."

I scoot up in the single bed, pushing back against the wall, right up to the old pink damask wallpaper I'd always hated. "I didn't. I didn't leave you, Sparrow. You know I'd never leave you. That thing tricked me."

She comes closer. She looks pixelated, like static. "She's angry now."

"Sparrow." My voice comes out cracked. "Go toward the light."

"There isn't any," she whispers. "They trapped a ghost in static,

45

and they broke a hole in time."

Her eyes glow black. Her voice, when she next speaks, sounds directly into my ear. That should be impossible, as there's a wall behind me. But then, nothing about this should be possible.

"Sparrow—"

She cuts me off. When she opens her mouth, all I hear is a high-pitched whine, like static.

Or birdsong.

She dissolves into static black noise, and I cry myself to sleep.

*   *   *

We moved here the summer before my freshman year. I don't remember ever feeling either comfortable or uncomfortable in the house back then. It was run down and dilapidated, but that was all my parents could afford with the price of real estate soaring. Things were normal enough to be boring. I settled in at school, found my place in the drama club, and even got my first boyfriend: Jimmy Duncan. Sparrow was growing like a reed and fully leaning into the role of cute but annoying little sister. Mom and Dad worked all week, then went to the Elks or the pool hall on the weekends with their friends. We hadn't explored the woods behind the house too much; Mom's paranoia about caves and sinkholes had rubbed off on both of us. Sparrow, particularly, was always scared that she would fall into a hole. So, we were wary enough to stay out.

At least, until the day our dog, Pippin, ran off.

I wish I could say I remember that moment as though it were yesterday, but honestly, it's blurry. I know Sparrow and I were in the yard. She was tossing a basketball into the hoop Dad had hung over the garage while I tried to teach Pippin to fetch.

Then a gray cat ran by, and Pippin took off after it. He was out of sight in moments, ignoring our calls. I remember this sinking feeling that we'd never find him, that he'd be out there by himself, lost and cold and hungry, and it was all my fault because I hadn't had him on the leash.

We both chased him, running through the unfamiliar woods. We walked for what seemed like hours, calling him.

Eventually, we came across a ruined white farmhouse. Pippin sat before it, growling. I was surprised, more than anything. It was deep in the forest, and there were no driveways or roads along our street that could reach it. Looking around the back, I spotted the remnants of an overgrown dirt path that must once have been a road.

"Wow," Sparrow said. "Is this ours?"

"I don't know. I'm not sure where our property line stops."

She walked up the crumbling porch and peered through a dirty, spiderweb-coated window. "There's stuff inside," she said. "A lot of stuff. Oh my god! There's the cat! It must go in and out through that broken window." She opened the door and went in before I could stop her. "Kitty kitty!"

"Sparrow!" I started in after her, but pulled up short at the door.

She wasn't kidding. There really was a ton of stuff inside. Aside from the layer of dust, the place looked like a time capsule. We, of course, couldn't help but snoop, creeping around like spiders, rooting through the remnants of someone else's memories. Dishes, clothes, tools: everything looked untouched.

The closet was full of dresses. There was one in particular, an Edwardian black gown, that I loved. It was everything I wanted to be: glamorous, chic, mysterious, beautiful. It was the kind of dress a girl only gets once in her lifetime; something made for someone else, but really meant for her.

"It looks like it'll fit you," Sparrow said.

"It will," I said, holding it up. "I know it will."

We heard something in the shadows. The faintest clink of glass on glass. Then a thud sounded somewhere below us. That moment was my first taste of true terror. We both froze. She looked at me, eyes wide with fear, mouthing the words, *What was that?*

"Come on," I told Sparrow. "Let's go."

The second thud was much louder. The floor shook beneath our feet.

I didn't have to persuade her to run. We were both terrified, and raced back to the house, Pippin trotting along happily beside us. Sparrow went full speed, though she usually moved slowly, still afraid that a cave or well would open in the ground and swallow her.

Perhaps one did.

* * *

I told my friends about the house the next day.

"Oh, wow," Jimmy said. "You went into the old McGrady house?"

"That place is haunted as fuck," Mark said. "Some say the gates of hell are in the cellar."

I hit the joint they were passing around. "Who were the McGradys?"

"Josephine McGrady," Mark said. "She was some kinda witch or psychic. Always having séances, conjuring the dead, all that. Then she took up with some scientist. I forget his name . . . some kind of government black ops guy. People started going missing. Eventually, someone noticed that the McGrady's were . . . off. The cops searched the place, found all sorts of weird occult stuff and a crazy mad scientist's lab, but no bodies. Someone decided to get revenge, and they killed her kid. She went complete batshit after that. Shot three men, then vanished."

"We went in there a few times when I was a kid," Jimmy said. "The last time, we went down into the cellar. Found all sorts of weird symbols on the walls. Looked like they were written in blood. And that's not even the craziest bit. Someone was living down there. There was a mattress and some food wrappers."

My heart froze in my chest.

In my dream that night, I was Josephine, angry and hurt and driven beyond the brink of humanity. She had trapped one of them in the attic, bound his flesh with chains and ropes, bound his soul with whispers and words and black magic.

I stayed away from the house after that, though I felt its presence there, just out of sight. That part of the woods seemed darker, colder, emptier, though perhaps it was just my imagination. I went on with my freshman life: drama club, the literary journal, choir, band. Sparrow was into all the sports that year. Mom and Dad joined a bowling league.

I wonder what would have happened if Jimmy hadn't asked me to prom.

If I hadn't gone back for the dress.

*   *   *

The first night Sparrow came back, I thought at first that it was really her. I even saw individual blonde hairs shining in the moonlight.

Sparrow was facing the other direction, talking, muttering, though her voice was strange and garbled. "The woods were taller then, and the shadows smelled of pine. There were faces in the shadows. Faces in the trees. The singularity hadn't happened yet, but the seed was planted here."

"Sparrow?" I sat straight up in bed, the wave of relief washing over me in that moment almost tangible. "Sparrow, oh my God, are you all right? Where have you been?"

She kept muttering.

I pulled the blankets back and swung my legs over the bed. "Sparrow, we have to get you to a hospital." I remember standing, yelling for my parents. *"Mom! Dad! She's here! Sparrow's here!"*

Sparrow turned slowly and looked at me. "Time-space convergence is the key to it all. Travel time gets smaller as technology advances. Time is a river. Usually it just carries us downstream, but sometimes there are whirlpools and eddies. Sometimes entire lakes drain through holes the size of a dime. Sometimes a river runs backward, and no one knows why."

I jumped out of bed and rushed to hug her. There was nothing there. My arms found empty space. The spot where she stood was freezing cold. My ears filled with static. I stumbled back, frightened and confused. "Sparrow? Is that you?"

"It's all of us."

I saw her mouth moving, but somehow her voice was behind me. She spoke into my ears.

Her eyes were black.

The terror that rooted in me at that moment was an ice-cold fist gripping my heart, dragging it through the floor. It was a demon breathing down my neck.

"You're not my sister!" I screamed.

She opened her mouth, and the room filled with birdsong.

Footsteps down the hall. Dad threw my door open. Chaos ensued. I think that was the moment that broke us. They never believed I wasn't toying with them.

The next morning, as I sat on the porch, bleary eyed and dehydrated from crying, the gray cat sauntered out of the woods, a bird in its mouth.

*   *   *

A few weeks after I returned to school, I was sitting in biology class. The teacher, a thin, pale-faced man, droned on as he flipped through slides on a projector. "There are only a few species alive now that were around in the Pleistocene. The bone deposits have given us the most information, but there have been some remarkable finds elsewhere, such as the remnants of a polar bear in Breck Smith Cave. Some of the creatures that once lived here include a beaver the size of a bear, ancient tapir, a prehistoric horse, and a bison with six-foot horns. Ancient elephants once roamed these woods, as did the mastodons, and the giant bison, and the ground sloth. Our local geography is unique. We have over one hundred and thirty caves, many of which have been found to—"

Something hit the back of my head. I heard a hiss and a giggle behind me as I turned. Two girls were whispering. "Jimmy says she killed her sister," one of them said. "Took her to that house, the old McGrady place where the witch and the mad scientist chopped up all those people."

I got up, walked out, and never returned.

*   *   *

Sparrow visited me randomly after that. I never did find a pattern or reason for her appearances, though it was always in the middle of the night. Sometimes it was the new moon, sometimes waxing or waning, sometimes full. Sometimes she came every night; other times, she was gone for months. I guess time moves differently for the dead.

I only returned to the McGrady place once. The windows were black as I approached, and the woods were silent. But I felt something in there. A presence. All of the strength I'd never had in those years came to me at once. I screamed into the shadows. "Let her go!"

The darkness, of course, didn't answer.

*   *   *

Sparrow changed with each visit. She spoke in static and birdsong, in starlight and smoke and dust, murmuring about the mysteries of time and space and eons past. She said the same thing over and over and over again. "We inhale seconds and exhale years, and we dissolve into static and only then do we understand what we are—*molecules, salt, water, fat*—and what we were—*humans, imperfect*—and what we shall be—*eternal*. Time only exists within us, as our atoms are moving and rotating."

Sometimes, in her mutterings, she accused me of leaving her. Those were the moments that broke me and left me sobbing.

The visitations stopped when I moved to Europe. They say ghosts and demons can't cross water. Memories certainly can, and trauma, and pain. But I had gone numb by then. I rarely spoke to Mom and Dad, and only saw them at weddings and funerals. I burrowed into my work: forensics. I think, since I never got answers, I wanted to help others find closure.

Looking back now, from a clinical perspective, I think something in me always hoped that I'd find her.

I never did.

*   *   *

The recurring dreams started when I returned to the States. In them, I am running through our house, only the house is changing, shifting. Closets open on halls. Our bathroom door opens onto a desert. Halls stretch and move and groan.

I hear a low growl behind me and turn. It's Pippin, but not Pippin. His hackles are raised, his teeth are bared, and his ears are flat. He lunges at me, nipping my leg. I race out of the room, slamming the door behind me, and turn to run down the hall, only to barrel into the wall.

Everything is backward. Everything is shifting, changing.

Eventually, I find the front door. Instinctively, I run for it. When I open it, I find myself again in the cemetery where we once buried an empty coffin.

Sparrow's funeral party stands before me, staring at me. She stands with them, pixelated but whole. I look down at the ground. A dead bird sits on the leaves.

In the distance, the sky is turning red.

For some reason, every time I wake from that dream, I remember a moment from my eighth-grade science class. My teacher, bald and pudgy, his glasses reflecting the glare of the overhead lights. "Some static—what you see as snow on your TV—is energy left over from the Big Bang."

Nothing can be created or destroyed, he kept telling us. *Things can only change form.*

In the intervening years, I managed to convince myself I'd had a break in sanity. That I'd seen something and blocked it out. I pretended the tension between my parents was the reason I'd fled the day after my eighteenth birthday.

Perhaps fled isn't the right word. They'd already left me behind. I just refused to rot here, refused to wait here. That was what they really wanted of me. They wanted me to stay in that house, alone, in case she came back.

They weren't wrong about that. After all, she did come back. But not as she had been.

*   *   *

I wake from disjointed occult dreams to strange, shifting light. The morning light is pale and pine scented. Pulling the old sheer curtains aside, I look over the trees and find a murmuration of birds dancing in the wind. They twist and turn as one, following some ancient choreography stamped into their DNA.

In the light of day, none of it seems real. By the time I shower and stumble downstairs, I've almost convinced myself it was just a dream.

Then I see the feathers spread out on the Formica kitchen table. They weren't there yesterday. I definitely would have noticed. Especially given what they spelled.

You left me.

I reach out to touch one of the feathers. It turns to dust in my hand. When I turn, I find the dress draped over Dad's old armchair. The bottom is folded into the ass groove he carved into the chair over years of watching football games and reading newspapers.

I should have been terrified, but instead, for the first time in years, a sense of peace falls over me. I quietly undress and put the dress on. It fits like a glove, though it looks a bit silly with my sneakers.

I walk to the back porch and stand staring out into the tangle of dead, gray-brown wood. From somewhere out in the woods, I hear the trumpeting roar of some massive animal that hasn't walked this earth for eons.

I know now what I must do.

I go to the garage, find the oil cans, dump the contents onto the kitchen floor, and set the place alight. My feet draw me into the shadow of their own accord as smoke rises through the air. Some part of my brain screams at me that I'm only going to my own death. The rest of me knows this is as it should be.

In time, I find myself standing before the McGrady ruin. The blackness behind the cracked, dirty windows is absolute, thick as oil and holding a menace I feel in every nerve of my body. I sense the dead things everywhere: ghosts in the air, ghosts in the mist. I can almost see them, but the shivering shadows melt away when I look at them directly.

Something moves behind the grimy glass.

She waits for me, inside, with the dust and the dead things. Her face is whole again, pale in the darkness. She speaks in that crackling static voice. "I knew you'd come back."

Sparrow. I mouth the word, but only staticky birdsong escapes my lips.

A second.

A minute.

A season (suddenly it is autumn).

I blink. And, just like that night, suddenly the house is lit up. The paint appears fresh, the steps are sound, and the property is neat and well-kept, not the tangled mess I recalled. The sound of music and laughter echoes into the night. Light glows from the windows. Figures move inside. Voices and laughter float out into the night, mingling with the tinny sound of the Victrola in the background.

A thick fog surrounds us.

"Sparrow?" I take a step forward, peering through the rolling mists. "Marco?"

And the reply: "Polo."

The mist clears a bit. Josephine stands on the porch wearing a full-length black dress, much like the one I have on, pale face smeared with blood. Behind her stands a group of children. Or things that were once children. Their eyes are black, and there are just holes in their chests where their hearts should be. But they aren't just dead children with her; there are others there as well.

People of all ages, colors, eras.

Sparrow moves forward and takes the hand Josephine offers. Josephine opens the door and steps aside, waving me in. "Come in. We've been waiting for you."

"Let her go." My voice is almost a growl. I hold my hand out. "Sparrow, come with me."

She shakes her head. "I can't. But you can come with me."

I hear the roar again.

"Mastodon," Josephine says. "Do come in, please. It's really not safe out here."

Static screams into my ears as I walk up the stairs. And then she is there. Real. Breathing. Atoms and molecules. Even the mole on her cheek, which I'd forgotten. Relief washes over me in waves. Decades' worth of pain vanishes in an instant. I fold her into my arms, sobbing. "I didn't leave you, Sparrow."

"You did," she says. "I went back once, and there was nothing there but an old burned-out ruin covered in vines."

The smell of smoke carries on the wind. I look back toward our house. The sky looks faintly orange. My throat is tight. "I never wanted to leave you."

"You were planning to, even then," Sparrow says calmly. "Always talking about going to college in another town. We all leave each other, in the end. Just as Mom and Dad left you."

"She's right." Josephine's voice is crisp. "We are all abandoned, are we not? In a grave, if we are lucky. If we are really lucky, even in the grave we aren't completely abandoned for a generation or two." She tucks a stray lock of Sparrow's hair into place. "She's come a long way toward understanding."

"I got trapped here, in the now," Sparrow says. "Because I stopped to pet the cat."

"That," Josephine says, "is no cat. Come in."

As I turn, I notice the photo framed on the wall. It is old, from the Victorian age: blurry gray and white. A young girl sits with a kitten on her lap. Her father stands behind her, handlebar mustache below sad eyes.

Dad and Sparrow.

I feel dizzy. "How can this . . ."

"Twists in time," Josephine says. "We inhale seconds and we exhale years, and we dissolve into static and only then do we understand what we are—*molecules, salt, water, fat*—and what we were—*humans, imperfect*—and what we shall be—*eternal*."

I stare at her as another roar echoes from the forest.

"Come," Josephine says. "Dinner is ready."

We follow her into the dining room. The feast is spread out on a long table set with expensive silverware and delicate china plates. Heaping salvers of food steam on the table: silver platters of hearts, brains, eyes, organs. About a dozen others are seated. The guests are finely dressed. Dead, all of them, I assume. Every now and then, the façade of life fades, and I see the dark eyes, the static, the pixilation. A Victrola plays big band music. It distorts frequently, fading in and out.

I take my seat.

Josephine serves us herself. "Sparrow?"

"A heart, please," Sparrow says.

"Good choice, dear." Josephine spoons a dark piece of meat onto the china. Sparrow immediately starts shredding it, using both the dinner fork and the dessert fork. "Use the salad fork, sweetheart."

Sparrow changes forks and continues shredding the meat.

"The heart," Josephine continues. "Passion, strength, and love. It's traditional for hunters to eat the hearts of their kill on the field. Doctor Arowisch?"

A man with thin greasy hair clears his throat. "Liver, please. And a bit of tongue in garlic sauce."

"The seat of the spirit. Houses our spiritual consciousness." She pauses. "I can't recall what the tongue is for."

"The voice of the gods." A thin, pale woman with dark eyes and curls escaping from her updo provides the answer. "I prefer kidney, myself. Sparrow, dear, you really should just cut it."

Sparrow ignores her.

Josephine looks at me. "And for the guest of honor?"

Sparrow looks at me, chewing. "Give her a heart, too."

"Don't talk and chew." Josephine serves me. "Would you like more champagne? I didn't set up the fountain, but there's plenty more."

"No, thank you." I say, taking a bite. The organ bursts in my mouth. It tastes of power and life and vitality. I know that it's dream food, but why can I taste it? Why am I aware of the fact that I'm dreaming?

"It's the singularity," Sparrow tells me. "You can feel hot and cold here. You can't in dreams. You only know the concepts of those things."

I stare at her.

"I can hear your thoughts now," she explains.

"We all can," Josephine says. There is a nuance of warning in her voice.

They all stare at me. More have filed in; they stand behind the table. Others filter into the parlor and living room.

Josephine pops an eyeball into her mouth, then daintily dabs her lips with a napkin. "Have you ever heard of the Bolton Strid?"

I take another bite of the heart. "No, I haven't."

"It's considered the deadliest river in the world." Josephine puts the napkin down. "It looks innocent, even pretty, when you see it. A peaceful, idyllic little brook, meandering and bubbling among mossy rocks. But that is the danger. It isn't what it seems. Due to a geographical anomaly, the river turns sideways. So, what appears to be a gentle stream is actually a very deep and narrow river. There's no bottom. At least, not that anyone has found and survived. They say the fatality rate for those who fall in is one hundred percent."

"That area," says Doctor Arowisch, "like this one, is riddled with caves, though that really isn't the point. Salt?"

"Yes, please." I take the silver shaker, sprinkle white flakes, look around at the dead. "I'm afraid I don't understand the point at all. What does this have to do with Sparrow?"

"Time folds here," Josephine says. "Like that river."

The cat jumps onto the sideboard, licking its paws. The other woman shoos it away with a clucking sound.

I remember Mom, reading us fairy tales. *Never accept fairy food.* My lips feel moist. There is blood on my hand when I wipe my lips. The rotting corpse in the corner isn't missing it, but I can see the empty, bloody cavity where the heart should have been.

"Thank you for dinner." I stand, wiping the blood from my face. "We have to go back now. Come, Sparrow. Let's go home."

Her face grows somber. "We can't," she says. "There's nothing left out there to go back to."

"What do you mean? Sparrow, let's go."

"She doesn't understand," Sparrow says. "It's all gone. The singularity happened after the appetizers. You missed those."

The others all put their forks down at once and turn to me.

The doctor doesn't look up; he's cutting his meat, which appears to be someone's leg. "Sparrow died—will die—in the Singularity, along with the rest of humanity."

Panic courses through me. I look back toward the door, and notice everything outside the window seems wrong. The light has changed. I shove my chair back, the wood scraping against the floor. Past and future flicker back and forth as I run through the house. I open the door.

A wasteland awaits us beyond. The sky is a sickly, sallow yellow-brown-gray. The landscape is desolate, barren. A murmuration of birds twists and dances in the empty skies.

"What happened?" I have to scream above the hellwinds. "What did you do?"

"They ripped a hole in time," Josephine says.

I stare at her. "*They?*"

"Oh, this wasn't us. We didn't do anything as drastic as this. We were just bringing back the ancient dead. Cleopatra. Aristotle. You know. But a few years before the singularity, things began to get strange. History changed. Reality changed. The moon glitched in the sky, and things began to unravel. You may have even seen a bit of it in your time. But that hole and our little hole, well, they've created a bit of a strid."

"Is that why you eat people? Because there's nothing out there?"

"Partly. Cannibalism also adds a bit of extra power to the rituals. You absorb those you eat, you know."

The birds form the shape of a Mobius loop. The irony isn't lost on me. The sky fills with birds. They are all dead. They cling together, flow together, a dance. Bits of rot fall from above, along with things that glisten and wiggle and crawl.

Josephine watches the sour sky. "The birds have returned—will return—quickly, because their lifespans are so short and they can eat the flies and maggots that are feasting on the dead."

"This is such a strange dream," I murmur. "I can smell rot and sulfur. I can feel the wind." I pull a piece of heart from my teeth, glistening on my finger in the sour sunlight.

"It's not a dream." Josephine holds out her hand. "Come back inside."

Something moves on the horizon. I'm not sure what, but the sight of it makes my stomach churn. "What . . . what is that?"

"The Singularity," Sparrow says. "Please, can we go now?"

I follow her into darkness. Her hand is warm in mine. Her pulse flutters like a bird's wings. I open my mouth, and birdsong emerges.

In the dining room, the others stop eating and stand in perfect synchronicity. Josephine leads them to a door, which she opens to reveal an old wooden stairwell leading down into the dark. She lights a lantern and carries it before her. Halfway down the stairs, she stops and turns. "The lab isn't here right now It's vanished again. We can do without it, though."

We follow her into the cellar, single file.

The basement is mostly unfinished, typical of many of the old houses that dot these hills. A Michigan basement, I think Dad called it. There is a layer of brick on the ground, but the cement walls are cracked, stained, and peeling. I see the sigils Mark and Jimmy told me about, and an old cot. In the center of the room is a carpet, worn and faded, over a piece of plywood, which she lifts to reveal a black maw.

A hole in the basement. Not just a hole. A void.

I look around and see a laboratory flickering in and out of existence.

"They conjured things," Sparrow said. "They trapped the dead. They sang into the void, and the void sang back. There was so much more."

The children surround us, chirping and tweeting and holding out their hearts.

"Why are they here?" I ask Josephine. "Did you kill them?"

"Of course not!" Josephine looks offended. "As the Lord says, thou shalt not kill."

"I do apologize, dear," Doctor Arowisch says. "But you've killed quite a bit."

I look at the older ghosts, the rotting ones.

"They killed her daughter," Sparrow whispers. "Broke her heart. So she took theirs."

"An eye for an eye," Josephine says curtly. "But no, we didn't kill them. Time washed them up onto our shores." She stands next to one of the children—a little boy—and brushes the bangs out of his eyes. "We found them floating in the void. We couldn't just leave them there alone. They don't mind giving us the organs. They're beyond need of them here."

I stare into the void. It's singing to me.

"Do not fear death," Sparrow says. "Fear time. Even death cowers before the passing of ages."

"Very good, dear," Josephine says.

The dead are ringed around her now, black eyes, their features fading, interposed over their bones, as Sparrow's was when I saw her. There are holes in their bodies where their hearts and organs once were. They flicker in and out of existence.

The cat sits on the edge of the gap, curling its tail around its paws.

"It was the age of séances and psychics," Josephine says. "We were experimenting with sound and static. The dawn of radio."

They trapped a ghost in static and broke a hole in time.

"Once," Sparrow says, "they dropped a plate down it. I waited to hear it hit. I never did hear a sound. I think it's still falling."

She holds out her hand. The dead around us are changing, becoming birds, circling around and around the small room. In the far corner, the radio lights up and begins emitting what I can best describe as a sour cacophony. It's playing backward, I realize.

The birds dive into the void, one by one.

Sparrow takes my hand. *Do not fear death,* she breathes, and her breath is cold pine wind; her breath is the ichor of a forest floor.

Fear time, I whisper back.

We hold hands and jump together, following the others into the void.

I've been told I'm not allowed to describe the singularity. And to be frank, I don't know if I could. Suffice it to say, we fell into darkness, and fell out of a blinding white sky. I am small, a winged thing moving through poisoned clouds. Far below, smoke curls from the place we once called home. I float and move in a synchronized dance with the others. Something draws me to the ground. Instinct? Hubris?

And then there is an impact that knocks me, breaks my fragile bones.

The last thing I see is the cat's face, fangs poised above me.

The Years' Dead Past
Timothy Flynn

Everyone has a door—
deadbolt locked, rusty nails
securing the mildew ridden planks
in place, wedged deep down in
the dark abyss of our minds.

Locked away to rot and fester,
memories fade like tendrils of
blue-gray smoke into nothingness.
You choose to forget the faces of friends,
unrecognizable, from the years' dead past.

Cryptic items litter that decrepit room:
cherished moments, sick with black mold,
thick cobwebs their only embrace.
As you erased decades of never-will-bes,
you can't yearn for what you have forsaken.

But *things* can seep through the room's door, ooze through aged
wood as hinges flex, a sharp
squeaky creaking: hints of familiar aromas stab your mind, vague
places pierce through
bloodshot eyes, and strangers on the street burn your insides
from unknown, eerie recognition.

Dead memories of scarred skin,

years of unused tears—mental prisoners in my door.
My key was destroyed; the door's lock
wedged with a finger bone, never to open.
The old me: a ghost of years' dead past.

Do you still have your key? Maybe you
dance with your skeletons in dark times,
morbidly tease through your hoard of
cardboard soldiers who protect mementoes
that make reality less bleak; colorless
Does it dangle around your neck waiting
to strangle you out of the utter fear of being
alone?

Rigby
Christopher Kelly

Curtis wakes in the guest room bed on sheets covered with blood and the various other syrupy fluids that oozed from his body while he slept.

The flow of crimson liquid dripping from his nose isn't heavy, but steady. Based on what he's read—when he could still focus on printed text—he supposes this is simply a matter of the soft tissue in his upper respiratory tract being slowly eaten away by the pathogen having its way with his insides.

Rigby sits a few feet away, alert, staring at the last surviving member of his human pack through two different-colored eyes. His pointy ears vibrate in a state of frantic attention, waiting for a signal from Curtis. At a look from the dying man, Rigby assumes permission to approach the side of the bed. The dog seems to consider before making the decision to jump up and join him. The mid-sized husky mix tries to stem the tide of hemorrhaging from Curtis's face with a series of licks to the nose. Curtis wants to push the dog's head aside, but his arms won't comply. He tries to yell, but he's too tired. Even with a blood-and-snot-stuffed nose, Curtis can smell the acrid urine stench emanating from the mats in the damned dog's white-and-gray-spotted fur.

How long had he been asleep? Twelve hours? Eighteen? Long enough for Rigby to have abandoned the disciplined restraint that once earned him constant praise from Nolan and Sheena.

Curtis directs all his decreasing energy toward the painful task of getting out of bed. It takes a minute or two, but the blood starts to flow into his limbs again, and with it, the assurance that his body still functions on some level. He gets on his feet and waits for the vertigo to pass. Once it does, he can almost believe he is getting better.

But he remembers all the news reports during the weeks before broadcasting stopped and knows this is probably just wishful thinking. What lies beyond his closed bedroom door at the end of the hallway makes him certain that, no matter what his fate, there isn't a way for any of this to *get better*.

Rigby, seeing his master on his feet again, jumps, wagging his tail with excitement. They head out of the room and down the hallway, making it to the back door in decent time, only stopping for Curtis to vomit gray-green bile once along the way. Curtis opens the door and Rigby bolts out into the backyard, dashing with urgency before finding the tree that smells just right to pee on. He continues in the raised leg position for a long time.

Curtis notices the yellow puddle near the door. The dog is getting older now, but he hasn't had an accident in the house since he was a puppy. It is large and likely consists of piss from multiple visits to the spot, multiple vain hopes that Curtis would let him out. He reaches for a pocket, intending to check the time and date on his phone, but he isn't wearing any pants. Even if he had been, he isn't sure the phone would still display that sort of information.

Watching Rigby finish his lengthy piss, the last remnants of the *maybe-I'll-be-ok-after-all* sentiment dissipate. An ache rises slowly within him, and he imagines for a moment his body is not composed of individual cells but of a trillion starving worms feasting on his soft insides. Back against a glass door warm from the noontime sun, he slides down into a sitting position on the floor.

A moment later, Rigby is at his side again. There is a pleading in the dog's kisses, his tongue desperately covering Curtis's face as if it might offer a miracle cure.

Curtis briefly considers leaving the door open so Rigby can get out to pee next time. Or so he can just get out and . . . what? Run off to a new happy home, maybe? Shed eight years of domestication, sleeping on soft cushions and eating processed food from his personalized dish, to revert to the predatory lifestyle of his ancestors? Curtis looks at the gate on the far side of the yard. It's latched shut. Even if he wants to, Rigby can't run off unless Curtis opens the gate for him.

The thought of crossing the yard to the gate makes Curtis's head hurt. But there's something else besides exhaustion keeping that gate locked: he's never been much of an animal person, but the dog is the only other living thing in the house, and Curtis can't imagine being alone. Especially at night, when he thinks about what's behind the door of his former bedroom.

A memory surfaces: a time he forgot to close the gate, and the dog, then only a few months old, ran off into the nearby woods. At that point, Curtis was so fed up with cleaning shit and piss off the floor, of being woken several times a night by the dog's immature bladder, and by barks and whines every time the neighbor walked by with her two Yorkies, he was not one bit sad about Rigby's escape. But Nolan would not stop crying. Not screaming, like from a sliced open knee after a fall off his bicycle, but a deep, existential wailing that made Curtis's heart ache in a way he hadn't known was possible before he'd become a father.

Curtis grabbed a flashlight and trekked through the swampy forest behind their property for more than an hour before finding Rigby in a thick briar patch, covered in mud and dried brambles. The dog ran to him, tail wagging and squeak-barking with elation. But Curtis, at the end of his rope, exhaustion, frustration, and worry for Nolan all swirling in his skull, slapped the dog across the face, hard. Even as Rigby squealed and fell sideways, Curtis was filled with regret. Or, more honestly, he was filled with dread, imagining how Nolan would have felt if he'd witnessed the assault.

Rigby tucked his head between his angry master's legs, begging for forgiveness, and Curtis rubbed the dog's ears. "I'm so sorry," he said, over and over. "You are such a good boy!"

Rigby looked up and gave him kisses. *I forgive you Dad, for you know not what you do.*

*   *   *

Curtis closes and locks the door. He thinks of Rigby's personalized dog dish and a disturbing question occurs: How long has it been since the dog's been fed? Sheena and Nolan had always split that duty; Curtis had never given it much thought. They were gone now, and he had been in bed for . . . how long again? It occurs to him there was no dog poop anywhere. He can't help but consider what the pathetic creature must have resorted to to stave off hunger.

He thinks of Nolan, and it gives him the juice he needs to crawl the twenty feet to the kitchen, where his dog's dishes and food await. Battling burning muscles and a quickly fogging head, he opens the cupboard and dumps a large pile of kibble from a bag showing a smiling cartoon beagle into a red dish marked with Rigby's name and a blue ribbon proclaiming *Best Dog Ever.* He pulls a half-empty water jug from the counter and fills the bone-dry water bowl to the rim.

Spent, Curtis rolls over onto the kitchen floor and lets the fog take him. He fades, watching the dog alternate between lapping up water and chowing down food, both with manic delight. Or maybe it's desperation from not knowing when food will be available again.

And as he drifts off into oblivion, he can't escape the thought that he is going to die on that kitchen floor. He wonders how long it will take before Rigby devours his shriveled remains.

*   *   *

He doesn't die there. He doesn't sleep, either. Not really. His eyes open to a tall figure standing over him, silhouetted but somehow also bathed in light. This must be an angel, he thinks. But there is only one angel that would be interested in Curtis at this juncture, and since this strange figure carries no scythe, he doesn't think it could be that one. Instead, it slowly reaches out to touch his head. The hand is warm, and moist, and the sensation it imparts is quite pleasant.

Curtis can't remember the last time he wasn't either freezing or burning up. Indeed, some part of him knows the divine figure before him is only there because a killer fever is cooking his brain. Whether real or imaginary, the angel's hand connects with Curtis and releases a flow of radiant energy into his body, an ethereal light moving through his head, seeping down into skin and muscle, past his cranium, and into his brain.

He closes his eyes, and it's like the houselights in a cinema going dark just before the feature presentation begins. Scenes dance in his consciousness, a surrealist's documentary of Curtis's life: random images of moments he'd long forgotten replay in ways they didn't actually happen, sometimes in places he's never been. It's hard to even know if Curtis is in the audience for these strange reenactments or if he's a player in the narrative, aware he's being observed without any sense of the observer's identity.

Perhaps some part of him makes a choice to turn the moving images into something more palatable because, after a minute or so, his visions change from experimental films to grainy old home movies.

. . . Sheena looks up from the toilet bowl she's been retching into, a puke-stained smile framing the words "You're going to be a daddy," . . .

. . . Baby Nolan laughs for the first time, echoing in Curtis's ear far more loudly than the carrying sound waves can account for. It is a song whose simple beauty Curtis knows will never be surpassed . . .

. . . Dr. Linda, the therapist, tells Curtis and Sheena that, even though he has never spoken a word in six years, Nolan is a very bright boy and has scored very high on the aptitude tests. Curtis hugs Sheena, not knowing how else to respond. Dr. Linda recommends even more therapy . . .

. . . Curtis is alone next to Nolan, who has finally fallen asleep. He slowly places the guitar against the wall, making sure the strings don't vibrate as he does; small sounds often cause Nolan to wake up screaming. He kisses Nolan on the head and leaves the room. The song he's just played for his son, a tale of a woman who dies alone in a church, hardly seems comforting, but its heavenly melody is one of the few things that can alleviate Nolan's nighttime fears . . .

. . . Sheena tries to talk him down from the mountain of rage he's climbed. "Don't you think we should have talked about it before getting a puppy?" he barks. "I would have," she says, "but this was unplanned. Look at them." Curtis can't hear it, but Nolan's lips are moving, forming words directed to his new friend. His forehead is pressed against the puppy and their eyes meet with something Curtis almost envies. As the boy sings what Curtis is sure, from the motion of his mouth, are Beatles lyrics, the dog licks him in return. Curtis climbs down from the mountain and makes no more objections to their new adoptee. He knows for certain what its name will be: if it is a girl, it will be Eleanor, if it is a boy . . .

. . . Rigby, now full grown, runs across the field on the first warm day of spring to catch the ball Nolan has thrown. The dog is slower than he once was,

but his passion for chasing flying spheres is undiminished by the pain in his hips. The smell of Sheena's lilies of the valley blankets them as the boy falls to the ground with a coughing fit. Curtis doesn't connect it with the scrolling headlines that have recently begun appearing on the bottom of the TV screen—something about cautions issued by the World Health Organization and the Centers for Disease Control . . .

Good Lord, it's getting uncomfortably hot again. Curtis begs the angel to take him away from that terrible moment. But still, the home movies play on.

. . . After puking up blood and chunks of what look like vital organs, Nolan screams for the last time. Curtis's legs give way. The fall to the floor seems to take hours, not seconds. He reaches to grab onto something, but his hands find only air. Thirteen-year-old Nolan will never get up again . . .

It feels as though his brain is beginning to boil. Curtis cannot think straight enough to end the parade of memories.

. . . Curtis presses END on his phone for the thousandth time; no one is answering the call. Does 911 ever close? Of course not. But Nolan's doctors aren't answering their phones, either. The hospital isn't answering. The ambulance service doesn't answer. Rigby comes over to the couch, head down, and begins to lick his comatose son. "Get away from him," Curtis screams and kicks the dog. And he kicks him again. Sheena grabs him, tries to make him stop, but he can't kick the people who are supposed to answer his calls. He can't reach out to hurt the world that's taking everything from him. He knows—somewhere—that Rigby is only trying to help, but rage is a beast that won't listen to reason . . .

. . . When the monster in his head finally lets go, Sheena is carrying their son to the bedroom, crying and calling him an asshole. The door slams, and Curtis will never see his wife and son alive again. Rigby leans into Curtis. There is fear in his eyes, but there is also love. He licks his master's hand. I forgive you, Dad. You know not what you do . . .

. . . Sheena lies on the bed, dead, holding her dead son. Trying not to look at the two motionless forms, he covers them with a sheet. Emergency services still doesn't respond to his repeated calls. He is numb with shock that his family, and the world they inhabited, have gone away just two weeks from the first time he'd become acutely nervous about a coworker's sniffles. It is that numbness that keeps him from using the Remington to blow his fucking brains out . . .

. . . Rigby stands outside the door of the master bedroom, unopened for almost a week. The dog sniffs the air coming from the other side, air that Curtis's phlegm-filled sinus cavities are mercifully immune to. A wave of panic strikes him. What does the dog want inside the room? Rage and fear drive him

to push the dog to the ground, his hands around its throat . . .

. . . A moment later, or maybe an hour, he hugs Rigby, crying. Screaming through sobs that he is so sorry, that Rigby is such a good boy. The dog leans his weight into Curtis's body, kisses the tears from his face. Curtis wants the dog to bite him, to extract justice but when he looks into his multi-colored eyes he sees only love . . .

The images of dead moments fade, and the angel still stands over him, touching his forehead with a warm hand. But as his eyes reacclimate to the low light of evening, the angel begins to disintegrate like a sandcastle in the rain. It is a slow transformation, but happening a step ahead of his mind's ability to comprehend what his viral-shot senses are detecting.

This is maybe that other angel come to take him, despite the fact that he doesn't believe in angels that come to take people. Maybe this is a wrathful god come to deliver judgment. He's less certain about that.

Either way, Curtis feels ready to go.

But the divine messenger is gone. Was never there. The hand that touched him was not an angel's hand, but a soft, graying muzzle. Rigby licks the sweat from his skin. The dog steps in front of Curtis, leaning his weight against his master. Curtis leans into Rigby. They rest that way for a long time.

*   *   *

Upon waking, Curtis finds himself curled in a ball in front of his refrigerator. Rigby is barking. The dog is normally easygoing, but right now he's enraged. Curtis looks up to see Rigby's back end, hackles raised.

Standing in the entryway between the kitchen and the dining room, a man points a shotgun at them. The man is young. He seems healthy; the dried snot hanging off his beard suggests he won't be for long. But his sunken eyes say sickness is a problem for tomorrow; today, hunger is his enemy.

The man aims the gun at Rigby, and Curtis cries out with his weak voice. "Please, no!"

"Then hold that fucking dog back and move away from the refrigerator."

Curtis tries to stand, but his legs give out and he slides back down. The gunman raises his weapon from dog to master, and with that, Rigby leaps, latching onto the man's arm.

The intruder delivers a quick boot to Rigby's ribs. The dog's yelp is piercing, as is the cracking sound somewhere in his body. Rigby makes a hard landing on the kitchen linoleum but is up again quickly. This will be the end of him. Curtis rolls toward the snarling dog and grabs hold of him.

Rigby continues delivering ferocious barks, but Curtis stays next to him as the gunman raids the refrigerator, dumping everything he can find into his backpack. He continues with the cupboards, even grabbing the last few cans of Rigby's food. For now, Curtis is only concerned with preventing his dog from charging into a blast from that scattergun.

When the man runs out the back door, Rigby breaks away from Curtis's grip and bolts outside after the fleeing intruder.

Curtis pulls himself up, willing his legs to work again, and they listen. But he can't reach the door before the dog runs down the back deck stairs. By the time he makes it to the glass doors, the intruder is exiting through the gate in the back fence, and Rigby is halfway across the yard.

Curtis stumbles out onto the deck just as Rigby reaches the gate. The fleeing gunman left it wide open. Curtis yells for Rigby. At least he *thinks* he's yelling. He's not sure if his voice is carrying, as his head is becoming cloudy again.

This is as good an explanation as any as to why he misses the first step and plunges down the stairs.

Some time passes before he entertains the question of whether or not he's been hurt. The dirt at the bottom of the stairs is soft, mostly, but *soft ground* is not a meaningful description when someone suffering from a virus that makes its living erasing body tissue has crashed into it. Curtis's muscles and fat have been eaten away and are unable to provide a cushion for bones exponentially more brittle than they were two weeks earlier. Curtis is sure his body has shattered irreparably.

As he gradually works his way into a sitting position, he realizes nothing is broken or twisted in an abnormal way. His aches are consistent with the pain he woke up with on his kitchen floor.

But his eyes burn. This is certainly because he's staring up into a bright blue sky, at a sun that has presided over countless extinctions on its third planet. Its habit of showering the Earth with photons isn't likely to change any because of this latest one.

The angel steps into view again, surrounded by beams of light raining down from the heavens. It doesn't bother this time with a sentimental slideshow of memories, reverting instead to the old husky mix who once saved his son's soul. Rigby whines and looks longingly to the open gate, but he tenderly sits, then slowly lies down beside Curtis.

*   *   *

Though he hasn't slept, Curtis can't recall how long he's been sitting against the steps leading to his deck. Much of his experience with this illness has been in a state of nowhereness; maybe the virus's one kindness is in preparing its victims for the oblivion it will sooner or later dump them all into. He's aware the sun is no longer beating down on him, and the sky has grown darker.

Those long bouts of fuzzy escape are punctuated with moments of retreat. His head has begun to clear and with it comes lucidity. Lucidity brings reality to the forefront of Curtis's mind. Like a baby being born, he screams to be let back into the dark place from which he'd recently arrived.

He expends the effort to lift his face to the sun sinking toward the distant horizon. There is a tall oak in the corner of the yard, the day's last light dancing around its many branches. Curtis has long meant to cut it down; at this moment, he rejoices that he never did.

The day before he collapsed in the hallway, Nolan had a strange burst of energy and was on his feet again. He wanted to climb the tree to get a look at what was happening outside of their neighborhood. Curtis said no. His son was angry but Curtis knew he'd done the right thing.

Thirty-six hours later, Nolan was dead, in his mother's arms in their bedroom. Half delusional with fever, she held him through the night and would not let go. She didn't see the sunrise the next morning, and Curtis wasn't sure if it was the virus that took her. He vowed to bury his wife and son under that tree, but that night a splitting headache turned into a fever, and he has never found the strength to fulfill that vow.

God, why didn't he just let his boy climb that tree?

Curtis no longer wants to look at the dying old oak.

Rigby is no longer by his side, but standing in the middle of the field staring at that open gate. It is hard to tell from his posture whether he feels a threat from the other side or if the dog simply longs to run free, beyond the walls of this home that has become a mortuary.

His heart drops. Curtis calls out to the dog. It's weak, but his dying voice is enough to get Rigby's attention. The mutt limps over and Curtis takes hold of the beast's collar and grips it tight.

Getting to the other side of the field is out of the question, so the gate will have to stay open. Curtis thinks he can make it to the couch, though. Man and dog hobble up the deck stairs and into the house. Curtis closes and locks the sliding door leading outside.

*   *   *

Curtis's last windows of life look out onto a shifting kaleidoscope of sleep, waking hallucination, and agonizing moments of clarity.

The latest opens at the end of a tunnel from the realm of sleep into the waking world of baking heat and swirling nausea. He sits up in a fit, disturbing Rigby. The dog has ignored protocol to jump up onto the couch and eat the massive pile of vomit covering the comforter in front of Curtis. It is somewhat chunky, somewhat slimy, and looks to contain diced offal.

Even though he's dying, Curtis finds ingrained reflexes taking hold, an all-too-quick backhand rising in reaction to his revulsion. Rigby cringes and shakes, knowing well the fury that has animated his master all too often. But Curtis sees how emaciated his dog looks. Even padded with his once-fluffy spotted fur, Rigby's ribs show and his eyes, blue and brown, are sinking into his skull. The poor creature has avoided the virus only to be held in the grip of starvation by way of the house's four walls and his unswerving loyalty to a man who doesn't deserve it.

Curtis pulls himself to his feet and stumbles toward the kitchen by way of the front hallway. The photographs lining its walls— awkward school pictures, scenes from cookouts and Christmases over the years—stare at him like spectators watching a gladiator march down the corridor toward an ancient Roman coliseum. The smiles of Sheena, of Nolan, condemn him. The laughter and joy of a dead era taunt him. The crowds chant in his head, *We rot in your bedroom because you don't even have the decency to bury us.*

He ignores the imagined stares, focusing all his energy into getting to the kitchen. When he arrives, his window of strength and clarity began to close. His legs tell him they're done, that he is going to fall down. He begs them for a minute more. He just needs to leave Rigby with something to eat.

But there is no food left. The gunman who invaded yesterday (the day before?) took everything, including the Alpo cans. He opens the refrigerator, but it's empty save for a jug of orange juice and bottle of ginger ale he picked up on the way home from work when Sheena texted him—about a million years ago—complaining of a sore throat. There are a few slices of bread left on top of the fridge and a bag of stale organic corn chips the intruder must have missed.

Rigby looks up at him, tail wagging, tongue hanging out and to the right, eyes asking for something to eat. Curtis pulls down the bread and picks off a few blue-green spots of mold before dumping it into the dog's dish. A second later, he adds the corn chips. A distant voice in his head screams the question, *What will you eat?* but he isn't hungry. He can't remember the last time he was hungry. It occurs to him with stark certainty that eating is something he will never do again.

The dog finishes the shoddy meal in less than thirty seconds. Habit moves Curtis to the door to let Rigby out, hardly noticing the puddle of piss on the floor as his bare feet splash through it. When he arrives at the door, Rigby shows excitement, but Curtis freezes when he sees the open gate.

No. The mutt will just have to piss and shit on the floor until I get strong enough to go out and shut that gate. Doesn't matter. It's what he's been doing anyway.

Rigby whines, but the window of lucidity is shrinking, and Curtis can think of nothing but getting to the couch. He arrives just as the window closes.

*   *   *

When the light returns to his eyes, it does so only partially. He's sitting on the kitchen floor, propped against the back door. How he got here, he has no idea.

Rigby sits, shaking, in the limited circle of vision remaining to Curtis. The poor dog has wasted away even more than the last time Curtis was awake, and his fur is falling out. Even still, his tail thumps weakly at the sight of Curtis's opened eyes.

Curtis pulls himself up and opens the back door. It is pouring outside, and for some reason that comforts him. He imagines for a moment the rain might somehow wash away the stained legacy he will be leaving behind.

Rigby looks outside, excited for what must have appeared to him as the beginning of his first walk in weeks, but Curtis cannot stand to walk with him. He struggles to pat his knee with his right hand, what used to signal walk time, but he can't find his voice to say, *Let's go buddy!* Rigby twitches with excitement every time Curtis moves, but doesn't vacate his spot five feet from the door.

"Come on," Curtis says, though he isn't sure his words are coherent. "You have to go outside now."

Curtis closes his eyes.

When he opens them again, the light is a little different outside and the rain is coming down harder. Curtis's right side is soaked from drops ricocheting off the floor.

Rigby springs from his lying position into a sitting one and his tail pounds the floor rhythmically.

Curtis gets to his knees, the dog's tail thumping more frantically as he pulls himself up.

"I can't take care of you anymore."

Rigby doesn't budge.

"Not that I ever really could."

Curtis clings to the door. The wind pushes the rain sideways into his eyes like flying quills. Rigby hops to his side, and the dog's slack face seems to smile up at him. Curtis reaches down and pulls the collar with all his dwindling strength.

Rigby has always been a good boy. Even when Curtis was too blind to see it, he knew it to be true. Since he was a young pup, Rigby always did as he was told and never fought against Curtis's commands.

Now, he fights with all his strength to defy the command to be free. The command to live. His claws dig into the hardwood as he fights his master's weak tugging. They struggle until both collapse to the floor. Curtis wraps himself around Rigby, releasing tears holding precious hydration. Rigby falls into him.

Curtis wants to die like this. Loved unconditionally. Forgiven. But he knows it can't be that way.

"I don't know what's out there for you, but there's nothing in here anymore."

He takes hold of the dog and squeezes him, ignoring the yelps of pain, and drags him toward the door. Curtis gets on his knees and wills himself the strength to toss Rigby to the deck outside. As the dog slowly rises, Curtis slams the door shut. Rigby limps back to the door and scratches fruitlessly at the glass. His sharp, whiny barks shoot through Curtis like poisoned darts.

For a moment Rigby stops, and they stare at each other through glass stained with dog-nose prints and dried blood and snot.

I forgive you, Dad. You know not what you do. Now, let me in so I can be by your side.

Curtis tries to stand, but his legs inform him that there will be no more of that. The virus has done its work on his leg muscles: his thighs are nothing more than skin sacks filled with liquefied meat.

It is his arms, and perhaps some part of him that can't be located temporally, pulling him to the end of the hallway as Rigby's frantic barks begin to fade.

At the bedroom door, he risks a look back.

Rigby has stopped scratching and now sits anxiously at the door, his eyes fixed on his master. His whine is piercing, but Curtis can't tell if that is real or just the pain in his head holding onto the sound. He pushes the bedroom door open and the miasma on the other side cuts through the ocean of mucous clogging his nasal passages, but only for a moment.

He pulls himself toward the bed. Curtis smells salty beach air, and movie popcorn. He smells Sheena's skin moisturizer, oily and lavender scented, and the citrusy glue from Nolan's model airplanes, and the maple syrup the boy loved so much on his French toast every Sunday morning.

Crawling toward the figures lying invisible beneath the covers, he takes a glance back toward the back door. In his blackening vision, he can no longer tell if Rigby is still waiting for him.

He climbs upon the bed and falls to lie beside the bloated figures waiting there.

He closes his eyes, able to rest now that Rigby has stopped barking.

Illustration for "This is Neverland" © 2024 Angi Shearstone

This is Neverland
Peter N. Dudar

Melissa Rogan turned her iPad on and propped it on the desk so the lens faced the child in the swivel chair. She pressed record. The tablet's light switched from red to green, and the timer in the corner of the frame progressed as she conducted her interview.

"Hello, Jeanie. My name is Doctor Rogan, but you can call me Missy if that's more comfortable. Is that okay with you?"

The little girl sat, arms crossed, gaze focused on some far-off dust mote or peeling paint chip on the wall; classic defensive posture for a criminal—or for a traumatized child like the one sitting here, in her office at the Department of Health and Human Services. Seeing it now in what should have been a normal, healthy eight-year-old felt unsettling. The child had brought her doll with her: a ratty old toy with a burlap face and body and straggly limbs, frayed strands where fingers should have been. The doll's clothes were caked with dried mud and crushed, dead leaves, as if it had been left outside overnight. The doll sat at the girl's feet, fabric face staring up accusingly at the tablet as if it were being interviewed rather than its owner.

"Jeanie, it's okay to talk to me. You're safe here. Your mommy and daddy are right outside in the lobby, and I'll get you back to them as soon as we figure out what happened to you. But I promise you, nobody is mad at you, and you aren't in any trouble. Do you understand me, Jeanie?"

"My name's not Jeanie. It's Corrina."

Melissa glanced at the tablet to make sure it was recording, then walked over and bent down beside the little girl.

"Your name is Jeanie Mayfield. Your parents brought you in here because you went missing for a few days. The game warden found you out in the woods, behind that big, old abandoned house in Cumberland. Is that where you live, Jeanie? Do you live in Cumberland?"

The corner of Jeanie's warm, blue eyes welled with tears; her lips pressed firmly together until the edges quivered.

"My name's not Jeanie, it's Corinna."

"Is this your dolly? She's very pretty, but her dress is filthy. Can you tell me what happened to your doll?"

Melissa bent to pick up the toy. The mistrust in the girl's eyes changed to panic, and she moved faster than the psychologist could have imagined, snatching up the doll and clutching it tight to her belly.

"Don't touch her! I need her! She's mine!"

Melissa hadn't noticed before, but the doll's belly looked bloated, overstuffed; as the girl's arms squeezed harder, like pythons crushing a small animal, the little dress lifted, exposing a row of jagged sutures where its abdomen had been haphazardly sewn together.

"I won't take your toy away," Melissa tried to soothe. "I just want to examine it. It looks like something happened to her tummy. Can you please be brave and show me your doll's tummy?"

The girl's eyes rolled back in her head, and a stream of gibberish poured from her lips. Melissa looked at the tablet again— just to be sure it was recording—then glanced helplessly at the child as her small frame shook and rocked in the swivel chair. For a moment, it sounded as if Jeanie/Corinna's voice had changed into another voice and a language Melissa did not speak—perhaps an island creole, like Haitian or Jamaican. The starkness of that change felt sinister and unnatural issuing from the lips of the child with the long, blonde hair and freckled, accusing face. The hairs on Melissa's neck stood on end. Jeanie turned to her, face riddled with fear and hatred. "I need this to pay off my debt, or the old man will throw me down the well!"

Melissa reached a trembling hand out to the doll and poked its belly, index finger pressing the ragged sutures. The thread popped and the fabric burst open. A stream of white powder gushed out onto the floor.

Jeanie/Corinna jumped out of her chair and shrieked. "Oh, God! Oh, God, look what you do!" The child dropped to her knees, cupping at the growing pile of powder, trying to stuff it back into the doll. A look of absolute dread filled the girl's face, tears streaming down both cheeks. She scooped frantically, dropping the powder back into the now-gaping hole in the toy's abdomen. Melissa watched, horrified, at first thinking the powder was cocaine or some other illicit drug. But as the white crystal grains sifted, the odor made her think of her own childhood, when she'd breathed in that sweet aroma as her mother mixed pitchers of Kool-Aid on those hot summer days.

The powder was sugar.

* * *

Sheriff Anderson stood at the edge of the Alfred property, gazing up at the old house. The three-story plantation home had been unoccupied since the Maine Historical Society had acquired it back in the late 1950s, when the last of Samuel Alfred's relatives had been foreclosed upon. It had been long before the sheriff's time, but like all old houses, this one had its own legends and mysteries. Anderson didn't pay much heed to superstition, but still felt something was wrong with the property—something fueled by dread and shame. Just standing in the shadow of the old house left him unnerved.

"The Historical Society should have burned this one to the ground," a voice called from behind him, at the edge of Stoneham Road. Anderson turned and watched as the old man retrieved a briefcase from the rear of his Subaru Outback and slammed the hatchback shut. Walter Pickford was a beast for both punctuality and frankness, and as the university's longest-tenured professor, those virtues had served him well. The old man walked up the driveway, free hand thrust out to shake with Anderson. "Good to see you, Mark. You look well."

"This is still an open investigation," the sheriff said. "Your help is greatly appreciated. And it's good to see you, too."

"We're not going inside, are we?" Pickford glanced up at the house. "I've been inside it once, a dozen years or so ago, and that was plenty. I can't explain what it is, but the moment you set foot through the door it gives you the impression of being inside a closed coffin. It's like the house sucks all the oxygen right out of the air and suffocates you. Stay in there too long and you start to feel like you're getting high. If you need to go in, I'll wait out here."

"No need. The judge hasn't signed off on a search warrant yet because no real crime has been committed. Of course, if I had probable cause . . ."

"Is this where you found the little girl?"

Anderson nodded toward the forest on the western side of the property. "It was the damnedest thing. Jeanie Mayfield actually lives in Falmouth. She went missing back on the ninth—her parents reported it and we issued an Amber alert—and somehow made her way here within a day or two. Nobody can get her to explain what happened. The local game warden discovered her out in the woods behind the house, huddled by an abandoned well, weeping and speaking in tongues. She shows no signs of abduction or injuries, so we think she just set off one afternoon and came here with no rhyme or reason." Anderson contemplated a moment. "Confusion is a symptom of dehydration and malnourishment."

The professor nodded. "Do you know the history of the Alfred house?"

"Can't say I do. Fill me in, and let's see if we can make some sense."

"This house was part of the Underground Railroad. The abolitionists relied on properties like this to receive escaped slaves so they could begin new lives. You see that lawn jockey statue up by the front steps?" Pickford set his case down and pointed up to the granite stairs leading to the sun-faded door. Its enormous brass knocker, blackened with age and weathering, glared at the two men like an accusing eye. "That was a marker coordinated by the abolitionists to show the house was safe. And that bell post over by the barn?" Pickford swept his arm toward the big red structure behind the eastern side of the house. "Same thing. There are probably dozens of telltale signs around this place if we look for them, but I suspect none of that will fit into your investigation."

"And Samuel Alfred owned the house back then?"

"Correct." Pickford knelt, opened his briefcase, and handed a stapled packet of papers to the sheriff. "I thought this might be helpful. It's some research I did on Alfred and this property. Old man Alfred owned a textile mill about two miles north of here. The mill sits on the Royal River and adjacent to the old railroad line. They could ship their goods out to the waterfront or carry them across the state in boxcars."

"So, how was it he offered his home as a destination for the Underground Railroad?"

The professor smiled as if the sheriff had just asked the twenty-thousand-dollar question.

"Because there was still money to be made. The slaves set off for the north to find freedom and shelter from the violence that came with being African-American, but the Underground Railroad still charged a price. The textile mills here in Maine were supplied by cotton grown down south just as much as the wool our own farmers produced here at home, so a lot of American businessmen didn't really want slavery to end. If southern plantation owners lost their slave labor and had to pay cotton pickers, the price of cotton would have gone through the roof. So, men like Alfred expected the Negroes to come north bearing resources like cotton as a donation for shelter and assistance. Of course, this was merely a token—a pittance. It made the slaves think they were paying their way out of servitude, but once they got here, they had no money or homes. Alfred put them to work in his textile mill at brutally low wages, but at least they were free. With the money he saved on these new employees, he could purchase more cotton and have it shipped directly to his mill. Does that make sense?"

"You bet. Let's take a stroll out back and see if we can't find that well. I want to know what would cause an eight-year-old girl to travel twenty miles on foot to find it and sit overnight in the Maine woods praying to it. The game warden—a fella named Richard LaPierre—told me the overnight temperature had dropped to the low forties, but when he found the girl, she showed no trace of hypothermia. That alone has me perplexed. It's not . . . natural."

*   *   *

The two men set off, unaware they were being watched from a window on the top floor of the Alfred house. The figure stood for only a moment, then darted off into the shadows, leaving the plantation house to its own devices. If there were indeed other inhabitants—mice or termites within the walls—the house would steal their breath soon enough.

*   *   *

"What is that?"

Professor Pickford lagged behind Sheriff Anderson by at least five yards, but was the first to notice anything unusual. Anderson doubled back to see what Pickford was talking about: a line of white powder, crystals spilled over the pine needles and dead leaves on the woodland floor, trailing off into the forest. Anderson knelt, wetted the tip of his finger, and dipped it into the white powder. He raised the finger, sniffed, then moved to set it on his tongue and taste, but Pickford stopped him.

"No! Don't do that."

"Why not? I need to know what this is."

"It could be arsenic. Or some kind of rat poison."

"Why would anyone use rat poison out here? The Alfred House is unoccupied, so it's more likely that illicit drugs have been smuggled through here. Maybe some dealer was trying to evade us and spilled some coke or heroin as he tried to make his escape."

"Let's just follow the trail and see where it takes us."

Sheriff Anderson stood tall and adjusted his hat. At full height, Cumberland's sheriff was an imposing man. "What aren't you telling me, Pickford?"

"I don't know. Something seems terribly wrong. I've felt it ever since we set foot on the property. Not like before, not like inside the house where I couldn't breathe. I could swear I feel eyes all around us. And I think if we follow the powder, it will take us to the well we're looking for."

"You said the house was foreclosed upon. Doesn't this Alfred fellow have kin around? How come none of his heirs have fought to reclaim the property?"

Pickford drew in one more deep breath, then started walking again, slower this time, more cautiously, craning his neck to peek through the trees. "Samuel Alfred had been gone for nearly a century when the house was foreclosed upon. Quite frankly, none of them wanted to inherit the property in the first place. They claimed they wanted no part of the cruel history of the Alfred legacy . . . but I suspect they, too, were afraid of the house. I also suspect they had plenty of money tucked away to live comfortably enough, but they couldn't find a buyer interested in the property so that they could move on."

"And the bank that foreclosed on it, they . . .?"

"The state foreclosed for failing to pay taxes."

"So the state wasn't able to sell off the property, either?"

"Have you ever been inside the house, Mark?"

Sheriff Anderson shook his head.

"I doubt even Dracula would want to live in that house."

* * *

They spotted the children long before finding the well: four boys and two girls, each carrying some kind of doll or toy. They traveled single file, heads turned down toward the dirt trail they followed. The boy bringing up the rear carried an enormous teddy bear in his arms, its face a worn-out grimace of mistreatment. The bear's rounded ears looked as if they'd been gummed down to the point of matted, threadbare material, its black button-eyes wide and unseeing. There was a hole in the bear's back, and from it poured a thinning trail of white powder. The powder spilled silently onto the woodland floor, but the boy carrying the bear had no idea its belly grew thinner with every step. Eyes wide and unblinking as his worn charge's, he followed the other children deeper into the forest.

"What the hell is going on?" Sheriff Anderson whispered. He hadn't been aware until now that his heart was pounding, his belly fluttering with butterflies of unease.

"I've never seen anything like it," Pickford said. "They look hypnotized."

"Or stoned," Anderson replied. They were at least thirty yards ahead, and he stepped forward to run and catch up with them.

Pickford grabbed his arm and held him back. "They're obviously unharmed. I want to see what happens. Let's follow them and see where they're going."

They pursued slowly, quietly, watching the kids march through the woods. The oldest, possibly eight or nine, led the procession with fierce determination. She clutched a faded Raggedy Ann doll against her chest with both arms, the filthy clown doll's face pushed tight against her blue cotton dress. She stopped. The other children came to an immediate halt, vacant eyes darting about the woods as if looking for some unseen threat. The moment passed. The girl waved one hand, clutched the doll tighter, and continued her trek. The other children followed suit, a feral lot in filthy hair and freckles, clothing tattered from the long journey.

"It's remarkable," Pickford whispered. "It's almost like they're reenacting the Underground Railroad. None of them are speaking or showing any signs of childhood vitality."

"You'd think they'd be laughing and playing," Anderson agreed. "You know, like in *Peter Pan*. The Lost Boys out having some grand adventure or something."

Pickford sighed. "I did a paper once about *Peter Pan*. Not the Disney version, but the book by J.M. Barrie. The story is actually a metaphor for childhood death. Neverland is heaven, where the Lost Boys never grow older and can spend all their time playing and having fun. These kids don't look like they're having fun at all. In fact, they don't even look like children."

* * *

Dr. Rogan watched the little girl scoop up the last of the sugar and carefully pour it back into the hole in her doll's belly. When she finished, Jeanie closed her eyes and clutched her arms around her knees, sobbing softly and rocking back and forth on the floor. Melissa thought of retrieving her sewing kit from her purse in the office closet to mend the doll, but was afraid the child might grow more hostile and more evasive to her questioning. Not that she was getting all that far to begin with.

She went back to her desk and pressed pause on the iPad's video recorder, then scrolled the video backward to the beginning. The footage ran, and Melissa gasped in horror.

The interview chair was empty. No little girl. Only the doll, floating in space as if held by hidden strings. As for audio, it was only Dr. Rogan's voice asking questions and getting no audible replies. Melissa turned toward the swivel chair to look at the girl and screamed. Jeanie/Corinna stood right behind her, pupils dilated into huge, inky disks. Her mouth hung open, canine teeth mysteriously longer and sharper than before.

Like fangs.

The child opened her mouth wider and lunged toward Dr. Rogan's bare neck.

* * *

"What are we missing?" Sheriff Anderson asked as they crept behind the children. His fear had grown palpable, disorienting, as if every step deeper into the woods led him farther from the world of the living. "This used to be the trail the Underground Railroad followed to reach freedom. They came to the Alfred House, and the old man offered what? Protection? A place to stay? You told me he offered them a paying job at his mill, but then what? What did this guy do to help them start their lives over again?"

Pickford was panting. The old man was a bit heavy around the middle, and perhaps not used to strenuously marching through long patches of the Maine outdoors. "Well, yes, most of the slaves who came from the south found work in his textile mill. It was a paying job, of course, but nowhere near real living wages or a chance at financial freedom. In a lot of ways they remained slaves, still working and toiling for the white man, but at least the rape and violence they'd endured had ceased."

"So . . . Alfred wasn't much more than a glorified slave owner, keeping these African-Americans as indentured servants? That's how he made his fortune?"

Pickford stopped in his tracks, causing Anderson to stop as well. "Not exactly. Alfred lived comfortably off the textile mill, but he made his real fortune selling rum."

"Rum?"

"As payment for his help with the Underground Railroad, the slaves were also required to bring molasses as reimbursement for his hospitality. He took the molasses and made bootleg rum back there on his farm. Many of the slaves were from Africa, but there were also slaves from the islands: Haiti, Jamaica, the Bahamas. Traders brought sugarcane to the States, and when they figured out how to extract rum from the sugarcane byproducts, it became enormously popular. Of course, the amount of molasses these poor souls had to carry couldn't sustain the massive empire Alfred had created, but just like the cotton, he could afford to import it, and the newly-freed slaves helped him to produce it."

"And yet Alfred's relatives couldn't pay the taxes, so the state took his house away. Where's the reasoning behind that? Did they piss away his fortune or something?"

"I have no idea."

"But Samuel Alfred was rich when he died. What exactly did he die from?"

"That's the thing. Nobody knows. Samuel Alfred's children claimed he'd contracted tuberculosis and died inside the house, but there's no death certificate on file. Nor is there any proof his body was interred anywhere. As far as history goes, Alfred just disappeared, and ownership of the property passed to his kids through probate. I imagine the scandal behind Maine's Underground Railroad Baron was all the more reason his kin just let the property be foreclosed upon."

"See, that sounds like foul play. Was there an investigation? Weren't any of his children questioned? How does one of Maine's richest entrepreneurs of the nineteenth century just vanish, and leave behind that huge freaking house and all this property? How has it never been sold? The Historical Society took possession, and yet nobody's made any effort to maintain upkeep and repairs. I don't get it."

The professor sighed. "Don't you see? This place is evil. It's been abandoned for a reason, and that reason is because it shuns the living. It wants to suck the life right out of us. Don't you feel it, Mark?"

Anderson started walking again, watching as the children ahead entered a wide clearing. The clearing was filled with tiny mounds of dirt along either side of the path, as if the land had been turned into a vast cemetery with no headstones.

"These kids are all carrying toys that appear to be filled with sugar. Is that somehow significant? Does that play in with the whole molasses thing?"

Pickford huffed and puffed, struggling to keep up. "I don't see how. Granulated sugar isn't used to make rum. Unless it's just symbolic, I don't see any connection yet. Are those graves?"

There were dozens of burial mounds around them, possibly over a hundred. The tombs clustered about the land like malignant tumors and sunken cavities on the forest floor. Sheriff Anderson wondered how it might be that this area had remained unnoticed, undisturbed for the past century and a half. He gritted his teeth and swallowed as he imagined countless slaves marching thousands of miles up the eastern coast looking for freedom, only to die at the end of the trail. He imagined these people: filthy, beaten down, reeking of body odor and seawater from crossing through the salt marshes of Scarborough to remain unnoticed in their travels. Had this been Alfred's work? Did he murder those poor people who could not pay him for his assistance at the end of the Underground Railroad?

My God, what a terrible fate, Anderson thought. *That little girl the game warden found, did she reek of that same saltwater odor when she was discovered?*

"Whatever is happening, we need to stop it." Sheriff Anderson had unsnapped his holster strap, hand resting comfortably on the butt of his service weapon.

Professor Pickford touched his shoulder and shook his head. "Not yet. The well must be up ahead. We're almost there."

*   *   *

Melissa Rogan's head filled with voices: strange, agonized screams and wails that made her skin cover with goose pimples. Her eyes welled with tears as the child sucked her life's blood from the gashed artery in her neck. Her head filled with chanting; foreign voices poisoned her mind with images of terrible cruelty and violence. She saw scenes of stripped torsos flogged by leather whips and red-hot iron rods mashing against black skin, as if these people had been nothing more than animals being branded. She tried to look away, but the spell held her frozen in place and time.

Eventually, she saw a dark figure emerge through the fiery embers swirling around the cacophony of human sacrilege. The man smiled a wicked grin of crooked teeth and forbidden knowledge, and Melissa knew the man to be the personification of vengeance.

"You will come to me," this strange man whispered, and Melissa Rogan immediately understood. She stood, grabbed her purse from the shelf in the closet, and walked over to the coffeemaker in the corner of her office. There was a half-empty bag of sugar in the cabinet below the machine. She pulled the bag out, dumped the sugar into her purse, and took the little girl by the hand.

"It's time to go."

*   *   *

The procession ended at an enormous hole in the ground, deep in the woods behind the Alfred House. Had it been a well, it had no earthly business here, far away from any home or livery stable where drawn water was a necessity. No, out here was nothing but a copse of dead maples, birches, and oaks, wooden skeletons swaying in the early autumn breeze as the sun began to sink over the western horizon. Pickford scanned the woodland and immediately noticed the strange sigils carved into the surrounding trunks. Markings of mixed origins adorned the dead trees, exotic symbols professing satanic faith. And if that wasn't disturbing enough, the ground was littered with abandoned toys. Dolls and stuffed animals, torsos punctured and drained of their contents, lay in heaps around the hole, as if hundreds of children had come to this spot to make their sacrifice.

"Oh my God, do you hear it?" Sheriff Anderson was moving faster now, handgun drawn and pointed toward the darkening sky. "It's coming from that hole!"

Pickford did hear it: the screams of the dead, issuing up from the seemingly bottomless well. The souls of the damned called forth, victims of a tyranny so terrible their departed souls could never rest. They wailed in endless suffering, waiting to claim new bodies and return to the world to feast upon it.

*   *   *

This is Neverland, Sheriff Anderson thought, watching the girl at the front of the procession raise her Raggedy Ann doll, pull the knife out of the doll's dress, and split the toy's belly open so the sugar poured down into the pit. *This is Neverland, and the Lost Boys are bartering with the devil to return to the land of the living.*

Pickford hustled up from behind, still panting but undoubtedly hovering on the same understanding as the sheriff.

"Shoot them! Shoot them all before it's too late!"

The girl's body arched backward, spine bending in an obscene contortion, then stood upright again. She tossed her empty doll onto the pile of discarded toys, stepped aside, and the second child approached the hole. He picked up the knife and sliced a gaping wound into his Winnie the Pooh and watched reverently as the sugar poured into the earthen maw. More screams erupted from the hole—only now, they sounded as if they were feasting greedily in rapt pleasure.

*   *   *

There was a terrible moment when Pickford watched as the second child reared backward—as if a soul had leapt out of the yawning well and into his body—and then the boy smiled a wicked grin and stepped aside for the next child. The boy turned toward them, and both Anderson and Pickford watched as the fangs appeared in his smile.

"Shoot them! Fucking shoot them!" Pickford jerked the Sheriff's shoulder as if Anderson had somehow fallen asleep and needed to be rescued from this nightmare.

Anderson raised his gun, pointed it at the first child—and froze.

A figure stood behind the well, a tall, dark entity that had materialized and now presided over the parade of children, his hooded robe reflecting white in the ascending moonlight. Pickford watched in growing horror, then understood this demon for what—who—it was.

Samuel Alfred. Alive and well, nearly a century after he should have been dead and lain to rest.

No, that wasn't right. Alfred had succumbed to tuberculosis in his late sixties. The Alfred house had been passed on to his children. Only . . . there was no real proof of that, was there?

Logic was slipping away with every passing moment.

"Ah . . . My children. Welcome home!"

The next child moved forward, took the knife in her tiny hand, and slashed the belly of her doll. Sugar rained down. Anderson leveled his gun at the first child and pulled the trigger. The woods resounded with the report, and the girl staggered, her damaged face filled first with surprise, then rage. Fangs gnashed in the growing darkness as the girl toppled into the shadow-filled well.

In reply, the screams from the well grew louder, as if the damned had been rebuked for wanting their vengeance. The dark entity glared at the two interlopers and hissed through teeth bared in a smile.

"You cannot stop me."

Its skin was pale, and Pickford immediately understood he was seeing Samuel Alfred—not the actual man, but a possessed puppet of the deceased baron of Maine's Underground Railroad. Whatever entity had possessed Alfred had remained in his home and perpetuated this evil perversion of history. This thing was centuries old and longed for retaliation for whatever evils had been cast upon its people. This was Captain Hook, wanting to steal Neverland back from Peter. This was Vengeance, and it demanded sacrifice.

Anderson raised his gun and shot again and again and again, each child falling dead to the forest floor. He took aim at the entity and pulled the trigger, but the hammer clicked; six empty casings lined the cylinder of his service revolver.

The dark creature grinned.

"You shall serve me for all eternity!"

The vessel that was Dr. Rogan descended upon Anderson from behind, fangs spread wide and punching into his throat. The child, Corinna, a soul freed from the well to bore into the little girl who'd once been Jeanie Mayfield, pulled Professor Pickford to the ground, bared her fangs, and feasted. Blood spilled onto the earth until the last of the living ceased to be.

*　　*　　*

This really is Neverland, Anderson thought as the voices from the pit spilled into his brain. The screams and wails of the tormented slaves whose bodies lay buried in the unmarked graves he and Pickford had just passed over now filled his soul. They had grown tired of waiting in this purgatory and wanted to return to the land of the living, to feast on human blood and avenge their deaths. His last action on earth was to rise to his feet, look defiantly at the demon, and cast himself down into the well they had come searching for, hoping to take whatever soul that tried to possess him back down to hell where it belonged.

*　　*　　*

The crate of rum arrived on the following Tuesday, marked with the usual waxed stamp of authenticity from the Alfred Distillery, in Maine. Twelve new bottles, their contents blood red and rocking at ninety-four proof, sat on Martin Alfred's desk, nearly two thousand miles south of the plot of Maine woods where it had been produced. The thrice-removed grandson of the Alfred legacy pulled a bottle from the crate, examined it, and smiled.

Eternal life resided inside each bottle, waiting to be purchased by some desperate billionaire longing to continue their time on the planet and willing to bleed those poor, useless fools of their lives in order to survive. That was how the world of privilege always worked, after all. When one had money, the rest of humanity bowed to their whims.

Martin had meant to put the bottle back, but changed his mind. Instead, he retrieved a corkscrew from his desk drawer, twisted the spiral blade into the damp wood, and retracted. There was a moment just after the cork popped free that he could hear the wails and screams of the oppressed, but the moment passed quickly. Martin Alfred poured himself a tumbler of rum and sipped.

Shisa Hachiko
Trisha J. Wooldridge

Morning Pages, 8/13

Jessi warned me she'd be working tons of hours. I *know* enough Japanese culture to have expected this, but it still sucks.

It's been a week since her job started, and I haven't seen her for more than a few hours at a time. I'm supposed to be grocery shopping, but really, I came back to this 7-Eleven for the shisa statue.

Jessi threatened to leave me in the parking lot over it last time we were here.

It was more of a threat when I had no idea where I was or that the apartment was a ten-minute walk away. But she wouldn't *actually* abandon me. Both our parents said they'd cut us off if we did this, and well, here we are.

In any case, I've spent the past week exploring the neighborhood, so I'm no longer in danger of getting lost. I'm annoyed and lonely. It's not Jessi's fault, but I can't help but want to defy her by doing the one thing she's ever told me not to do.

So here I am, writing my Morning Pages beside this shisa statue. We can be lonely together. Maybe he'll help fill my mandatory journal pages as I work through *The Artist's Way* again. My advisor *suggested* I go through the whole twelve-week program (even though I've done it twice before, once in undergrad and again when I decided to get a masters in painting) and email her the weekly check-ins and tasks from the book as part of my academic leave.

I'm sure she hopes it'll help me figure out what to do with my life. I should've graduated two years ago, I haven't even got a full semester's load of credits left, and now I'm on *sabbatical* to Okinawa with my girlfriend for her video game art design dream job.

But sure, why not? I can hope too. Like, maybe I can sell a painting of this lonely shisa for millions of American bucks and postpone dealing with my future life indefinitely.

Manifest, baby! Why not? I'm already anthropomorphizing a statue. Let's see where this inspiration takes me . . .

Some years ago, *Futurama* had this episode that could bring anyone to tears, particularly if their childhood already bore the collected trauma of *The Brave Little Toaster*; Atreyu's horse, Artax; and Littlefoot's mom. "Jurassic Bark" was based on a real story from 1920s Japan. An Akita named Hachiko waited every day at Shibuya Station for his human, a university professor, to return from work. One day, the professor had a cerebral hemorrhage and never came home. For the rest of his life, Hachiko returned to Shibuya Station to wait for his beloved person.

Most people didn't know the story behind that episode. It wasn't even well-known in the Anime club I belonged to, which includes all sorts of Japanese-everything-loving nerds. But Hachiko's a national treasure in Japan, with memorials around the country and his taxidermied self preserved in the National Museum of Nature and Science. In Tokyo, Jessi and I saw people lined up to take pictures with the statue at Shibuya Station.

Yet the poor dog died thinking he'd been abandoned by the person he loved most.

And Shisa are the famous dogs of Okinawa—originally Ryukyu, before a bunch of colonization and wars. Shisa are usually in pairs—an open-mouthed male to scare away evil spirits and a closed-mouth female to keep in good spirits—but some single shisa stand watch at various places. There are multiple myths of shisa saving towns and kingdoms, and you see them *everywhere*: businesses, private homes, town borders, hanging out on any red-tiled roof . . .

And in an empty, overgrown lot beside a 7-Eleven.

I have another page to fill, so let me sing the praises of the Japanese 7-Eleven. They are *convenience stores* (*conbini* in Japanese) elevated to peak perfection: cheap food, from fresh and packaged groceries to prepared grab-and-go deliciousness to multiple coolers of frozen snacks; all the coffee and tea anyone'd want, hot or cold, fresh made or packaged; fresh fruit smoothies; post office; business center; ATM *and* currency exchange machine; drug store; package store; souvenirs, periodicals, comics, manga, and toys; and clean bathrooms no one gives you side-eye for daring to use.

Awesomeness within notwithstanding, the outside of a Japanese 7-Eleven looks exactly like an American 7-Eleven. Put it in a shabbier section of town (as *shabby* as Japan gets, which wouldn't even trigger my mom to hiss "Lock your doors" as we drove through), add an abandoned and overgrown lot right behind it, and it almost felt like home.

Except the random shisa, of course.

Jessi didn't even notice him. When I pointed him out, she was like "No big deal, they're everywhere," then got defensive because I wanted to go see him. "Don't be one of those ignorant Americans galumphing into a sacred space."

Like I would! I know more Japanese culture than she does, and her dad's Japanese!

Then she threatened, "Get in the car or I'm leaving without you." That pissed me off more, so *then* she was all, "It's our last night together before I'm working crazy hours . . ." *Kiss, kiss, kiss.*

Well, that worked. She should've led with that.

All of that is to say I'm naming my 7-Eleven shisa friend *Hachiko.*

And I'm pretty sure he just ate my last onigiri.

*   *   *

Morning Pages, 8/14

Yesterday's weird thing with the shisa is still on my mind. When Jessi asked why I seemed so distracted, I mostly lied. I don't think I've ever lied to her.

Maybe I ate that second onigiri and just forgot. Totally plausible for me. Except the wrapper was lodged under Hachiko's front paw. Not easy to pull free, so how would I have put it there?

I know better than to litter in Japan. So I was pulling, pulling, pulling . . . but *carefully, carefully, carefully* because possibly sacred statue, right?

As if on cue to scold me for loitering, a policeman came out of the 7-Eleven, bento box in hand, and made a scowling beeline for me as I nearly fell over freeing the wrapper from under that stone claw.

My very American ass—that *wasn't* missing any extra rice ball sandwich—held me upright, like one of those bobbling toddler dolls you can't knock over. My journal, sketchpad, copy of *The Artist's Way*, and half my backpack spewed around me.

So much for not making a mess of a potentially sacred space! Jessi would *kill* me if I got arrested! I'm not sure what's left from her signing bonus, but it probably wouldn't cover criminal fines, much less bail.

There I was, shoving crap into my backpack, when the officer pales and his expression goes slack. He makes an about-face and gets into his little black-and-white car that I can't, in good faith, call a *cruiser* because it looks like a toy.

What the . . .?

I looked at my stone companion.

I don't recall where his open mouth was pointing before, but at that moment, he was roaring at that tiny police car.

My tongue went dry and my stomach went cold. I stuffed everything into my backpack, one eye on the cop 'til he drove out of sight.

But then I had to get weirder. I gave the stone dog a scritch behind his lion-puppy ear.

"Thanks, buddy," I said, hoping to amuse the eerie chill out of my stomach. "Glad you liked the onigiri."

I shook out the old flannel I was using as a blanket, then looked again at Hachiko. I swear, his roar even more resembled a doggy grin. And his stone pupils pointed at me.

Because I can't *not* take any joke too far—even with myself—I petted his head and said, "I gotta get some groceries and bring them home to Jessi. But I'll be back. Sayonara for now, Hachi! You're a good boy."

That eerie feeling still sat in my stomach, but I was inexplicably *happy*.

The old woman behind the 7-Eleven register welcomed me back in English.

I vaguely remembered she'd spoken English when I'd grabbed the two onigiri, the hot maple pancake thing, and the milk tea. I properly greeted her in both English and Japanese.

When she regarded my shopping with not-quite-judgy eyes, I explained I was grabbing groceries. She asked why I hadn't grabbed groceries when I'd come in half an hour ago.

I explained I was an artist and had wanted to sketch the shisa in the back. But then the police officer had looked at me like I was in trouble or something. "Is there something sacred back there? Was I accidentally doing something wrong?"

Her face went pale like the cop's, and she said, *slowly*, in English, "It's not a sacred space, no. But it's dangerous. You shouldn't go back there. You could get hurt. Bad things happen back there."

Speaking Japanese, I prompted her to explain.

She frowned and said basically the same thing in Japanese.

I thanked her very much, she wished me a good day, and I left with my groceries.

I couldn't help but wave goodbye at Shisa Hachiko. The way the sun played between the wind-dancing tree branches, I could've sworn he wagged his tail.

*   *   *

Morning Pages, 8/18

Jessi is working *another* weekend!

She was supposed to have this one off. We'd made plans for a little *Karate Kid* sight-seeing tour, but noooooooooo, her stupid boss needed her to make some stupid changes and come to a stupid meeting.

Fuck me.

So, I'm heading back to the 7-Eleven and Hachi. I was going through my sketchpad over breakfast and noticed something weird in the drawings I made of him yesterday morning. All my shisa statues are in different poses. And the lines look more like fur than stone. So yeah. Weird Part One.

But then Jessi started flipping through my pictures—without asking, I may add. Rude. Especially since she'd *just* yelled at me for looking at what she was working on for the video game because NDA blah-blah-bullshit. And something about that samurai-armored horse *still* itches my brain. Probably thinking how I could fix it for her. The proportions were off, and I can *feel* my hands drawing the lines to make it right.

Anyway, Weird Part Two: she *forgot* we'd even seen the shisa before! And our argument! She tried to play it off like she eventually remembered, but I know better.

But, weirdness aside, I'm abandoned again. And I want to see how Hachi really is posed . . .

* * *

Nakata Sachiko paused in the parking lot before her Sunday shift at the Umusa 7-Eleven. Unexpected movement caught her eye, so she looked to the abandoned lot—something she normally avoided.

The shisa glared. His roar was for her, she was certain. It had been for nearly a half century.

She accepted this. It was kinder than she deserved.

Why anything in that lot beckoned *her* attention, she didn't know. Or would prefer not to know. Or not be beckoned at all. The things she didn't want to see in that lot had only grown in number over the years.

Flapping book pages. That shouldn't need her attention, yet the fluttering paper drew her feet and cane closer.

The shisa continued glaring. She didn't *hear* his growl, but tones deeper than mortal ears could perceive resonated in her gut, her bones. A *pressure* hindered her approach.

"I will not cross the boundary," she grumbled, gaze on the pavement. Age already bowed her body, but she kept intention in her posture. "I will not upset *her*."

The resistance lessened.

"Ah, so I am being summoned."

The air fluttered, as did the sensation in her stomach.

"Summoned or drawn. I suppose it is your call, shisa-sama, if I continue. Should I heed what pulls me or your roar?"

Nakata nearly fell forward. Though bent, the woman hardly used the cane she carried. Her steps moved surely over uneven pavement as it surrendered to patches of packed dirt.

The book was right beside the shisa.

Sunlight still fell upon her within a few paces of the statue, but Nakata shivered as if entering shadows. A wind—likely *more* than a wind—blew from the trees and flipped the small, bound book. A corner landed on the parking area's blacktop pebbles.

Using her cane, Nakata pulled it toward her as gently as she could. When the whole book was on blacktop, she picked it up.

This Journal Belongs to . . .
Rachel McAllister
TAW Morning Pages 2007

Pictures of the shisa, birds, tree branches, bitten onigiri—exquisite, even for doodles—bordered the identification box and many pages. If Nakata hadn't recognized the given name, the art clarified to whom the journal belonged: the red-haired American artist girl who spoke Japanese. She was infatuated with the shisa statue, had sat with him the other morning. It appeared she'd returned, despite Nakata's warnings.

Frowning, the old woman slipped the journal into her purse, begrudgingly bowed to the shisa, and returned to the store for her shift.

*　　*　　*

Dear Ms. McAllister,

I found this and brought it inside to keep it safe. I opened it to search who it belonged to, saw your name and art, and set it aside with a note so it may find you again.

While I am pleased to return your work, I am disappointed you returned to the lot behind the store. Please allow me to stress that it can be very dangerous. There are many great sights to draw in Okinawa, many other lovely shisa statues. I am happy to give you suggestions and maps. Please remain safe and continue to draw beautiful things.

Most respectfully,
Nakata Sachiko

*　　*　　*

Morning pages, 8/20

I was so worried I'd lost my journal, but thank goodness Mrs. Nakata rescued it for me!

The note reiterating *the lot is dangerous* and *remain safe* is a little unsettling. Her English is great, though. Maybe I'll swing by tomorrow and visit with her. Maybe I can find out what she *really* means when she says that lot's dangerous. At the very least, it'd be nice to know what else I can do while Jessi works. I've wandered every inch of the neighborhood and walked all the way down to the ocean, out to Nago Park, and even to Nago Castle (where there are, in fact, *many* shisa statues!)

But I don't want to *not* visit Hachiko. We're abandonment buddies.

Maybe if I paint something nice for Mrs. Nakata . . .

*   *   *

Morning Pages, 8/23

After I dump Jessi's uneaten curry in front of Hachiko, I dive into my backpack.

"Fuck me sideways!"

My sketchbook and Mrs. Nakata's painting aren't here. They're in the bedroom. Even if I wanted to walk the ten minutes back, it's pointless.

I mean, Jessi didn't *kick me out* kick me out. She just made it clear I wasn't welcome in the bedroom—her office—'til she somehow shitfacedly sends her boss some ideas that she and some Keiko chick shared during a get-drunk-with-dinner business meeting that *I know* is normal business SOP in Japan. But I hate it.

Glancing at the celestial, sacred messenger stone lion-dog, I feel like I just swore in church. "Sorry."

"It's all right. I've heard worse."

I just about jump out of my skin. Did the statue just talk? In a little kid's voice? In my imagination, he sounds like Keith David—Goliath, from *Gargoyles.*

A little girl with pigtails and powder-blue, home-sewn corduroy overalls pops around the dog and says, in perfect English, "Sorry, I thought you were talking to me."

"Oh, sorry too! I, ah, didn't see you there and that was kind of rude of me. Um, hi?"

"Hi!" She smiles brightly and waves. "I'm Emiko."

"I'm Rachel." I wave back. She's tiny, with similar features to Jessi. Half American? There are lots of U.S. bases in Okinawa. It's possible she's older than she looks, but even if she's twelve or thirteen, it's late for her to be out alone. In a *dangerous* abandoned lot. "Nice to meet you, Emiko-kun."

"Nice to meet you, too. Why are you upset, Miss Rachel?"

"Upset?"

"What you said after you fed Shisa Hachiko. That you apologized for."

I open my mouth. How does she know what I named the shisa?

Emiko cocks her head, much like a dog. "The f-word sideways."

"I know what I said. I just . . ." I look at the shisa and notice nothing's left of the curry.

"He really liked it. He also likes onigiri, especially salmon. And the name you gave him."

"Oh." Well, that answers some questions. And opens way more I'm *not* ready to entertain. "I-I'll remember salmon next time . . . And I forgot my sketchbook. Why I swore."

"Oh, okay." Emiko climbs onto Hachi's back, stretching to scritch between his ears. "He thinks you're a good artist too."

Unexpectedly honored by the opinion of a stone dog and/or a little kid's magically-shared imagination, I blush. "I appreciate that. Thank you."

"He says you're welcome. Can't you hear him? Oh, never mind. Right." The girl's whole posture slumps.

"What's wrong?"

She shakes her head. "I'm just glad you're talking to me." She sits up prettily. "Can you draw me sometime, Miss Rachel?"

"Sure, I guess. I haven't drawn many kids, so it might not be that great."

"Hachi thinks your portrait will be great."

"I appreciate the vote of confidence." I lay down my flannel and sit. "It's darker over here than I figured. I probably couldn't have drawn much tonight."

"It's normally dark at this time," Emiko says.

"I thought the 7-Eleven lights would spread more. But it is late." I raise my eyebrow at Emiko, Mrs. Nakata's warnings loud in my mind. "Do you live near here?"

She stares for an uncomfortable moment before shrugging. "This is my home."

"This lot?"

She hits me with that special childlike disdain reserved for particularly stupid adults.

"Sorry. Dumb question. Actually, what *is* this lot? Like, why is there a shisa *here?*"

"It used to be an apartment, but was damaged by an earthquake, and then got torn down. His mate got broken, so the construction workers took her too." Emiko wraps her little arms around the lion-dog's neck.

"I'm so sorry." I can't help but pet Hachi to console him too.

"But I keep him company. And he keeps me safe. Why are you here?"

He keeps me safe. I glance around nervously, but perhaps the stone lion-dog guardian who likes my art will keep me safe too. I'll just ignore all the fairy tale and mythic red flags. "Well, I was going to draw. And I wanted to do something with the curry . . . I figured Hachi would like it."

Emiko nods solemnly, then asks, "So, if you had dinner, did you have dessert yet?"

"Um, no?"

"Hachi really likes ice cream. If you were going to get some, that is, Miss Rachel."

I raise an eyebrow but can't repress a grin. "What about you? Do you also like ice cream, Emiko-kun?"

"Yes! I love Suika bars. The ones that look like watermelon."

"And does Hachi have a favorite?"

After another head tilt, Emiko says, "Chocolate and milk waffle cone."

I frown. "Chocolate's not good for dogs. Or cats."

"It's not?"

"I mean, I don't know specifically about celestial stone guardian lion-dogs . . ."

"He says he'll be fine."

Chuckling, I stand. Fighting with drunken Jessi wasn't even the worst part of my day. And she did throw money at me—a disturbingly *large* sum of yen. Becoming a manga or fairy-tale heroine might be a change for the better.

Why not?

Who am I to argue with a celestial stone lion dog about dessert?

*   *   *

Morning Pages, 8/23 (part 2?????)

WHAT. THE. FUCK.

I left my journal home with my sketchpad and Mrs. Nagata's painting last night. I have no memory of writing in it. But that's my handwriting. It *sounds* like me and I certainly did imagine that if Hachi talked, he'd sound like Keith David.

Did I sleep journal? Wake up whenever Jessi did, write my Morning Pages, and fall back to sleep? I mean, the journal and sketchpad are right on my nightstand. Jessi probably put them there because I'd tossed them on the bed when I ripped through my backpack searching for my bank info to see if there was any money I could send to my mom before she sold off everything in my US bedroom.

Right. That also happened yesterday.

I got my first email from Mom in weeks—to fucking say she and Dad were emptying out my room since they didn't know when I'd be back and mom wanted a fucking study.

Fucked up or not, the journal's accurate. More accurate than I'd probably write, what with having actual dialogue, proper verb tense, and everything. But accurate: spooky but adorable kid who talks with a shisa statue asks me to get her and said stone lion-dog ice cream.

But wait! *There's more!* Because why not use Morning Pages to document the ever-climbing benchmark of WTF that is my life?

No wrong way to do morning pages, Julia Cameron says.

So, I go into the 7-Eleven sans sketchbook and painting but with—surprise—rage-chucked 30,000 yen at almost eleven o'clock at night, and who's working?

The sweet Mrs. Nakata of course. Clearly not a woman who ascribes to old person (or Japanese, for that matter) early bird stereotypes. And man, she looks concerned. In fact, she asks if I'm all right.

I burst out laughing. And crying.

The old woman brings me a hot tea and pulls over the business area chair. Sitting on her stool behind the register, she asks what happened.

I tell her about my parents getting rid of my stuff, Jessi coming home late, us arguing about her hours, and then her throwing money at me like I'm some . . .

I don't finish the sentence. I don't have to. Mrs. Nakata gets me a piece of chocolate cake from the cooler.

I sniffle, thank her, and fumble for money.

She waves it away and suggests I send the money to my parents to get a storage facility. I can do that. Because you *can* do all that in a Japanese 7-Eleven. At half-past eleven at night.

All that accomplished, I thank her profusely and remember why I'd come in. I grab the requested ice creams, plus one for me and another Jessi likes, and insist I pay for those.

She doesn't question my indulgence, which is good, because thinking of what I'll say if she asks sends this deep, foreboding rumble in my belly, but Mrs. Nakata does walk me to the door and waits like she's seeing me off.

Well shit.

I head down the street and cut behind the neighboring building (a *resort & business hotel* with cardboard in all the windows). Their parking area abuts the shisa's lot.

I make it to Hachiko without getting accosted—except for tripping over an old umbrella. Emiko's nowhere to be seen, but it is nearly midnight. I unwrap both treats and leave them in front of the shisa.

*   *   *

Morning Pages, 9/2

Missed morning pages yesterday. Don't wanna today. Too shitty.

I got invited to dinner with Jessi's team on Friday. A good thing, I thought. I've lost almost ten pounds, so even though my good dress was a little big, I looked *haaawwwt!*

And Jessi wore this sexy, coral jumpsuit that brought out the coppery sparkle in her eyes, complimented the blue streaks in her hair, and hugged her in all the right places. Every. Single. Curve.

I could've just watched her move in that all night.

When I asked when she got the jumpsuit, she got all defensive. "How could you forget when I got this?"

I didn't know.

Then she did that annoying sitcom wife/girlfriend thing of never telling me what I forgot, so we ended up not talking in the taxi ride to the restaurant.

Should've been my first clue.

Besides no one being interested in manga, comics, or anime

(despite them all working on what I know, stupid NDA notwithstanding, is a Japanese-themed video game), most of them grated on my nerves. Her boss, Taira Hiroshi, kept listing all the awesome things to do in Okinawa—as if he gave any time to go and *do* said things. I managed to hold my tongue.

And then there was Keiko. Jessi always only calls her by her given name, and *she's* the one coming up with ideas requiring Jessi to put in extra hours. *She* sat on Jessi's other side. Far. Too. Close.

I don't *recall* saying anything . . .

Hell, I could've disappeared into the furniture. The waiter kept looking surprised whenever I asked for more water—which never got refilled. And the hibachi chef, who was cooking *in front of all of us* kept forgetting to serve me!

. . . but Jessi claimed I made a fool of her, and she went to sleep frigid and angry.

I went to sleep frustrated and horny.

Then yesterday morning, she's like, "Let's go to the aquarium!"

"But I thought you had to work this weekend," I said. "That's what you all were saying last night."

"Keiko's covering this morning. And haven't you been complaining we haven't had time together in weeks?" Then she got all kissy and kittenish, we had the fantastic sex I'd wanted last night, and I was ready to follow her anywhere.

The aquarium was as awesome as everyone says. I got some good sketches, really good ones I want to paint, and then we came home and had more great sex.

And this morning, she was back to being a pissed off ice queen for no reason whatsoever. Well, no *logical* reason. She *said* I didn't remind her to set an alarm or give her time to work yesterday, so she had to run into the office early and get shit done.

So here I sit, not wanting to look at yesterday's sketches. I don't even want to leave bed. Maybe I'll spend the day re-watching the first volumes of *One Piece* or *Ah, My Goddess!* on the computer . . .

* * *

Morning Pages, 9/3

I turned yesterday around when Jessi called to say, "Don't bother making me dinner," and, "Use some *petty cash* to get something nice for yourself."

At first, I was even more depressed and pissed. Then I noticed the rose-gold sunlight streaming through the shades. It was gorgeous outside! I had to capture whatever the sunset would look like!

After making Great Big Plans, I realized I hadn't eaten all day. So, back to the 7-Eleven. I got some food, chatted with Mrs. Nakata, and snuck out while she spoke with another customer so I could bring food to Hachi.

The shisa was glorious in that light!

I'd packed a camera with my art supplies for taking reference photos. I grabbed that—and wondered if it were rude to just start snapping pictures. At this point, I kinda *knew* this celestial, sacred lion-dog.

"May I take your picture, Shisa Hachiko?"

"He says you may, Miss Rachel."

"Emiko-kun! Konnichiwa gozaimasu!" I greeted with delight, though I didn't see the girl.

"Konnichiwa, Miss Rachel. I'll stay out of the way while you take a photograph of the most handsome Shisa Hachiko."

I thanked her, put down my things, and took several pictures before tripping over the bags of food I'd bought with my *generous* helping from Jessi's petty cash.

As I placed two salmon onigiri and a chicken stick before the shisa, Emiko appeared, hair and clothes exactly as when I'd last seen her, a hungry look in her eyes.

"Fried chicken stick?" I offered.

"Yes, please. Thank you so much, Miss Rachel."

"You're welcome, Emiko-kun."

"You may call me Emiko. Or Emi," she said over a mouth full of chicken.

"Yobisute de ii," I respond. "And I prefer just Rachel, no *Miss*, please."

"Thank you, Rachel! I'm so glad we're friends."

After we ate, I pulled out my sketchpad and asked Emi if she still wanted me to draw her.

You'd think I offered a PlayStation 3, an Xbox 360, a pony, and all of Christmas in one shiny present. When she stopped gleefully vibrating, she sat even more still than professional models.

I got lost in drawing her.

"Are you almost done?"

Realizing I no longer moved my pencil, I looked at the picture. "Wow." I'd never felt so good about a rough sketch.

"Can we see? Can we see?"

I held up the pad.

Her response—hers and Hachi's, she promised—was full of more squeals and joy than I remember from my whole life of sharing pictures. I basked in it until I couldn't see my own lines on the paper.

"You're not getting in trouble for being out this late?" I asked as I packed up.

Her face was unreadable. "No."

"Your parents aren't going to be worried?"

Emiko said nothing for an uncomfortable amount of time. Finally her façade crumbled some and she looked away. "My parents are gone."

Gone?

Before I could ask more, a deep *growl* hit my stomach. Hachiko's face was more roar than smile.

I took the hint. "I'm sorry, Emi."

She shook her head. "It's been a while . . . Do *you* have family worried for you?"

Would Jessi be home yet? I checked the sky as if I could tell time from stars and guesstimated it was probably well past dinner. "My girlfriend might be, actually."

"*Girl*friend?"

If Emi's guardians didn't care how late she was out, they could handle me explaining my relationship. "I like girls better than boys. Boys don't deserve me, and I'm pretty sure most of them never outgrow their cooties."

"Oh. Okay . . . I don't want to worry your girlfriend." Disappointment colored her face.

"I'll come back. I have to show you my finished painting of you, right?"

That cheered her up. "Yes! Please! Thank you!"

*　　*　　*

Nakata Sachiko looked up from pricing tubs of Ramen when the door chimed.

Tearstained and holding back sobs, Rachel McAllister, the

106

American artist, stumbled over a black umbrella the old woman had been *certain* she'd thrown in the trash, and then headed to the cooler cases.

Sneering at the tattered umbrella, she rolled the business center chair over to the register and went to make some tea for the girl.

Not a *girl.* Rachel was probably close in age to Kazumi when—

That was the last thing she wanted to think of.

"What has happened?" She gestured to the chair as Rachel returned to the register with an armload of food.

The *young woman* burst into tears, blubbering apologies in English and Japanese.

Nakata collected the groceries in a basket, urged Rachel to sit and accept the herbal tea, then waited patiently on her stool, holding out a box of tissues.

Your own daughter would have appreciated such kindness.

It was far, far too late to do anything about that.

After more apologies and gratitude, Rachel shared her misery. "My mom sent back the money order. No explanation. Nothing. Just a *return to sender* stamp or whatever. I never got a response to the email I sent when I got the money order. I checked my spam and everything. So I used my emergency phone card to just call her. She said she never got my email and the money came too late. She'd already donated or sold things to pay off the loans she and Dad had gotten when we split the cost of my bachelor degree. Just like that. All I had back home is . . . *gone.* Like they don't even *want* me to come home. How can parents be like that?"

Nakata would have preferred the girl stab her with a knife, a plastic fork even, than with such a question. While Rachel blew her nose, she composed herself and said, "I'm sorry that happened to you. Sometimes parents make terrible decisions they later regret. They are human, too."

"Do you have kids?" Rachel sniffled.

Nakata flinched.

"I—I'm sorry. That was out of place to ask. I didn't mean—"

"I had a daughter. And it is fair to ask after hearing me make such a weak excuse for cruel behavior."

"I don't mean to make my parents sound cruel. I mean, they paid for half my undergrad costs that weren't covered by scholarships. I just never met their expectations for what I'd do when I graduated—"

"Listen to me, Rachel-san. What they did *was* cruel. And selfish. When you choose to have a child, to create another life, you make an agreement to love and nurture that life. No matter what they do." She headed to make another cup of tea and hide the tears of her hypocrisy.

"It's not just the college loans. They didn't want me to come here with my *girlfriend*. They think I'm going to hell anyway."

Nakata froze, stifling a gasp until she yelped when hot water ran over her hand.

Rachel came to her side, wrapping towels around the scalded hand. "You should go to the bathroom and run cold water over that. I'll clean up. It's the least I can do for all your kindness."

In a haze, Nakata did so.

I am not kind.

When she returned, Rachel had wiped up all the water. The old woman bowed and murmured, "Thank you."

"No, thank you. For . . . everything. Are you all right?"

"I'm fine. Thank you very much." Numbness still chilled her voice.

Rachel studied the floor, face red and fresh tears threatening.

Nakata reached for the young woman's hand, shaking. When Rachel grasped her fingers, the woman blurted words she hadn't spoken for over half a century. "My sister married an American serviceman and moved to the United States. My parents disowned her."

"I'm so sorry!" Rachel said.

"That was what happened then." She closed her eyes. The image of a man in an American Navy uniform played behind her eyelids . . .

. . . standing on the doorstep of the small family home Sachiko's father left to his only heir, the unwelcome American declares, "I love your daughter. I will marry her—"

"Stay away from Kazumi!" Sachiko tries to slam the door in his face, but her daughter pushes by.

Tears run down Kazumi's face, which is rounder, chubbier, brighter than usual. "Mother, I'm pregnant—"

"Get out of my house!"

Nakata rubbed the wrinkles over her throat as if she'd *just* screamed those words. "Okinawa has a complicated history with American military."

Rachel nodded. "I learned about that some in school."

Tell her the rest. Tell her you're no better.

"And your . . . girlfriend? Is she taking good care of you?"

Rachel's face fell. "She has a lot of work, so she's not around much. But she gives me money and she brought me here."

Nakata pressed her lips together, wishing she couldn't read the young woman's words and expression so well. "You know, there are clubs in Okinawa for Americans. A lot of military, but also their family, students, and others. I will make you a list next time you come in. You need more friends here."

"Thank you." Rachel didn't look cheered. "I . . . Is there anything else I can do to help?" She looked toward her basket at the register.

"You have already helped so much. Thank you again. Will your girlfriend be waiting for you?"

Rachel looked toward the clock over the business center. "She might be home by now."

"Do you have long walk? Your ice cream has been out for some time." There were several ice cream options for just one person. "Here, go get fresh ones."

"It's fine, really. I don't want to waste anything." She shrugged and grabbed behind herself where she normally carried a backpack. Shocked dismay reshaped her face as she patted her body and pockets, hissing out a long *ffffff.*

"Don't worry." Nakata pulled her own purse from the shelf under the register. "I have this. A gift to help with such a painful day."

"Oh, I can't—"

"I would be offended if you refused," Nakata said sternly. "And before you worry, I have money. I work here because . . . because I would rather not spend my evenings alone."

"Oh . . . sorry . . . And thank you. Really, um . . ."

Tell her.

"Go on." Nakata bagged the food and handed it to Rachel. "But go straight ho—"

The door chime rang extra loudly, drawing both their attention. No one entered, but the umbrella no longer lay inside the door. She scowled at the empty space it had occupied.

"Wind?" Rachel offered, turning and bowing deeply. "Thank you so much, Nakata-san. Truly. I appreciate your kindness."

Another wave of guilt kept the woman from speaking further. As she tried to leave the register to follow, her cane hit something that made her stumble.

A tattered black umbrella.

"You. Really?"

The umbrella didn't respond.

Nakata snatched it up and headed to the back door, by the dumpster and where she could see the shisa's lot.

The door chime rang again. She recognized the customer who waved and bowed on the way to the self-serve food. He was here an hour earlier than normal.

Nakata greeted him back before glaring at the umbrella and throwing it into the little trash bin behind the counter.

Why didn't you tell the girl what you did to your daughter? And her daughter? The honest reason you say the lot you know she's heading to right now is so dangerous?

"No more of your mischief tonight, kasa-obake," she hissed, heading to help with the microwave's inevitable malfunction.

*　　*　　*

Morning Pages, 9/9

Jessi was working late again, so I headed to the 7-Eleven.

I only saw Emi around sunset. Yet another red flag related to interacting with spirits and *other*beings. But I was *doing* favors and kindnesses, not receiving them. *If* I believed in such things, I should be fine.

I'd finished the painting of Emi. And one of Hachiko I especially liked. I rearranged my backpack to make sure they—and Mrs. Nakata's painting of ducks on the Yabu River—didn't get wrecked.

Mrs. Nakata wasn't working that night. I'd worried about her seeing the paintings of Emi and Hachi with how she kept stressing I stay away from the back lot. And I thought she'd said she'd lost a daughter—I definitely remember her saying she lived alone. Something in my head connected that with the picture of Emiko possibly upsetting her, but whenever I thought about it, something distracted me.

In any case, I got food and headed to the lot.

Emi, sitting on Hachiko, waved as I approached. Once we were eating, I pulled out the paintings and reveled in Emi's delight—as well as a warm, but distant, happiness I'd come to recognize emanating from the shisa.

"I have a gift for you, too, Rachel," Emi said, neatly folding her dinner trash. She stood and reached for me. "But I need to bring you. Come with me?"

I glanced at Hachiko, getting the emotional resonance of a poker face. Not comforting, but not a warning.

"Okay . . ." I took Emi's hand. It felt fragile, not really there, almost like my grandmother's when she was in hospice care.

Releasing a joyous squeal, Emiko pulled me with a strength beyond what such dainty fingers should possess. We jogged through more overgrown grass and scrub trees than I expected. Every so often, something moved in the corner of my vision. A flash of darkness, a blur of light. If I hadn't been struggling to keep up with an energetic kid, I'd've been more unsettled. When she slowed, I saw only old trees and bushes—and a half-crumbled, stone lantern lighting a gnarly opening between massive azalea bushes.

Emiko pulled me through that wild doorway. I didn't even get a look at how that old lantern was lit. In the center of a . . . yard? . . . stood a little old, paper-walled building that belonged in a manga or anime. Or a Studio Ghibli film. The surrounding garden beds were overgrown mixes of weeds and dead plants, and the house looked like a good wind might blow it down at any moment. Between rotting wooden slats, torn holes in the paper winked like little eyes.

Emi bounded up the stairs, unafraid of their creaking cracks. When I hesitated, she offered, "You can wait here. I'll be right out with your surprise."

Once she disappeared inside, I slowly turned around, heart pounding. No way I was still in that abandoned lot. I had to be dreaming. Maybe I'd eaten something bad and was still in bed.

Another broken lantern—the same one?—illuminated this side of the azaleas. A variety of trash littered the untended beds. Another ratty umbrella—did everyone just leave those around?— stuck up as if planted, and unmatched sandals leaned on garden walls and plant stalks.

Little Emi returned with a milk crate piled high with manga and placed it in front of me. "You were sad when your mom got rid of your manga and books, so I found this for you!"

I stared at the familiar, worn—familiarly worn—titles. *Sailor Moon. Ranma 1/2. Nausicaä of the Valley of the Wind. Fruits Basket.*

"Here!" Emi patted a plaid flannel on the ground. Not the one I'd left by Hachiko, along with my backpack and the food, but another that shared the books' familiarity.

I sat beside her and gently shuffled through the soft-edged books. Hardly looking, I grabbed the first volume of *Sailor Moon.* "Do you know this one?"

The girl snuggled against me. "Will you read it with me?"

My own heart fluttered warmly, protectively, and I put an arm around her. The volume fell open to the first page. Surprisingly, the one stone lantern cast enough light to read. We picked characters and performed their speech bubbles to each other. When we got to the end, Emi begged we read the next one.

I hardly noticed. I was preoccupied with the fact that we were surrounded.

The umbrella stood a few feet away on its curved handle. In the folded material, a single eye blinked above a grinning mouth, and from the mouth a cartoonish red tongue dangled almost to the handle.

The mismatched sandals sat to one side like a school of kindergarteners, little legs out in front of them, single-eyes raptly settled upon us.

Directly in front of us, the lantern crouched, legs curled underneath itself. Its beaming face collapsed with the stone housing: one eye (of two) squished and sunken between rock pieces and its smile unevenly spread over cracks.

"It's okay." Emi patted my arm. "They're my friends."

My mouth was too dry to respond. I nervously fingered the manga's paper and felt the imprint of writing across the last page—first page, if it were an American book.

I turned there.

Rachel McAllister was scrawled in middle-school cursive.

I dropped the book and scrambled to stand. My hand tangled in worn flannel threads. I shook free. Easily. Muscle memory recalled the worn fray of the old shirt I'd stolen from an ex and couldn't throw away.

"Can we go back, please, Emi?" I whispered.

"You don't want to read another?"

"Not now, please. Emi? I-I want to go back. Please?" Manners.

Manners were always important in stories.

The girl's lower lip trembled. There was something familiar about her, too, but . . .

"Please, Emiko-kun? Emiko-san?" I bowed respectfully, certain I wasn't speaking to a child. "Please may we go back?"

"Okay." She sounded ready to cry, but took my hand.

"Thank you," I whispered.

The . . . haunted things . . . moved out of the way. Once we passed through the azaleas, we were back in the lot. And it was still sunset. Had it been that dark in the trees? Or had I been away . . . longer?

I managed to not run from Emiko. That would've been rude. Crossing that small lot was both much faster and slower than when we jogged to her *home*. I was just as out of breath. As I neared Hachiko, my anxiety doubled. Or rather, his joined mine. I don't know what we said while I packed up and left for home.

Maybe I don't want to know.

*   *   *

A large black folder leaned on the side of the 7-Eleven, close to the shisa's lot. After a concerned glance toward the guardian, Nakata Sachiko headed toward the unexpected item. It was on the parking lot; she wasn't crossing any boundary.

Like a file folder but larger, the heavy cardboard caught the wind like a sail. Each gust nearly pulled the woman off balance, but she got it into the store without falling.

She placed the folder behind the register and was surprised each time she saw it.

Between ten and midnight, she was overcome with a sense of expecting someone, but she couldn't recall who. Flashes of a young woman flitted through Nakata's mind—visited in shadow images around the store. A chubby American with red-blonde hair and green eyes who carried a backpack dangling a purple-plaid shirt.

I know her, she thought several times before promptly forgetting such insights.

When she tripped over the black folder, Nakata put it on the counter. There were no other customers. She had time to look inside.

Three paintings, each wrapped with tissue paper. The first was a serene view of several ducks floating on the Yabu River. On the back was a thank you to her. *Nakata Sachiko.* The signature on the bottom was *Rachel McAllister.*

"Rachel-san," she murmured with a clearer picture of the young woman.

The next picture was the shisa in the lot. The back read *Shisa Hachiko.*

"You named him? Oh, Rachel-san . . ."

Her hands shook as she unwrapped the third painting. Though her stomach sank, she was unsurprised at the beautiful, ghost-child's beaming face. She didn't have to flip it over.

Teardrops landed on the paper, blurring details and calling to mind a newspaper clipping too worn to decipher, but like the painting's name, she didn't need to read.

Surveyors and police found the crushed remains of a young girl in a condemned Umasa apartment. The apartment, which has not had residents for years, was critically damaged by last month's earthquake and neighbors have been worried it may collapse, damaging nearby residences and businesses. No identification was found with the girl's body. If you have any information . . .

Nakata caressed the painted cheek she'd never touched in life. Unaware what surname the girl had been given, she whispered the only name she knew. "Emiko."

*   *   *

Morning Pages, 9/16

I don't remember the walk home or even entering the apartment. All of a sudden, I'm in our bedroom. I hear Jessi in the bathroom. Her computer monitor is on, and there's a pile of drawings on a table next to her desk. The pile of art echoes the uncomfortable pang of the box of manga and the worn flannel, so I look at the screen. That feeling gets worse.

Sickening familiarity.

Illustrations of Asian weaponry. Action studies from the jujitsu dojo. An unfinished rendering of a horse in samurai armor.

I spread the sketches and finished works over the bed. *My* pictures. That I did *not* pack to bring with me. In fact, I remember having a panic attack, telling Jessi I'd forgotten them on my shelf in the third art closet. I worried they'd be thrown out while I was away. Jessi told me she'd made sure they'd be safe. I figured she'd spoken to someone.

She'd *taken* them?

She was *using* them? For *her* video game work? That *she* was getting paid for? Credit for?

I hear the toilet flush. As soon as Jessi comes in, I face her. "What! The! Fuck?"

Jessi doesn't even look at me. She stares at the spread-out art. "Rachel?" she murmurs.

"Yeah. Me. *My* art. What the *fuck* are you doing?" Stupid question. I can see what she's doing. What she's been doing.

She walks right by me and begins gathering the pages. "You're gone. You've *been* gone. For a week."

"What?" I slap the pictures from her hand. They fly around with hurricane force.

Jessi gasps and shakes her head, face whiter than mine.

"Goddamnit, Jessi, look at me! Fucking look at me!"

"No. No . . . I can't do this right now." She stalks out of the room. "This isn't happening."

"'This isn't happening'?" I screech. I want to follow, but my feet are frozen. Years of my art settle on the floor like a flock of birds. Something else catches my attention. On my nightstand.

My feet move around the bed and I see my open journal. There's no pencil, but lines in my handwriting tell me they are happening and I'm leaning over to read . . .

I back away. From a distance, I still see *my* writing filling the lines.

I'm at the 7-Eleven. I'm in front of Hachiko.

"What's happening to me?" I demand of the shisa. I *hear* his growl as well as feel it down to my bones. Emiko peeks around him. "What did you do to me?" I scream at her. Am I even experiencing this or am I reading my journal? I don't know.

Hachi growls louder. His eyes glow like little fires.

I don't care.

"I-I-I was trying to be your friend," Emiko whimpers, cowering behind the shisa.

My whole body shakes. A pressure pushes against me, pushes me away. I'm too furious, too terrified to be moved.

"No. Nononol!" Everything is unreal. Living shisa statues. Little girls with no parents who have the childhood my mom threw away. Fucking living umbrellas, sandals, and lanterns? My journal writing what's happening by itself? Nothing makes sense. That has to be it! "This isn't real. None of this is real!"

"Don't say that!" Emiko shouts back at me with the unholy fury of a scorned child facing down the unfairness of the universe. "We are so real!"

Hachiko's growl—did I really name a fucking statue?—rings in my ears. Twists my stomach like I have to puke. How long since I've eaten? Did Jessi say I was gone *a week?*

"No! You're not real! None of this is fucking real!"

The shisa's roar shoves me back, knocking the wind from me as my ass and shoulders skid on pavement. My ears ring so hard I can barely see. I push myself up, expecting to fight the shisa off me, but he sits on his stones many feet away on the abandoned lot.

Just a statue. A statue I can't go near. Everything is silent but for a child crying.

A child I can no longer see but who I will never, ever forget.

The Ballad of Johnny and Carmen
Elaine Labbee

"Come on, Johnny Boy, she wants ya. What are you, a chicken shit?"

"Yeah, thought you wanted to be a Pharaoh so bad. Well, this is it. This is what we do. Now get your ass in here and go to town on this chick."

Johnny Delmonico slumped against the cold cement wall in the basement of the abandoned tenement as his buddies egged him on. Over in a dark corner, two junkies huddled, far beyond caring what else went on in that dank, forgotten place. A feral cat meowed somewhere on the other side of the building, and he imagined it hunkered over a litter of blind, slime-covered black kittens, wriggling like worms as they searched for their mama's teat. The aroma of stale sweat, piss, cat shit, and blood permeated his nasal cavities. He thought he might puke, but he couldn't let these guys know that.

Carmen D'Agostino lay on a yellow-stained mattress, legs spread and hands above her head; one forearm faced the wrong way, and he could see her purpled elbow swelling. He pictured her with pompoms, yelling football cheers, but no hurrahs sprang from her lips now. Her screams and sobs had stopped a few minutes ago, while Davey Longmire had taken his turn with her. Now she just lay there staring at something none of them could see. That fancy beauty parlor hairstyle had come undone and her shiny blonde curls were in disarray. The satiny layers of her pretty pink prom dress, shredded and blood- spattered, bunched up under her backside, rhinestones littering the floor. Blood dribbled from her lips—one of the guys must have bitten them. The top of her dress splayed open; Freddy P, leader of the gang, had torn it down the middle as soon as he'd jumped on top of her.

Just a little while ago, the gang had been hanging out in the alley behind Ernest W. Throckmorton High School while the senior prom frothed inside. The sounds of Barry and the Boys playing "This Diamond Ring" had blasted out from behind the barred gymnasium windows as they'd waited for a couple to sneak away from the festivities for a little private action. It hadn't mattered who.

They'd planned to shank the guy and take off with the girl, drag her through the rotted door just down the alley and into this party palace. Johnny had nodded along. To prove himself to this group, he'd already helped rob a corner store and steal a car, but that had been small change compared to what they'd been fantasizing. Still, he'd do just about anything to be hanging with this bunch of guys.

The plan had worked like a charm, and Johnny mindlessly went along, somehow disassociating himself from the events even as they'd happened. They hadn't known the guy, but Johnny'd recognized Carmen from homeroom as soon as they'd gotten her into the weak light of the basement. She'd recognized him, too.

"Johnny! Johnny! Don't let them do this to me!" she'd begged as two of the guys had tossed her down on the mattress. "You know me. We're friends! I gave you my pencil that time, so you could finish your math homework before class. You've got to help me!"

That had stopped him cold for a sec. They weren't friends, but he did remember when she'd loaned him her pencil. He'd asked Joey Danvers across the aisle, not even daring to speak to the princess sitting in front of him, and she'd turned around, all Pepsodent smiley, and offered him hers before Joey could even respond.

"Here," she'd said in her sweet, privileged voice. "You can keep it. I've got plenty." Then she'd whipped back around, curly blonde ponytail bouncing. Johnny, stunned by the fact that she'd even noticed him, let alone spoken to him, had thought briefly that she looked like Betty from the Archie Comics, then hurried to finish his assignment before time ran out. He couldn't even remember if he'd thanked her.

That cheerleader's cuteness had disappeared under smeared makeup, and her honeyed voice had sounded ragged as she'd pleaded with him. Deep down, he'd wanted to help her, but couldn't. What would these guys do to him if he didn't take part in this horror show?

Freddy P had turned, appraising him. "You two know each other, huh? What . . . you date in junior high or somethin'?" His laugh was short, deep barks. "Maybe you should go first, then, since you're acquainted with our date here."

Johnny had instinctively stepped back. Freddy P'd responded with a smirk, saying, "Oh, okay. Little virgin here wants to see how it's done. Well, I'll show ya." Then he'd turned away and things had gotten going. Carmen had stopped pleading with Johnny and started screaming like he'd never heard a woman scream in his life.

He felt ashamed that all the violence had turned him on at first, especially seeing Carmen's boobs pop out when Freddy'd ripped her bra, but now those milky jugs were tainted by bite marks, bruises, and streaks of blood, and no longer pretty. One of her nipples was clean gone. Johnny didn't know if it had been bitten off or sliced off with somebody's knife. While everybody had stood watching Freddy and cheering him on, Johnny'd turned away to stare at the graffiti-covered wall and hadn't looked back until the other three guys had finished. His hard-on had embarrassed him, but as the screaming increased and he'd heard the punches, the erection had died.

Johnny *had* wanted to be a Pharaoh, like his big brother Jake, for so long. Jake had been cool as a cucumber, going around wearing a leather jacket emblazoned with the gang name on the back. But one day, Jake had skipped school, taken off on his Harley, and never returned. They'd found his body in a ditch by the railroad tracks, his bike totaled, his head bashed in. Nobody knew exactly what had happened.

That had made Johnny want to be a Pharaoh more than ever. It would be cool to step into his big brother's shoes. But Jake had been built big and strong like the rest of the guys, while Johnny— short, skinny, and pale—could barely lift the half-kegs at the convenience store where he worked. He honestly didn't know why they'd let him in at all.

He wondered now if Jake had done shit like this. He'd bragged about robbing a couple of gas stations and jacking some cars, but he never mentioned raping any girls. Johnny couldn't imagine Jake crossing this line. Now he questioned whether *he* could cross it.

An image of his mother invaded his thoughts. She'd raised the two boys on her own since their dad had left her for some chick he'd met at a bar. Unlike the mothers in stories, though, Mom hadn't worked two jobs and raised her boys to stay on the straight and narrow. She hadn't had a series of bad boyfriends, either. Instead, she'd gone on welfare and sat in her recliner all day, eating crap until she blew up to three hundred pounds and needed an oxygen tank and a scooter at the grocery store. Eventually, she stopped going out and asked Johnny to do the shopping. They lived on cheap frozen pizza, potato chips, and Black Label.

Still, even though her motherly skills were lacking, he didn't think she'd be too happy if she found out he'd raped a girl.

"Let's see that snow-white ass of yours." Davey hit him on the back, then leaned in and said, almost in a whisper, "Stop thinking about it and just do it."

Freddy P took two steps and got right in Johnny's face, giving the boy a front-row seat to his pockmarked skin and crooked, cigarette-stained teeth. Johnny almost gagged from the smell of stale Marlboros, beer, and a sausage sandwich with onions. "Look, you fucker, you'd better not be thinking about running out on us. Because if you do, that means we can't trust you no more. And guys we can't trust no more end up like your asshole brother."

"Shut the fuck up, Freddy!" said Denny Amato. "He don't need to know about that." Amato, the guy who'd come to Johnny after Jake's death, offering to use his influence to bring Johnny into the gang, put his muscly arm around the younger boy now. A pack of cigs fell out of his sleeve to the gritty floor. He ignored it. "Look, John." He wiped his nose with the other hand. "I'm guessing this is your first time doing anything like this. But you've fucked girls before, haven't you? That's all this is. Just another piece of ass." His tone changed as he shoved Johnny down on his knees between Carmen's legs. "Now do it."

Terrified, Johnny tried to do as told, but his body didn't want to cooperate. His limp dick didn't even twitch. No way could he let the guys see that, so he fell flat on top of Carmen and furiously rubbed against her pussy until things came to life. Then he slid inside her, squeezed his eyes shut, and pounded away as fast as he could. Carmen didn't make a sound, and she didn't move—just like the other girls he'd been with. But just as he felt himself about to shoot his wad, Carmen came back from wherever she'd been and looked him right in the eyes, and as he came she cried, "Why'd you do this to me, Johnny? I thought you were my friend." Then her head lolled and she didn't say anything else.

He fell back down upon her, exhausted and covered in sweat. The other guys were whistling and clapping, and Freddy P said, "You got more balls than your brother, I'll give you that, kid. Now get up and let's get the fuck outta here."

Johnny couldn't get up, afraid to look at Carmen again. She lay quiet and still, but somehow different. He could feel the warmth flowing out of her body, and he knew Mr. Death had come calling, just like in those cheap pulp paperbacks his mother liked to read. He turned and looked at Davey, sweat and spittle dribbling down his chin, and said, "I think . . . I think she's . . ."

Freddy P let loose with a bellowing guffaw. "Oh shit. You fucked her to death? Oh my God, Johnny Boy, you're gonna be a legend. Now, let's go."

As he tucked himself back in and zipped up, a bit of graffiti from the wall popped out at him, like when he'd worn those 3-D glasses at *House on Haunted Hill* at the State Theater. It said, *Abandon hope when you come in here.* Hadn't he heard something like that in a horror movie once?

* * *

A couple of weeks later, alone in the rattrap apartment he shared with two of the other guys, Johnny took the opportunity to jack off. He'd been doing it at least twice a day, every day, since he'd had his turn with Carmen. He did it in the scuzzy john at the store where he worked, he did it at night when the other guys were sleeping, and he did it in his rusty Chevy Corsica, parked at the rest area just up the road on 95. He didn't need his magazines anymore, just the memory of Carmen . . . but he didn't envision the warm girl he'd slid his prick into. No. Instead, he could only picture her dead, and as soon as he conjured up the feeling of a cold, marble-walled pussy, he exploded. He'd started worrying about being some kind of perv, but then the thought of her and those glassy eyes staring into heaven hijacked his brain and he just had to do it.

The night before, he'd been at a party in some girl's basement, and a hot babe wearing a tight yellow halter top had come on to him. Her lips had been bright red and she'd smelled like strawberries. Just the sight of a girl like that from across the room used to be enough to get him going. She'd wanted him bad, sitting on his lap, rubbing her heart-shaped ass against him, but he hadn't gotten hard , not even when he'd seen her nipples popping through the flimsy material of the halter. He'd felt her up and . . . nothing. So he'd gotten angry and tossed her off him, leaving the party to be alone with Carmen and spank the monkey in the woods behind the house.

Something *was* most assuredly wrong with him. He had needs now that could only be satisfied in one way. He'd given up hope of things ever being normal again.

So here he stood, picturing cold, dead Carmen and yanking hard, when he heard the front door downstairs open and close. The maintenance crew at Messalonskee Paper got off at five, and October afternoon light still shone through the windows; his roommates wouldn't be home for at least an hour. Still, it was better to be safe. He zipped up his pants and went into the hall.

Someone was ascending the stairs, heading for their apartment—the only one on the third floor. *Who the hell would be coming up when I'm the only one here?* The old staircase echoed with the clacking of shoes—girls' shoes, high heels—taking the steps in painfully slow fashion.

Johnny held his breath. The footsteps stopped on the landing outside his door. Something rustled—a familiar sound, one he'd heard before. He wracked his brain for a second, and it came to him: the skirts of the taffeta prom dress when the guys had bunched them up under Carmen's backside.

Knuckles rapped, light and quick. Johnny hesitated to open the door. The air in the room had turned sour, a terrible stink of stale sweat, piss, cat shit, blood, and . . . something else. Something like the pound of hamburger that had gone bad in July, when they'd lost power for three days after a thunderstorm. He put his hand over his mouth as his stomach spasmed and threatened to return his lunch.

Oh God. What's happening? There is no way in hell I'm answering this door.

A honeysuckle whisper slid through the keyhole. "Johnny, you sexy thing. You have to open up. After all, it's all these powerful fantasies you've been having that made me finally get up and come see you."

He held his breath and didn't move. Whoever this was, they didn't know for sure he was there, and if he didn't respond they might just go away.

"You abandoned me in that basement, and I've been lying there all alone for two weeks now. Well, except for the rats, but they're not as nice as you. I did have a visit from that flea-infested mama cat. She was starving and needed to feed her kittens, and after all, I had no use for the meat on my broken arm anymore, did I? But mostly, I lay there lonely until your thoughts came to me on the wind, along with a vision of what you've been doing. So here I am, Johnny. Wouldn't you rather have the real thing?"

This was starting to piss Johnny off. "Who the fuck are you? You couldn't possibly be who you say you are. There's no fucking way a dead girl could walk over here in broad daylight without somebody calling the cops."

She laughed, tinkly and girlish. "Oh Johnny, you silly boy. Don't be foolish. Nobody can see or hear me but you. Now let me in. I've got what you've been dreaming of, and it's cold as ice."

Johnny may not have been the sharpest tool in the shed, but he could recognize a prank. That skank Tina, Freddy P's girl, stood on the other side of his door. Only she was skeevy enough to do something like this. "Go away, Tina. What the hell are you doing here? Freddy P put you up to this? And what the fuck is that rotten smell?"

The girl whined. "Johhhnnnnyy, you're hurting my feelings—"

"And how the hell do you know what I've been doing, you stupid cu—" He yanked the door open, expecting to see Tina's fat face, her greasy bangs hanging down over that pimple-studded forehead of hers, zits so red and huge they looked like volcanoes about to blow. Freddy P must put a bag over her head to do her. He had time to think all of this before his brain could comprehend what stood before him.

The rat-and-cat gnawed corpse of Carmen D'Agostino leaned against the door frame, one arm up and the other—the twisted one, now devoid of a good hunk of flesh—hanging akimbo. She wore the tattered prom dress. Blood caked her mouth and breasts but the bruises were gone. Instead, her skin was a dark, mottled green and her chewed-up lips were black. One socket oozed a sable and scarlet muck; a substance Johnny presumed had once been her eye had dried across her cheekbone in a gritty paste. The other cheekbone had been bashed in. Somehow, she'd put her silver strappy shoes back on. Johnny thought they'd come off during the struggle in the abandoned basement that night. Her stink assaulted Johnny, and his gorge rose, but he managed to hold it back.

"Johnny, why did you do this to me?" she whispered, stepping into the room and reaching for him with cold, blackened hands.

Johnny got hard.

Roots Grew Where She Planted Her Feet
Cindy O'Quinn

I called on the keeper of dreams, but she was on duty elsewhere.
I clattered the tail of a timber-jack and used it to rattle one in.
It blew in the cricket song and carried me off to sleep.
The skinny, old reverend shook a feathered life and spread it beneath my feet.
He didn't have use for the things I believed.
Mattered not to me, for it was the bees that hummed away his disease.
Flew me up a holler on the vibrations of scarred wings.
Searched for my childhood room in the house Daddy built without guarantee.
They dropped me on the wicker bed Momma got for free.
I painted it red, then whistled in the glow bugs to light the braided edge.
Created a waterfall of blood and named it, Jubilee.
The crickets struck in tune and whisked me to a place out past the pond.
I curled like a cat and screamed into the deep canyon beyond.

A smile carved into my face convinced me I was where I should be.
After lavender's second season, he'd come for me.
Harvest all the beauty in the world and wear it like an undead queen.
I sat around hell's campfire and listened to the coyotes sing.

Between notes of a flute duet and paper, I bled.
A handsome man once told me I was a writer, so that is what I believed.
I wrote about an ancient dream and told the story of her, and her, and her.
The lies murmured from brutal men before they deceived.
Life was a complicated woman, cuffed to an unforgetting world.
Together, they created a daughter of stories.
Look into my eyes and you will see. She is me.
Alone and without need.
Roots grow where I plant my feet, and where I write is where I bleed.

Ready Player None
Salvantonio Clemente

Born, we matter
So ancient handprints on cavern walls tell us
Born lucky, into an age we barely comprehend
A new and infernal appendage clutched in our fists

Inside, the predator lurks and learns everything about us
Things we don't even know about ourselves—
All the dark holes waiting to be filled
As we press home again and again

And doubt our own eyes
Doubt the Earth
Our mothers
Our fathers
Our loves
Our worth

While in monstrous masses, we slouch toward X
Without paper or pen
Alone in the dark-mode glow
Writing psalms in the Substacks
And dreaming we've left a mark

Turn off, I tell myself. Pull away!
Throw your hands—your real hands—back into the clay!

Before you lose the strength to even wave

Or clang the bell and hit the thumb
And pray, if you like, to any god you choose
They won't answer
They never have
They never do

You may, however, hear a hum
Beneath the ring of tinnitus
Within the white noise thrum

The hopeless lament of the already lost—
Desperate to find a buried melody—
Amidst the buzzing echo of extinct bees

Escape to the Ruins Following His Mark
R.C. Mulhare

She had to steal away, away, she had to steal away: out of the dormitory in the stronghouse, where the other tripping maids and lumbering bumpkins quartered, slipping off into the night to hie away. She had to stride away, across wastelands of sere grass and blackened snow. Stands of bare-branched trees reached their starveling branches toward the black stars wheeling in the pale sky, falling into the constellations heralding the arrival of her lord and king.

Hardest of all, to slip past her superiors—Wilde, the newly-appointed head butler in particular, so calm and congenial yet keeping each servant in their place and serving their role. She waited 'til evening, when the servants retired to their small chambers. When the first pale moon had passed its zenith and the black second moon had just risen, when the maid who shared her room had fallen asleep, she pried open the aging casement and, slipping between the hard veil keeping out the beasts wandering the blasted lands, dropped to the frozen ground. Her ankle burned with a sudden sharp pain, but she pressed on in spite of it.

The first moon silvered the roofs of the manor and crenellations of the stronghouse of House Aldonces, on the shore of dry Lake Hali. She gazed across the hollowed lake to an island in its center, the second moon rising behind the weird shapes of the hall of Carcosa, rising from the shivering sands. She paused on the shore of the dry lake bed, gazing about her. Alone, alone at last, at last. Alone to find her way to the halls of her lord and sovereign's domain.

Years feeling like months, feeling like days, had passed since first she'd come to this place, after heeding the call of her pale lord, since first she had had her mask removed and replaced with a new one. But the infidels who'd sought to silence her lord's call, the usurpers who had exiled her to the servants' quarters in one of House Aldonces's holdings, had tried to stop her ears and separated her from household and court, casting them to the four winds. But his voice could make itself heard in any place, through any walls, in any time and any clime, if one had the eyes to see and ears to hear and voice to call back in reply, regardless of barriers raised by usurping captors. His sign had shone on the face of the second moon every night since it showed itself anew.

She would find the way; she would find the word. She would find his darkness that brought light. This time in seclusion as a handmaid, stripped of power and birthright, had made her strong again. To know greatness, to know *his* greatness, one must know humility, purge oneself of selfishness, clear oneself of entitlement. Even still, she must cleanse herself of the last traces of the mask clinging to her face. Pine for him, find for him, bind her mind to his mind, away from all humankind that is not kind. Only Hastur, wise Hastur, kindly Hastur, would bring her to what truly made one great.

She strode forth across the burning sands, eyes fixed upon the castle.

*   *   *

"Ingrid was there when we did a bed check at midnight and again at three a.m.," Mitchells—one of the night nurses—said, a mask of concern almost hiding the detached look in his eyes.

Dr. Alice Wilde, the new head of the secure ward of Sefton Mental Health and Rehabilitation, sighed, sitting back in her desk chair and rubbing her temples. "Was there any indication she wished to leave?"

"She hasn't hinted recently that she wished to leave in search of her lord," Sang-Hoon, the other senior night nurse, replied. "She didn't show up on the surveillance cameras in the hallways. The window in her room had been opened. The snow was brushed off the outer sill, and security found footprints roughly her size in the snow below it."

"The windows are supposed to open only so far, and there's a thick wire mesh over them," Mitchells said.

"The mesh was worked loose, and she's a small woman," Sang-Hoon said.

"The window was locked when we found her missing," Mitchells argued.

Sang-Hoon remained calm. "Her roommate admitted to closing and locking it."

"Had Ingrid said she wanted to leave?" Dr. Wilde asked.

"Last month she was asking if anyone had come to visit her, or if her master had sent his messenger, but not this month," Sang-Hoon said.

Wilde sat forward, tapping at her terminal, pulling up patient files. "She's on some fairly high doses of anti-psychotics."

"As long as she's taking them, she shows no agitation," Mitchells said. "But if she goes off them, she starts trying to literally take your face off, claiming you need to remove your mask."

"Aggression has only happened twice since I started here ten years ago," Sang-Hoon replied.

"The notes say she has a history of refusing or palming medication from time to time," Dr. Wilde said.

"Maybe once in a long while," Sang-Hoon said. "She's also spoken of a master coming to take her away and lead her to a new world, something about his sign on the moon and black stars rising over Lake Holly, or some place of that name."

"He's going to take her to Santa's Village?" Mitchells asked. Sang-Hoon glared at him.

"A rather elaborate delusion," Dr. Wilde said, trying to stay on top of the conversation. "Is there a reason she's here in a locked facility and not a care home?"

"Besides the fact that she's inconsistent with her meds?" Mitchells asked.

"She has no one to speak for her," Sang-Hoon said.

"No one? No family? No friends? Not even a legal guardian?"

"No," Sang-Hoon said. "She fell through the cracks. Been here since the late 1980s, as far as I know."

A police officer entered the office, looking puzzled and

concerned. "I hate to barge in like this, but we may have a lead on your missing patient."

Dr. Wilde stood. "What is it?"

"We found three college students on the access road to the old asylum, loaded down with cameras and ghost hunting equipment. They wouldn't talk to us, but said they'd talk with a hospital administrator present."

"All right. Where are they?"

"We've got them outside, on the side of the access road."

Dr. Wilde reached for the coat hanging on the tree beside a filing cabinet. "I'm on the way."

On the side of the access road leading to the woods that had grown up around the disused buildings of Sefton Asylum, she found two more officers and three college-aged people in black hooded jackets with a green ghost-like logo and thermal pants, some with GoPro-type cameras strapped to their heads or shoulders.

One panned around them with an EMF meter. "This place is lousy with activity."

"Todd, there's cop cars and shit everywhere with radios. You're probably picking up that," said a girl with a shoulder-mounted GoPro. She eyed Dr. Wilde. "Are you the doctor in charge?"

"I'm in charge of one of the secure wards, yes." Dr. Wilde introduced herself.

"Morgen Shadowwalker with GhostPhasers," the girl replied. "Don't arrest us, but we came here last night, looking into the legends of the haunting in the old asylum."

"You mean the old mental hospital?" the third of the group asked.

"Chanelle, the mental hospital is the modern building where they treat patients. The old building they don't use is the asylum, and from all the stories we've heard it's probably the poster pic for the horror movie asylum," Morgen said, then turned back to Dr. Wilde. "We've got some footage from last night. We picked up something we thought was a haunt, but then we heard about the escaped patient. We wondered if it could help you find her." She took a phone from her pocket, held it up to show a video file, and hit play.

The screen showed a slightly angled, grainy video, tracking unevenly as the operator walked. The beam from a handheld floodlight panned over a stretch of floor strewn with fallen leaves and branches along with discarded bits of nameless trash.

Though he wasn't in the shot, Todd's voice, slightly tinny in the reproduction, came from the phone's speaker. *"Is there anyone here?"*

"Are there any spirits here?" Morgen's voice now, closer to the microphone.

Chanelle's voice, a little farther away: *"Are there any spirits of departed patients?"*

The flashlight beam panned up with the camera, showing scribbles of graffiti on the walls, love declarations and poorly spelled occult references alongside seemingly random scrawls. Something shuffled from the shadows, shouting at them incoherently. The scene tilted slightly, the view expanding as the camera backed up.

"Pause that, please?" Dr. Wilde asked.

Morgen tapped the screen.

"Could you enhance this?"

"It's not exactly a high-tech video program, but I'll do what I can." Morgen enlarged the image. The screen showed a blurred, vaguely female-presenting form standing half in the shadows, half in the floodlight beam.

"Is that your missing patient?" the officer asked.

"It could be. It's hard to tell," Dr. Wilde said. "I've only recently started as director on one of the secure wards. I could ask one of the veteran nurses to take a look. When did you say you took this video?"

"Last night. We came here around midnight, when the paranormal activity starts to ramp up," Morgen said.

"Also when the not-paranormal activity ramps down," Todd said, earning amused glares from Chanelle and Morgen.

Dr. Wilde paged Sang-Hoon, who came down after a long moment. Morgen played back the video for him, pausing it when the mysterious figure appeared.

Sang-Hoon frowned at the screen. "It's grainy and hard to see, but I'm certain that's Ingrid."

To the officer, Dr. Wilde said, "At least this gives you a lead."

"We can call the search team off the woods and tell the locals they don't have to look in their sheds or basements anymore," the officer replied.

"Let me guess," Todd said. "You've had a bunch of dumb calls from people seeing her under their porch or rummaging in their trash cans."

Morgen looked at him like she wanted to slap him upside the head. "Not funny, Todd."

"I'm afraid I can't elaborate on an open case, but you wouldn't be wrong," the officer replied.

"Are we in trouble for trespassing?" Morgen asked.

The officer eyed Morgen's camera and the green indicator light on the side. "I got more pressing things to resolve. Just get permission to poke around abandoned locations next time? I think you found out the hard way this isn't exactly *Scooby Doo*."

"Not like we thought it would be," Chanelle replied as Morgen lead her and Todd away.

*   *   *

The tracks in the snow faded as the search and rescue team crossed the grassy field behind the main building of Sefton Mental Health and Rehabilitation, separating it from the now closed Sefton Asylum, an aging nineteenth century structure which some would call *Gothic*, but architecture experts would label *Kirkbride style*. It stood surrounded by a chain-link fence erected so long ago wild grape and bittersweet vines covered it, hiding both wire mesh and the barbed wire atop it. A band of snow ran along the base of the fence, melted in places so the searchers could barely discern if someone's footprints had broken through.

"It's been over twelve hours since she vanished," said Hildreth, the mental health advocate from the Arkham PD, as the team crossed the field, approaching the buildings. "She's going to be hungry, if not dehydrated and hypothermic. Based on Dr. Wilde's assessment, she may react poorly, even in a hostile manner. Don't make any sudden moves. Don't act hostile or confrontational. She may talk about a mask. She may talk about her master or seeing his sign. Whatever you do, don't try to humor her delusion. Never say you know her master or he sent you to help her."

"If she's even alert," Sanjay, one of the EMTs, said. "Temps dropped to near zero last night, even without the wind chill, and she wasn't exactly dressed for the weather."

"She could have found shelter," his partner said. "She might have found a vent from the steam tunnels, or even the tunnels themselves."

One of the hospital security staff spoke up. "We looked in the tunnels first, at least the ones that haven't been blocked up. Lots of escaped crazies end up trying to get in there, especially this time of year."

"Let's not use words like that," Hildreth said. "This is a person in need."

"She might be a person, but I wonder if she's lost her grip on her humanity," the same staff member said. "You ever hear of the Yellow Massacre of 1981?"

"I have." It was Sevren, one of the officers. "My father was on the force in Manuxet back then; he took that call. He had a hell of a time just seeing the steaks in the meat case at Market Basket for a long time afterward."

"Do I want to hear the reason behind that?" Hildreth asked.

"A group of kids from the art school at Miskatonic U started a drama club. Seems they got into some bad cannabis or something and went nuts. They put on some old play, broadcasting it on a public access channel during the overnight shift. Turned into a literal bloodbath. Viewers thought they'd gone over the top with the makeup effects 'til one sharp-eyed nurse on the night shift spotted things no one should have to suffer and called it in. My father had taken that night shift, so he and his partner drove to the studio—a studio full of seriously messed-up kids. The actors had skinned each other. Some didn't make it from blood loss or shock. Our girl survived with some facial damage. The medics had to sedate her heavily to keep her from prying at *their* faces," Sevren said. "The court psych docs found her incompetent to stand trial, so they commuted her to life in a locked ward. She kept claiming some *Yellow King* or a *Tatty King* or something had told her to take the masks off the people around her. Insisted her name was Camilla or Priscilla, something old-timey like that."

"The way you tell it, it sounds like an urban legend high school students would share," Hildreth said.

"It's become the stuff of local legend," Sevren said. "A VHS tape turns up in evidence, and some old timer at the station asks if it has a yellow label on it. Seems a copy of the show ended up on a yellow-labeled VHS tape in the archives at Manuxet Public Access TV before it went off the air."

"Do you know if anyone else made a tape of the play?"

135

Hildreth asked.

"We're ninety-nine percent sure someone at MPA-TV did, but no one's ever proven it," Sevren replied. "They closed down after the channel changed hands, and the new manager failed to live up to the job description. The building and its contents were seized for failure to pay taxes, and some of the contents were auctioned off. Developers bought out the building, tore it down, and planted a bunch of townhouses. The tapes are probably in the wind."

"And Ingrid Blaxton was in the play?" Hildreth asked.

"Pretty sure she played some kind of fairy-tale queen, or wannabe fairy-tale queen."

"From what Dr. Wilde and Nurse Jim Sang-Hoon told us, she's in a constant dissociative state where she believes she *is* the character she played. The court-appointed psychologist deemed her incompetent to stand trial. She was remanded here after her injuries healed." She took a slow breath to clear her head. "The world moved on and forgot she exists."

*   *   *

The Yellow Sign pulsed on the face of the second moon, yellow against black as the satellite rose behind the twisting towers of Carcosa.

One slipper fell from her foot, vanishing into the dark. Very well. She cast off the other as she approached the holy ground of Carcosa, lost Carcosa, dark Carcosa descending onto the waters of the dead Lake Hali, covered in rime mist and frost.

She padded across the sere frozen ground, heedless of the cold, her frostbitten footsteps a fitting offering, her soles burning so they bled. Blood for the blood, and let the blood purge her and her path of all impurity she may have acquired in the house of the usurpers, whom she would have sacrificed—or brought to enlightenment— given half the chance.

She approached the iron vine-clad walls surrounding Carcosa, towers glinting in the light of the twin moons, black stars casting their weird light on the looming edifice.

She climbed the wall of thorns, heedless of how the plants rose and extended their tendrils to seize her, clambering despite the toothed coils. She shook free, but the thorns tore into her flesh nonetheless, tendrils lashing as she scrambled up and over and into the wild lands behind the wall. Gore painted her limbs, a fitting mark of devotion to her lord, that she would offer her blood as sacrifice,

She entered the outer court, traversing the overgrown flagstones leading to the gates.

Approaching the gates, she knocked upon them in the pattern prescribed by her lord, whispered to her as far back as the day of her awakening. The door did not open. She beat upon it harder, 'til she felt the fabric of the door part and shatter. Heedless of the edges closing on her, cutting into her flesh, she climbed through, leaving more blood behind as another offering to her lord.

She entered the halls, feeling the warmth of her Lord Hastur's presence pervading his domain, and heard his voice call to her, his mind to her mind. *Farther up and farther inward,* she thought. Attendants approached with festal garments. They gently divested her of her now ragged servant's garb before dressing her in the festal clothing, silken robes embroidered with the yellow sign and a coronet set with yellow and russet stones.

She turned to approach her lord's court, piping voices of strange intruders whispering and chattering. Lights stabbed into the hall, through the veils covering the windows and the tapestries lining the walls embroidered in fading figures of birds and beasts and plants unknown to humans, in colors unnamed in human tongues—known only to those with eyes to hear and ears to see. The skittering footsteps of the intruders rustled on the rush-strewn floor.

Tall, tenuous forms wavered out of the gloaming. The guards closed about her, drawing their swords and raising their shields in a phalanx between the intruders and their lady. She stood tall as their shadows fell over her, and cried out: "Begone, you shades, you vagabonds in the Yellow King's domain."

She spread her arms, robes of state trailing from her wrists. The wights scattered, cawing and gurgling as they fled into the murk, the dull light swallowing them. Her courtiers gathered about her, speaking their assurances and smoothing down her robes.

"A test, perhaps," she said. "My lord may have allowed or shaped these shades. Or some unworthy would-be devotees found a way in without my lord's invitation."

"You know his will and ways of testing the members of his inner circle better than we, and you know well his ways of dealing with such nuisances,"

the tallest of her attendants said, smoothing her hair and straightening her robes with a tendril arm. Courtiers approached, guiding her down the grand hall, then to the foot of the dais, atop which awaited her Lord Hastur.

Her lord and lover sat enthroned above her. She raised her eyes to his lithe form, clad in tattered robes the color of a summer sky obscured by a dust storm, the face above unveiled entirely, his mask lain aside that she might gaze upon his naked aspect.

Halfway up the steps, she sank to her knees before him. Hastur rose and approached, standing over her, the shredded train of his robe pooling around her. She lifted her face and raised her hands, extending them to her lord.

Camilla, my love, my lady, you have found your way to me, he said, mind to mind. He leaned over her, tendrils extending from beneath his robes, twining around her in a firm embrace and lifting her up. He brought his flat visage down to her, features indescribable in human terms coming closer to her simple human face, and pressed the segment that served as his forehead against her forehead. His eye opened, and her inner eye opened in response as he gazed into her, awakening knowledge she dared not accept and thoughts she dared not think, imparting to her his knowledge of sights and spaces humankind dared not imagine, nor could grasp with their tiny comprehension.

She sank against him, and into him. He unfurled his webbed wings, folding them about her, drawing her closer. She spiraled down the turns of his wisdom. She felt the heat of him intensify, burning her 'til she foundered, black stars wheeling and whirling about them as she sank into the void, swooning with the majesty of him.

*   *   *

Their flashlight beams lit up a torn green scrub shirt and a gray thermal undershirt lying on the floor of the dust and leaf-litter strewn hallway.

"This doesn't look good," Sevren said. "Think she was lured up here and assaulted? We need a crisis team in here?"

"I doubt it. It was single-digits cold last night. She may have been in end stage hypothermia, which can cause changes in peripheral vasoconstriction resulting in something called paradoxical undressing," Sanjay said.

"High-score words in Scrabble. Can you say that in words someone who didn't go to medical school would use?" Sevren asked.

"People in very cold conditions with inadequate clothing can have their body temperature drop so low it becomes life threatening. At that point, their system pulls the blood from their arms and legs and into their torso, making them feel boiling hot. Hypothermia also causes mental confusion, so they start taking off their clothes," Sanjay explained.

"Up here," the search party's radios crackled. The searchers converged on the main stairwell to the upper floor.

A female person knelt on the first landing, limbs and sides badly scratched and bloodied. Her arms had curled under her torso, one reaching across the tiles, as if she had sought to embrace a being they could not see. Before her, on the aging green plaster below a smashed-out window, someone had spray-painted a large double spiral in black and yellow.

Sanjay knelt beside the woman. "Ingrid? Ingrid Blaxton?" He reached under her jaw, feeling for a pulse. "Can you hear me?"

Hildreth also knelt, gently shaking her shoulder. "We're here to help you." The woman did not move.

Sanjay turned the patient over. The woman seemed frozen in position. Sanjay took a stethoscope from his supply bag and listened to her chest. "If she's alive, she's in a deep coma."

"What could have drawn her here?" Sevren asked. "That weird graffiti. Did she put it there?"

"Probably not," Hildreth said. "Her file says she's barely left the facility since she got here, outside of some court dates and hospitalizations for surgery and other treatments they couldn't arrange in the ward."

*   *   *

Something reached under her jaw. A tendril lifted her from her lord's arms and onto her back. She willed to raise her hand and push them away, with their blank faces and unseeing eyes. She willed to cry out and drive them away, but her lord restrained her.

No. Do not resist. They mean no harm, his voice soothed.

She sank into his embrace even as the intruders raised her up.

Between the two, her lord and the interloper, they bore her through the crumbling halls of lost Carcosa, out of the fading light and into the welcoming darkness. Waves of shadow and nameless colors embraced her as they laid her upon a palanquin and closed her in with its tattered yellow veils, covering her face with a mask to hide the radiance of her knowledge from the prying eyes of a populace whose eyes had yet to open. She sank back, her lord at her side, as the interlopers gathered around the palanquin, bearing it from the halls of the fading palace and rising into the darkening sky above.

* * *

"She's not going to make it," the newly hired EMT said as Sanjay performed chest compressions. "Temp's at fifty-six."

"Still no pulse," Sanjay said. "Only reason the temp is rising is she's thawing out."

"How could she have gone so fast, besides how cold it got last night?" the rookie asked.

"Moving her could have caused her heart rhythm to drop."

"Going to call it?"

"No, keep going 'til we get to the hospital. I've seen miracles happen. We had an ice fisher drop through on the Manuxet River last winter and come back from the verge of death once we got him into the hospital and started running his blood through dialysis. Old saying I learned from my instructor: You aren't dead when you're cold and dead. You're dead when you're warm and dead."

Penetralia
Kurt Newton

Penetralia I

Deciphering signals sent from deep inside the Earth's mantle,
examining data structures that hint at intelligent design,
mapping coordinates using 3D AI modeling,
revealing the existence of a vast subterranean city . . .

A team was assembled to determine the best entry point,
based on proximity and existing cave systems,
along with theories regarding once-flooded regions,
now emancipated by the planetary drought.

Chevé Cave in the Sierra Juarez mountain range—
believed guarded by the mystical *Señor del Cerro*—
the *Lord of the Hill* who cures troubled souls
and those of spelunkers looking for lost civilizations.

Cutting through the cloud forest to a cleft in the hillside,
entering the mouth of Chevé on the eve of a new moon,
lighting the way using phosphorescent torches—
downward ever downward till we reached rock bottom.

Penetralia II

The impenetrable floor was just another ceiling:

an entry hatch plugged by a seamless two-ton stone.
A decision was made to blow the pre-Cenozoic artifact—
better to ask forgiveness later in the name of science.

It was here our journey into unnatural history began.
A stairway of unusual size and dimensions
designed for legs both large and long of gait,
each stair tread requiring a miniature rope descent.

Here we witnessed the erosion of times the water tables receded
throughout millennia.
Another mile and a half down, our signal grew stronger;
we were now closer to the source than our home base above.

An echo in the hollow chamber of the great stairway.
The soft susurration of a great body of water.
When we finally reached bottom, we stood on the threshold.
A massive city landscape on the dark shores beyond.

Ophiolatreia

We traversed the banks of a seething black ocean
where watermarks striped the walls like an apocalyptic growth chart
upon a walkway of megalithic steps each the size of a Baalbek stone
toward the mirage-like metropolis in the distance.

We were prepared for every fantasy we had ever imagined—
a welcoming committee of the highest order,
a meeting of minds and perhaps new species—
with technology playing the great equalizer.

As we walked through the gates of the great subterranean city,
a ghostliness echoed in our footfalls.
No signs of life among the alien architecture,
it was an eerily abandoned prehistoric Croatoan.

Immense structures once inhabited by a race of gargantua,
replete with obelisks and statues honoring reptilian-shaped
Gods . . .

Bioluminescent lichen limned each surface
like a velvet canvas of a city bathed in perpetual moonlight.

Necropolis

We could have explored for days but we found our answer.
At the far outer edges of the silent city sprawl,
another impressively-engineered landscape:
a burial ground created wholly from the bones of the dead.

Here we discovered the sad truth of its creators:
Written in the glyphs of their arcane language,
a eulogy of a culture forever lost to the world.
They had waited out time until there was time no more.

Our translators told a tale of desperate survival:
The surface of the planet, increasingly uninhabitable,
an impending doom of catastrophic proportions,
brought them down–deep down–into the folds of Earth . . .

Waiting for millennia through one cataclysm after another.
Watching the rise and fall leave its mark on the cavern walls.
While the graveyard grew like a great sequoian spirit forest.
Until the last procession crossed the ultimate threshold.

Cephacolossus

But the signal that brought us here continued to chime.
Like a beacon, it led to a vast chamber beneath the city,
to a fortress of doorways and gates fallen to decay.
to a familiar loci set thick into the floor.

Only this massive plug had been partially breached.
Another civilization, we pondered, even deeper below.
Imprisoned by their reptilian overlords above;
confirmed by what we were about to witness.

As if awakened by our presence, there came a slithering sound.

A tentacled arm shot through a fissure in the stone,
encircling one of our crew, pulling them down into the dark—
to a chorus of screams mercifully silenced.

We ran for our lives and for the good people of this Earth.
For the unknown legacy of our reptilian protectors.
We ran from the slithering and the bellowing rumbles
as the cries of the ancients broke from their long-held captivity.

Penetralia III

We ran, but our pace was no match for our pursuers.
Our size was not meant for such massive architecture.
They slithered up and filled the streets of the abandoned city,
spilling over into the depths of the seething black ocean.

Magnificent creatures of every shape and dimension:
tentacled descendants of a once proud and dominant beast,
from an epoch, no doubt, of forming, embryonic Earth—
savage and wild and unyielding in its infancy.

They cornered us on the great steps that led down from Chevé:
their entry point to our world in the breach above.
But in the zeal of our quest we had not forgotten our duty:
our search protocols demanded a doomsday contingency.

Explosive charges had been placed at critical junctures
to close the doorway should a worst-case scenario present.
Our crew held hands as the ungodly horde overwhelmed us.
We sent us all back to a time now forgotten.

The Road to Heaven is Paved with Bad Intentions
Laura Cooney

Mary woke to the sound of mewling, so loud and sad and demanding it shook her out of a peaceful sleep, the dream she'd been having popping like a balloon. The digital clock glowed green. It took a few moments for the time to come into focus. Three minutes past midnight. Sam snored evenly beside her. The high beams of a passing car shone through a tear in the yellowing shade, casting light on Sam's large red nose, dripping like a leaky faucet, watery mucous shimmering in the dark.

Poor kitty, Mary thought. *You must be so cold and hungry.*

Mary slid out of bed quietly, so as not to wake Sam, and padded across the hardwood floor. Sam continued to snore. The bedroom door creaked open and softly closed. The mewling was much louder in the living room. She wondered how Sam could sleep through it.

Sam didn't like cats, and would be angry at her for bringing one into the house. But the poor thing sounded so desperate. Maybe she could let it inside just long enough for it to warm up and have a bowl of milk?

Mary unlocked the front door and pushed it open. A frigid wind cut through her; she was dressed only in a thin nightgown. The crying was the loudest she'd ever heard. A bright red wagon, a child's toy, was on her doorstep, and something moved inside it. Mary bent and, like in a fairy tale, saw a baby wrapped in a blue blanket, face red and wrinkled from endless crying, tiny arms and fists moving like a robotic doll.

"Oh, my goodness," Mary said. "Poor sweet thing!"

She put her arms around the baby and hugged it to her chest. The child continued crying as Mary brought it into the house. She sat on Sam's black recliner and kissed the tiny forehead. The crying grew softer as Mary cuddled and loved on the infant. Her silent tears fell on the blue swaddling blanket. She had wanted a baby for so long.

God is good, Mary thought. *God is love.*

*   *   *

"We have to report this to the police, Mary," Sam said.

Mary put a plate of fried eggs and bacon on the kitchen table in front of him. "God sent him to us. You don't reject a gift from God."

"For Chrissakes, Mary!"

"Yes, exactly."

"How do you expect to explain this sudden appearance of a baby to our friends? To the neighbors?"

"God will provide," said Mary. "We just need to have faith."

"Look," Sam said, salting his eggs. "I know you've been wanting a little one all these years, and I'm sorry, real sorry, that . . . circumstances . . . prevented it. But we need to do things legally. Apply for adoption and whatnot. Maybe, if no one claims this baby, we can put in for it. I'm sorry, sweetheart, but I *am* going to call the police."

"No sir, Samuel Mayhew. You will not. Or I will never forgive you. Ever."

"You're a Christian, Mary," said Sam. "And my wife. You'll forgive me. Now, can I get a drink?"

"Get your own damned drink!" Mary shouted. "*And choke on it!*"

"That's it," Sam said. "I'm calling the police as soon as I finish my breakfast."

"You will *not!*"

"This baby is making you crazy. You never in your life spoke this way to me or anyone. You should be ashamed of yourself."

Mary turned her back to him and went to the sink. She

wrenched on the hot water and began washing the dishes.

"Well," said Sam, "you aren't going to stop me from enjoying my breakfast." He picked up a long strip of bacon and stuck it into his mouth like a cigarette. He gnawed on it slowly, as if to stop himself from saying anything more.

Just as Sam was about to swallow the bacon, the baby let out a powerful cry. Startled, Sam gasped. The bacon followed the gasp into his airway and lodged there, an immovable mass of masticated meat. Sam tried to cough, over and over, but couldn't push air out any more than he could pull it in. Face reddening, he reached across the table for a cup of coffee or glass of orange juice, but the longed-for drink had never been poured.

Mary turned from the sink and watched her husband struggle, head bent over his plate, chest heaving. Her hands gripped the edge of the sink behind her. She sniffled and shook but didn't move from where she stood.

Sam went silent, eyes glassy, lips blue. He fell face down on the blue willow china. Mary remained frozen except for her mouth, which formed a perfect O. Time moved in slow motion: the whole scene couldn't have lasted more than five minutes, but it felt like an hour. The baby cried the whole time—until it suddenly went silent, and Mary was able to move again.

She ran to Sam, slumped over the kitchen table, and gently lifted his head from the plate. A fried egg yoke covered his left eye and a piece of bacon lay under his nose. Sweeping the food off his blue-tinted face, she forced his mouth open and managed to fit her small hand inside and down his throat. Her fingertips gripped the tip of the bacon and pulled it loose. Mucous followed it up and out of his mouth as her husband loudly passed wind.

"R-really, S-sam . . ."

Sam's blue eyes were open, registering nothing. Mary didn't try to revive him.

In her imagination, she heard a doctor's voice say, *Call it.* She read the time off the microwave: "Eight seventeen a.m." She went into her bedroom. The baby lay cooing on her bed, wrapped in the blue blanket. Mary smiled.

"Precious angel."

*   *   *

147

Mary told her friends and neighbors the baby belonged to a long-lost relative, an unnamed sister who'd brought the child to comfort her in time of grief. People went silent whenever Mary spoke of her family. It was well known that she'd been estranged from them since she was a teenager, and that she'd been horribly abused by her father—something about a broomstick, and that she could no longer bear children. Most people who heard that inquired no further. Those who did were shown the door and never spoken to again.

Mary left town holding a small yellow suitcase and with the baby wrapped in the blue blanket. She said she was moving to another state to live with her sister, the baby's mother. Whenever anyone tried to ask anything more, Mary got a look in her eye that reminded them of the story about her father; then they'd just get quiet and rub her on the arm.

In the new town, Mary was a widow with a baby and no living relatives. She told people she'd moved to get a fresh start, and was quietly grateful for Sam's large life insurance policy. She hired a financial advisor to take care of her investments, which allowed her to stay at home and take care of the baby.

Mary picked the baby up out of the crib in her new home. He had the same beautiful violet eyes as Elizabeth Taylor, one of Mary's favorite actresses, whom she admired not so much for her acting or movie roles, but for her spirit and attitude. Liz had taken what she wanted and never let a man push her around. She'd fought back against men who'd tried to control her, but at the same time remained generous and kind. At least, it seemed like it from what Mary had read in the tabloids about how Liz had helped her gay men friends years ago. Mary wished she had a gay male friend, even though the Bible spoke against homosexuality. Mary believed it was straight men who were bad. They wanted women for sex, but didn't want to give anything in return. They hadn't wanted her to have her sweet little angel. Not her father and not her husband.

"Men just want to use you," she said to the babbling baby in her arms. "They say your private parts are ugly, when all they want to do is get inside and rip them apart. Make your insides bleed and hurt. Take control of your body and mind."

The baby laughed as she lifted him up in the air, making kissy noises at him.

"No," she said. "We don't need men. Not for nothing."

Mary put the baby down on her new couch. It was blue velvet, like the song. Blue like the baby's blanket. It couldn't have been a coincidence that blue was also her favorite color. She'd almost called the baby Blue, but it seemed too silly. When Mary received the documents her lawyer had procured, she'd thought hard about names and their importance. She went to the Bible to pick out his name: Moses. Both Moseses had been sent off by their mothers as babies, to women who could give them a better, safer life. Sam hadn't understood that Mary had been entrusted by God to care for little baby Moses. That was why he'd died.

Moses's middle name was Montgomery, for Elizabeth Taylor's gay actor friend, Montgomery Clift. She hoped little Moses Montgomery Mayhew would be gay, so he would never break the heart of a woman. Then she took the thought back because she didn't want the baby to burn in hell. Having a name with three *M*s would bring him good luck, Mary thought. Good things come in threes.

*　　*　　*

"Baby, so innocent and pure. I'm tainted, I'm a whore. Give me the innocent, give me the pure. Sweet baby, whom I adore . . ." Mary sang, off-key and out of tune.

The baby gurgled, then laughed.

Mary didn't know what she was singing. Were they real words to a real song? Or something she had sung in her heart for years? After she'd run away when she was sixteen, everyone she'd told her story to said her father was a bad man. She agreed—both with words and by nodding her head—but in her heart, buried deep down, she felt the truth of what her father had said: women were evil, put on Earth by God to tempt men with their bodies, their fake smiles, and their sweet-sounding lies.

"Eve," her father would say, "is short for *evil*, and woman is the reason we got kicked out of Eden. Eve put a stain on the hearts of men. And I'll be damned if you're going to use your sick flower to ruin men."

But it was a confusing thing, because he'd used her sick flower and then blamed her every time. According to him, she was the whore who had seduced him. She wondered why he had named her after Mary—the only woman born pure, without the taint of original sin. She understood he was sick and bad, but couldn't get the things he had done and said out of her head. Little baby Moses was the only one who could redeem her.

She'd cut herself off from everyone; she would never speak to her old friends again, just as she'd never speak to her family. Her whole life would be church and Moses.

Mary went down to the local church, five blocks from where she lived, and met Father William. He was ruddy skinned and short, with white hair and thick, unkempt eyebrows. She wanted to get Moses baptized, but didn't know what to say when Father William asked her about Moses's godparents.

"I just moved here," Mary said. "I don't know anyone. Except you, Father."

"Do you not have any family or friends?"

Mary had a lump in her throat. When she'd first devised the plan to isolate herself, she didn't know it would feel so bleak and empty. For a moment, she felt like she wanted to die—then was ashamed, because she realized she was not alone.

"I have Moses and God," Mary said.

Father William smiled at her with sad eyes. The little room that was the priest's office felt very warm . . . too warm. Not hot enough to be Hell, but somewhere along the way. The child lay asleep in his carriage. Father William walked around his desk to bend and stare at little Moses. The baby stirred. The priest put his hand to his chest, gasped, and fell to the floor.

Mary screamed. This time she would get help. She fumbled her cell phone from her pocket and dialed 911.

It was a curious thing that all through the noise of the ambulance, and the EMTs running into the room, shouting and trying to revive Father William, little Moses slept like . . . a baby.

* * *

After that—watching another man die right in front of her—Mary decided not to go back to church and not to have baby Moses baptized. The feeling in that room right before Father William had collapsed told her something was wrong with the church. Moses, she felt, was like the Blessed Virgin: he was an immaculate conception and didn't need to be washed free of original sin.

But it was so lonely without a job, or friends, or family, just money and Moses and too much silence, except for the noise in her head and the cries and laughs and gurgles of the baby. Mary discovered a lovely park not far from home, with beautiful green lawns, willow trees, colorful flowers, and a lake with swans. She took Moses there in his stroller almost every afternoon to sit and watch the swans.

One day, a deep voice said, "What a beautiful baby."

Mary turned from the lake and looked up at the man standing over her. He was dressed completely in black except for a blue scarf, long enough its fringes kissed the asphalt path. He was in his thirties and looked a little bit like Montgomery Clift. She would have ignored him except she thought—hoped?—he was gay.

"What's his name?" asked the man.

"Moses," she said. "Moses Montgomery."

The man smiled, waving his hand at Moses. "That's quite a name you have, little man."

The baby smiled, hands reaching toward the stranger. She'd never seen Moses do that before. It must be a sign from the Divine, Mary surmised. The man crouched in front of the stroller, twiddling his fingers at the baby. Moses grabbed his index finger, babbling happily. The man smiled at Mary.

"I hope you don't mind," he said. "I just love babies."

"Me too," Mary said.

"I'm Abel, by the way."

"That's from the Bible," Mary said.

"Yes," said Abel. "Alas, it didn't end well for my namesake. And you are?"

"Mary."

He let out a long whistle. "Wow. Biblical royalty."

Mary blushed. Abel stood, then stooped and held out his hand. Mary shook it.

"Very nice to meet you and Moses, Mary."

"Would you like to sit down?" Mary said.

"I would," Abel said, sitting next to her on the bench.

Mary and Moses spent the rest of the afternoon with Abel. She hadn't realized how much she'd missed the company of another adult. The thought felt like a betrayal of baby Moses. Even worse, she ended up spilling her guts to Abel as they fed stale bread to the swans.

"Wow, girl," said Abel. "Just wow. You are one impressive lady. Remind me to never get on your bad side."

"Oh, no," Mary said. "I'm not like that. I'm quiet and dull. Nobody in their life has ever been afraid of me."

"That's because they didn't know you. But Moses knew you'd protect him. That's why he came to your door. I can see it just looking at you."

Mary blushed. It was embarrassing how many times Abel had made her blush in the few hours since they'd met. She hoped again that he was gay. She didn't want any hetero men around her.

"Do you know who Montgomery Clift is?" she asked.

He smiled and nodded, eyebrows raised. Mary felt like they were sharing some intimate secret.

"Old movies, old black and white movies," he said, "are my weakness. And my strength."

"I love them, too," Mary whispered.

"Beautiful, tragic Monty."

Mary nodded. They stared out at the lake. The sun was going down, the sky a soft, pinkish gray. Abel looked over at the child. Moses was chewing on his yellow sweater.

"Omigod. Is he named after Monty?"

Mary nodded eagerly. "Yes."

"Moses Montgomery. Love it."

"Moses Montgomery *Mayhew.*"

Abel's mouth dropped open, and he laughed. "Three *mmmms.* Like something delicious. And Mary Mayhew. MM. Like Marilyn Monroe. You're just all kinds of royalty, aren't you?"

Much to her embarrassment, Mary blushed again. "Oh, no, I'm nothing like Marilyn. She was a goddess. I'm nobody."

"Are you nobody, too?" said Abel.

"You're—Are you making fun of me?"

"It's a poem," he said. "Emily Dickinson."

"Oh. I don't—I've heard of her, but I don't understand poetry. I never graduated high school."

"Of course, sweetie. How could you have, after what you went through? How old were you when you ran away?"

"Sixteen."

"Sixteen. That's so young. So young. But you survived. And look at you now, in the park with your little boy. Making it all on your own."

"On Sam's insurance money," she said. "God bless him."

"Hush, your mouth, Mary. Give yourself credit. You're living each day, taking care of this baby by yourself with no friends or family or spouse. Isn't that what you told me? 'I haven't a friend in this world.' Well, you do now. Perhaps God directed me to you."

"Oh, my goodness," said Mary. "Yes. I wonder one thing though. Something I've been asking God for."

"What?"

She shook her head, blushing again. "I can't. It's personal . . . embarrassing."

"I want us to be the kind of friends who have no secrets," said Abel. "Nothing between us will ever be shameful. Understand? It may *sound* shameful, but not between us, because we get each other."

"My God," she said. "That sounds like a beautiful dream."

"Trust in the dream! Tell me."

Mary covered her face with her hands.

"Tell me."

"I—I can't."

He gently peeled her hands from her face and looked her in the eye.

"Tell me."

"It's a question," said Mary.

"Tell me your question."

"Are you . . . I can't!"

Abel's forehead wrinkled. "You're not asking . . . if I'm gay?"

"You hate me now," said Mary.

"What kind of little snowflake do you think I am?" He leaned in. "I'll tell you a secret. I'm just about impossible to offend. And why would someone thinking I'm gay offend me? I wouldn't want *me* for a friend if I was like *that*."

"So, you are? I mean, I don't know if you are. I don't want to assume."

Abel laughed. "Look at how upset you are! You're adorable. Such an innocent. I don't really consider myself anything. I don't define who I am in those terms."

"I hope I don't sound stupid," she said. "But I don't understand what you mean."

"I just don't believe in limitations. I believe all things are possible and none of them are right or wrong. You know that, right? Gay isn't bad. I know the Catholic Church is a bit backward on that, but, my Lord, look at what your straight Christian father did to you. The worst things have been done in the name of religion. The second worst things have been done in the name of heterosexuality. I don't know if you need to hear this but . . . loving tits and loving women are two completely different things. Also, if you love the woman's hole too much, you cannot love the whole woman."

Mary burst out laughing.

*   *   *

Mary opened her refrigerator, and a little breath of cold touched her arm. The light shone brightly on little round packs of yogurt, peaches in a paper bowl, a green bottle of sparkling water, and glass jars of baby food with all their variety of colors and sizes and shapes. She was overtaken by the beauty of it all. Before meeting Abel, oddly, the contents of her fridge had given her a crushing feeling in her chest. Now, she stood there holding open the door and couldn't remember why she'd opened it in the first place.

Abel came up behind her, standing close without touching her. "What's good?"

"I can't remember," she said.

"I'll give you a primer."

Shutting the refrigerator, she faced Abel, who was, as always, dressed in black. Sometimes she called him Johnny as a joke, and never had to tell him she was referring to Johnny Cash. He already knew.

"I can't remember what I went to the refrigerator for," she said. "Mom brain."

"Aw," said Abel. "You know what you need? A day where someone takes care of *you*!"

"Oh, no."

"Oh *yes*."

And there it was. Mary went to a spa while Abel looked after little Moses. When she returned home, Abel and Moses were in the living room watching TV. Standing in the doorway with her fresh, glowing skin and her new haircut, she felt she was interrupting some secret thing between man and child. But Abel quickly stood, greeting her with a smile and a kiss on the cheek.

"You look beautiful."

"Thank you, dear. I hope Moses wasn't too much trouble."

"Sweetheart," he said, "you must learn to be more *selfish*! I'm serious."

He helped her off with her coat and put it in the closet. Mary rubbed her hands together, biting her lip. Abel led her over to the leather recliner and made her sit down.

"All your life, you've been serving people. It's time someone served you."

Mary felt a little odd hearing these words. Abel had told her she needed to have more confidence and learn to love herself; only then would she be able to give a full, strong, healthy love to baby Moses.

"What I'm proposing may seem radical—cruel even," said Abel. "But I think it's the only way for you to take back what was stolen from you. You need to confront your father."

Mary felt a chill and her stomach started hurting. Despite feeling cold, she was sweating. Shivering, she asked Abel to get her a blanket.

"I know you're scared." He picked Moses up from the couch and put him on Mary's lap. She put her arms around the baby, feeling immediate warmth and comfort as Abel wrapped them both in a fuzzy blue blanket.

"I don't know if . . . my father," she said. "If my father is . . . alive."

"He is, sweet cheeks," said Abel. "I did a search on him and your whole family."

"Why would you do that without telling me?"

"I've been thinking about this for a while," Abel said. "I wanted to get all my ducks in a row before I came to you with it. Moses wants this for you also."

"Moses? He's only fifteen months old."

"Do you know, really, how old he is?"

"Based on what he looked like when I found him and what the doctor said, yes I have an idea," said Mary.

"He's a very old soul," said Abel.

"He's a baby," said Mary.

"He's special."

Mary hugged Moses.

"Mama scare," Moses said.

"See?" said Abel.

"He's babbling. He heard you say that."

"I've got the address for your mother and father," he said. "They live in Florida now."

"I'm not going to Florida," said Mary.

"You've got to," said Abel. "For Moses's sake."

*   *   *

Mary sat in a window seat with her child in her arms. Every other jaded passenger had their window shade drawn; Mary lifted hers to uncover the brightly shining sun and white fluffy clouds that looked to her like a soft, cottony, carpet to heaven. She stared out longingly, feeling like she'd missed her stop permanently. She imagined taking off her shoes and walking across the clouds to paradise.

Instead, in a few short hours she would be walking on burning coals toward hell.

"Are you okay, mairzy doats?" said Abel.

"Oh, I like that one," Mary said. "Bing Crosby."

"I love how you get my references."

"Doh!" said Moses.

They laughed and the baby laughed back at them.

"Silly boy," said Abel, pinching the baby's cheek.

Moses's face turned bright red. He let out a loud cry that couldn't be soothed into silence. Not with whispers, not by bouncing him on Mary's knee or by stroking his thin blond hair.

The businessman in front of them turned in his seat to stare back in disapproval. "Shut that kid up."

"I'm sorry," said Mary. "I'm trying."

The man rolled his eyes. "I didn't pay for this shit."

"He's an infant," said Abel. "What's your excuse?"

It was very sudden, the way the man collapsed. He fell across the lap of a well-dressed, elderly woman, who slid off her seat and ran, surprisingly fast, up the aisle.

Mary was impressed by how prepared the crew was for the medical emergency. Sadly, even with a defibrillator, two MDs, an EMT, and an LPN on board, nothing could be done to save the grumpy young man who, up until about twenty minutes ago, had thought the worst thing that could happen on a flight was hearing a baby cry.

*   *   *

Mary strapped Moses into his seat in the back of the black rental car. She'd wanted red, but Abel had wrinkled his nose and said a red car was "too flashy." She'd *wanted* to be seen as loud and flashy and vulgar when she met her father, but black was Abel's favorite color.

Abel mounted his phone to the dash and a very proper-sounding British voice gave him directions to the retirement community Mary's parents lived in.

"It's so weird," said Mary.

"What's weird, Mare?"

She looked at the squat palm trees flashing past along the highway. They didn't look like they belonged alongside concrete and technology, but on a deserted island somewhere, listening to the waves. The little trees here seemed sad; there were tears in their leaves.

She said, "Not to be morbid . . ."

"I love morbid."

"The day after I got Moses, my husband dropped dead right in front of me. Then Father William, and now this rude man on the plane. That's a lot of death for a little baby."

"Are you saying that," Abel said, "Moses Montgomery Mayhew has . . . powers?"

"I didn't say *that*. It's just weird, is all. What if it scars him?"

"We've all got scars, honey," he said. "Our scars make us beautiful."

*   *   *

Street after street, row after row after row, the square beige bungalows all looked alike but for the curtains: some had blue, some had white, some brown or matching bungalow beige. The same sad, plump palm trees sat in every front yard alongside assorted greenery, which all appeared to be plastic but was actually real, living plants.

As the voice prompted Abel's rental car onward, baby Moses

talked a nonsense blue streak in the back seat. Mary's nervous stomach rumbled and gurgled, sounding like a dying lawnmower. Meanwhile, Abel hummed the old Gloria Gaynor chestnut, "I Will Survive," which made Mary think once again that he was gay even though he'd said his sexuality was *undefined*.

Abel stepped on the brake just as his phone spoke its final sentence: "You have reached your destination."

Mary looked out the window at the bungalow; the number above the door read *999*. She felt like she should get out of the car and turn the numbers upside down.

"If you stand on your head," Abel said, "you'll see the mark of the beast."

Mary nodded. "Just as I suspected."

"Bee," said Moses from the back of the car.

"Should we bring Moses?" Mary asked. "I don't want him to be exposed to that man."

"You have to. Show your father that, in spite of what he did, you are a mother, and you have a beautiful son."

"I don't know."

"You can't just leave him in the car, girl. Or are you afraid he'll witness another man's death?"

"He's a *witness*," she said. "Not a *catalyst*. Don't you think so?"

"Do we care if beast daddy dies?"

"I don't want Moses seeing it a fourth time."

Abel got out of the car and walked around to open Mary's door, holding out a hand to her. Mary took off her seatbelt and they opened the back to get Moses. She held the baby close with one hand and Abel's hand with the other as they walked to the front door. The welcome mat was straw, with a cartoon drawing of the Cheshire Cat grinning his huge grin. Underneath the smile it read *Welcome* in big blue letters.

"A very merry unbirthday," said Abel.

"I'm afraid," said Mary.

"Allow me." Abel knocked loudly.

There was movement in the window: someone peeking through the blinds. The door opened. An elderly, gray-haired man with a very large, round belly and a long, ZZ Top-style beard stood before them dressed in light blue corduroy shorts and a blue and white Hawaiian shirt.

The man pointed to the sign to the left of the door. "No

soliciting."

"That's all you have to say," Mary said, "after twenty years?"

The man took a pair of folded glasses from his collar, put them on, and stared at the couple with suspicion. "Twenty years? What's that supposed to mean?"

"You need a stronger prescription," Abel said.

The man looked like he wanted to punch Abel, but didn't; Abel was forty years younger and sturdily built.

A woman's voice came from inside the house. "Who's at the door?"

"Fuck if I know," said the man. "Who the hell are you two?"

"You don't recognize your own daughter?" said Mary.

"Mary?"

"Aren't you going to invite us in?"

He looked over at baby Moses. "This your kid?"

"Moses," Mary said. "My son."

He stepped back to let them inside, frowning at the baby, who'd started to cry. An apple-faced elderly woman with clown-red dyed hair stood in the middle of the living room, nervously watching them. Mary stared down at the hideous, olive-green carpet to avoid looking her mother in the eye.

"Mary?" The woman sounded uncertain.

"Yeah," said Mary softly.

There was an uncomfortable silence in the room until the baby started crying again.

"Is he yours?" her mother asked.

Mary's father rolled his eyes. "C'mon, Penelope."

"Well," Penelope said. "How am I supposed to know? I didn't think she'd be able to . . ."

"Shut up," said Mary's father.

"I have really powerful sperm," Abel said.

Penelope looked down at his crotch in confusion. Mary's father again looked like he wanted to slug Abel, but limited himself to clucking his tongue.

"I'm Abel, by the way." He extended his hand to Mary's mother. She shook it without saying anything.

"You two married?" said Mary's father.

"We don't believe in marriage," said Abel.

"What'd I tell you?" Mary's father said to his wife.

Mary hugged Moses close to her chest, rubbing his back, her

heart beating fast. She pushed his face into her neck.

"Raymond," Penelope said. "That's your grandson."

"No way he's biological," Raymond said.

"He's biologically mine," said Abel.

"Yeah?" said Raymond. "Who's the mother?"

"Raymond!" said Penelope.

"Ruth," said Abel. "Ruth is his mother."

"Ruth!" Penelope and Raymond said, almost in unison.

"Ruth?" said Mary.

"You knew Ruth," Abel said. "Didn't you Mary?"

"She—" Mary's face felt hot. Her throat tightened.

"Ruth died years ago," Raymond said.

Mary hugged the baby tightly.

"Did she?" said Abel.

Penelope loosed a weird, high sob, then knelt on the carpet, hands clasped in prayer. "Oh, Lord Jesus, forgive me."

Mary had blocked her younger sister, Ruth, out of her mind for years. The guilt of leaving a ten-year-old girl alone with her father had been too much for her; she'd willed her sibling into nonexistence.

"Are you serious?" Mary said. "This is Ruth's son?"

"He's full of shit," Raymond said. "Ruth died eighteen years ago."

"No," said Penelope. "She didn't. Mrs. Worthington took her."

"That bitch you used to clean toilets for?"

"I knew once Ruth got her period, you'd be doing to her what you did to Mary," Penelope said. "I couldn't have another daughter suffer like that. I asked Mrs. Worthington to take her in. She was well off and could give her the kind of life we couldn't. She'd always wanted a daughter, and Ruth was so pretty and sweet."

"I saw the coffin," Raymond said.

"You saw *a* coffin," said Penelope. "But you never looked inside."

"You told me her body was all burned up from the car crash."

"There was no crash," Penelope said. "Mrs. Worthington and her husband arranged everything to make you think she was dead. I told them about Mary. Why she'd run away."

"You're fucking full of shit," Raymond said.

"Where is Ruth now?" asked Mary.

"She died giving birth to him," said Abel, indicating Moses.

"He's not a regular baby."

"Get out of my house," said Raymond. "I'm not listening to any more crazy-ass lies."

A feeling of light-headedness came over Mary. She sat in the nearest chair with Moses in her lap. The baby had settled down, quietly playing with strands of Mary's brown hair. What Abel had said couldn't be true. Her tummy started hurting and her throat was sore. She looked over at her mother, who had dropped from her kneeling position to sit on the floor. Time hadn't been kind to her. Why would it, with the kind of life she'd lived?

Her mother had always kept her at arm's length. Even as a small child, Mary would cry and reach out her arms, but her mother would tell her to wipe her face and stand up straight like a big girl. And whenever she'd said, *big girl,* Mary had thought of how Alice, from her favorite book, *Alice in Wonderland,* had grown bigger when she ate some kind of cake. And Mary'd felt like she was swallowing something too, every time her mother had rejected her and told her to be big. She'd swallowed a lot, all through her childhood, all through her life. It sat inside her like a cold, dense mass that never left her. Ever. Swallow. Swallow. Swallow. Her life was just a series of swallowing up stuff she didn't want to eat.

Moses was kissing her face. Her stomach felt really sick. Nauseated. Like something was going to come up and she couldn't stop it. Moses's little feet kicked at her stomach. It didn't hurt, but made whatever was inside her move. And then the baby was rubbing her throat with his little hands like he was petting a cat.

Mary suddenly noticed how silent it was, her parents and Abel staring at her with the odd expressions of people watching something horrible. Mary's mouth opened, and everything she'd swallowed in her thirty-six years came up with a burning sensation in her chest. Every hug she'd not been given, every kiss she'd been refused, every kind word she'd never heard, every bit of respect she'd been denied, spewed from her mouth like fiery lava.

Mary closed her eyes but still heard the screams, and what came out of her smelled like a dead thing rotting. One moment, she was sitting, baby Moses on her lap; the next, she was on hands and knees, retching out bile, all that was left inside of her. She collapsed onto the green carpet in exhaustion, the vomit hot and sticky beside her. Things were silent once again. Mary opened her eyes.

The bodies of her parents lay on the floor, their flesh seared off as if they'd been burned. Abel was completely black. Mary didn't know how, but he stood, slowly and weakly.

"The power was inside you," Abel said hoarsely. "All this time."

Mary got up off the floor feeling like she'd been punched in the stomach. She looked around for Moses, but he was nowhere to be seen.

"Where's Moses?"

"Blessed are you among women," said Abel. "And blessed is the fruit of your womb."

"What does that mean?" said Mary.

"You're just all kinds of Biblical royalty, Mary," Abel said.

"No," Mary said. "I'm not."

"God bless you," Abel said.

And Mary felt like Alice. Too big. Too big for this little house. Too big for herself. She went outside and it was dark and soundless. She was blind and deaf. She wondered if it was the world this had happened to or just her.

The Secret of St. Augustine
Aaron White

"You sure this is the right way?" Kristen asked. It'd been a while since she stopped trying to spot landmarks—it was black beyond the windshield. There'd been one last streetlight, sputtering as they drove beneath its flickering cone of light, but that was miles back. Now, it was dark.

"Yeah," Tyler muttered. "I mean, there haven't been any turns for a while, and we were on track before the GPS shit the bed." He glanced at his cell phone, held by something suction-cupped to the dash. There was a blue arrow in a field of gray. The screen hadn't updated for some time.

Every now and then the edge of the headlights briefly illuminated the hard angles of some empty and forgotten house— windows boarded up, lawn lost to wild grass and overgrown vegetation—then their fleeting facades were gone, like the ghosts of the families who'd lived there. Kristen had the sense that this whole section of town had been abandoned. During the day it would be depressing, but at night . . .

"So we're just supposed to find some . . . house, just because some guy you knew in college said so?"

"I think it's more like a warehouse or something, but yeah, we'll probably know it when we see it." He cautiously glanced at her. She was ignoring him and getting annoyed. "Look, it's kinda weird meeting a friend I haven't seen in like ten years, but . . . I don't know, I thought it'd be cool. And I thought you did too."

"I didn't know we'd be driving through some backwoods

shithole. Does anyone even *live* out here?"

"Maybe that's the point—to get away from civilization."

"Whatever."

He glanced at her again but couldn't see much. The lights of the dash touched upon her nose, angled cheekbones, and the choppy black hair framing her face. The rest was lost. He reached for the radio dial.

"No, don't," Kristen said softly. "I like the quiet. I might shut my eyes for a bit."

He withdrew his hand, heard the crinkle of Kristen's leather jacket as she settled into the seat. One of the tires hit a pothole and she mumbled something, then all was silent.

The dilapidated three-deckers gave way to overgrown and neglected fields—the rusting husks of cars beside rotting barns, the owners of both long gone. The moon was lost behind a thick layer of clouds. Beyond the glimpses of old wood and flaking metal, there was only darkness. It was a rural apocalypse.

"It's like the end of the world," Tyler muttered to himself.

"Did you say something?" Kristen mumbled, half-asleep.

"No," Tyler lied.

Soon the buildings petered out, and it was just the car, the ruined road beneath it, and the night. Tyler gritted his teeth as the Chevy pitched over what was left of the asphalt. The high beams licked crumbling storefronts and moved across empty parking lots. A sharp curve in the road led to the outskirts of a long-dead industrial park, the sprawling brick and concrete buildings like the petrified corpses of giants.

Tyler slowed the car to a crawl. He was close. He turned into a parking lot, following the long contours of an empty warehouse covered in graffiti. A hard corner and he spotted lights in the windows of a nearby building, pulsing in rhythm and shifting colors. As the car moved closer, he heard the steady beat of a kick drum, like a mechanical heart.

* * *

"Hey. *Hey.* We're here."

Kristen stirred, wiped her eyes, and peered through the windshield at the lights strobing in the broken windows. "Is this a fucking rave?"

"It's like a . . . some kind of multi-media installation or something."

Weeds had reclaimed most of the parking lot. Cars of various makes, with no lines to guide them, were parked haphazardly. Tyler steered around them until they were too cluttered together to drive any farther. He pulled the car close to a low brick wall and threw it in park. Behind the idling engine, a bass drum throbbed from somewhere in an adjacent building.

"You ready?"

Kristen sighed, rubbing at a temple. "*Well*, I've g—"

She'd been about to tell him about the headache threatening to well up behind her eyes, but knew he needed this, so bit her tongue. He hadn't said anything, but she knew he was lonely. Never a social animal, she'd noticed him going out less and less, and it troubled her. Maybe a run-in with an old acquaintance would do him good. She forced a crooked, tired smile. "Sure, let's check it out."

That dim optimism began to fade soon after they left the vehicle. There were other people milling about—between cars, some lying atop hoods or roofs—all strangely silent. Kristen had assumed there'd be at least *some* conversation, but there was nothing. They barely moved. A fire burned in a large metal barrel against one brick wall and a group of young men surrounded it, each with the same blank, comatose look on their faces—jaws slack, eyes heavily lidded, like they were sedated. They just stood there, watching the flames dance, skin glistening with sweat. And while it gave Kristen the creeps, there was a gnawing hunger in her that wanted that—to get lost in the dark, to go blind and numb to a careless and cruel world. It was a hunger she'd had to turn her back to before.

"I'll have what they're havin'," she muttered to Tyler, trying to make a joke of it. He knew about her past, but didn't seem to hear. He didn't appear to take in their surroundings, just strolled up to one of the doors dotting the length of the warehouse and tugged one of the doorknobs. The door opened.

Before he slipped inside, he turned and gave her a look. It was charming, the mix of excitement and nervousness in that almost-sad smile, the sheepish-yet-hopeful look on his face. Time paused, and as she drank the fleeting moment in, she had an absurd thought that she embraced anyway: *If something were to happen to us, this is how I want to remember him—just like this.* And then he was inside.

She pressed close to his back, not trusting the shadows and already mildly annoyed at the music, equal parts amateur techno and experimental noise. The racket dramatically increased: voices raised in competition with the music, much louder inside the building. The only illumination came from strobe lights, lasers, and various videos projected onto walls layered with years of graffiti. She came to a halt, not quite realizing she'd stopped, gazing at a strange symbol painted onto one of the walls.

An upside-down triangle attached by its bottom point to something that looked like an inverted ankh, surrounded by a wavy circle that could've been a snake. It resembled one of those planetary symbols, the ones associated with the zodiac, only with an eye painted in the middle of the triangle. The words scrawled around the outside of the serpent—in red paint that dripped like blood—read: *CARO EST VAS DIVINUM.*

"Hey, Kris, what the hell are you doing?"

Tyler's voice snapped her back into focus. He was some twenty feet away, a puzzled look on his face. There was a doorway behind him and a room beyond. Purple and red lights throbbed to the beat of a drum. It took her a moment to respond.

"What is all this?" The question was vague but she didn't care.

He smiled and shook his head. "It's just art school shit, y'know?" He approached, took her hand. "I thought you were into this stuff."

"Well, yeah . . . I just . . ." She realized she was at a loss for words because her emotions weren't making sense. The apprehension, the unease, it wasn't like her. Before any more words shaped themselves, a voice from behind Tyler cut her off.

*　　*　　*

"Ty . . .?"

He turned and saw a young man standing in the doorway, a scrawny silhouette against the strobing lights. Tyler knew the voice, but the rest was unrecognizable. Colored lights played along gaunt and sunken features. The figure approached and stepped into a pool of shifting light.

"Hey, man, it's me. It's—"

"Jesus, *Barry*?" Tyler blurted, unable to keep the surprise out of his voice. The ghost of his old friend was there, lost in the walking corpse standing before him. Barry looked *sick*. Dark circles ringed his bloodshot eyes. His mane of black hair had been hastily shaved close to a skull that looked disproportionately big for his skinny body, a body from which dark, paint-spattered clothing hung. His skin looked taut, waxy.

"*Tyler*, man, I'm glad you made it!"

Barry offered a hand, and Tyler was not surprised to see track marks dotting the crook of his elbow. He took it, afraid for a moment that he'd crush the fingers like a fistful of twigs.

"Who's this?" Barry asked, gesturing toward Kristen with his chin.

"Oh, yeah, this is my girlfriend, Kristen."

Kristen took the extended hand. Even through the mix of emotions seeing his old friend stirred up, Tyler thought her smile was a little forced.

"Nice to meet you," Barry said.

*   *   *

The three moved slowly through the crowd. Kristen strayed a few steps behind, letting the boys catch up while her gaze wandered across the walls and over the faces of strangers. They were all high in some way. There was pot smoke in the air, and behind that, something almost chemical, like burning plastic. Clips from horror movies played on loops, projected onto the grimy concrete walls. Sometimes the almost cartoonish gore would freeze and fragment into colorful geometric shapes that spilled onto the ceiling or floor. They were almost hypnotic, these loops, and as she watched, Kristen wondered what her deal had been on the way up here, why she'd been so tense and on edge.

The drumbeat's tempo ramped up and a frantic distorted synth faded in. The people around her began to move to the rhythm, swaying, eyes closed and lost to the moment. The images on the walls began to change with the beat: a devil's red face, a blood-soaked hallway, a burning church. She spun in a slow circle, taking everything in, and realized she'd lost track of Tyler and his friend.

"Tyler?" She knew her voice didn't carry over the music filling the warehouse. "God damn it, *Tyler*!" She scanned the room. Three doors lead into other spaces. She wondered which one they'd taken. Moving through the room, she had to push with her shoulders and elbows against the crowd, grimacing as her arms brushed skin dripping with sweat. She didn't remember there being this many people a moment ago, and fought a rising panic. Beyond their wet, bobbing heads, she caught a glimpse of a figure in white, its lower face covered by something like a fabric mask. And then it was gone.

Kristen moved backward, pushing against the humid bodies around her, scanning the crowd. Something wasn't right. She turned, pushing her way into the horde, ignoring stray hands that seemed suddenly animated. She did this with her eyes glued to the floor and didn't stop until she no longer felt slick flesh against her palms.

She was in another room—a darker room lit only by pulsing red LEDs lining the walls. There, in a back corner, Tyler was talking with Barry. Their body language looked almost conspiratorial.

"Hey!" Kristen called. "Tyler!" His eyes suddenly darted in her direction and she wondered if he really looked guilty. Barry turned toward her, face expressionless. "Where the fuck you been?" she asked.

It took Tyler a moment to gather himself. "We . . . we were just in here, babe. I thought you were . . ." He gestured to the room behind Kristen. "I don't know, dancing or some shit. You okay?"

Kristen took a breath. "I just need some air. My head is pounding." That much was true—her temples throbbed to the rhythm of the music.

Barry's strangely lifeless face suddenly animated, and he smiled at her. "Hey, yeah, good idea! Follow me."

He led them out of the room and down a hall that turned a corner and led into a different space. At the far end there was a red EXIT sign above a door. He shouldered it open and let them through.

*   *   *

"People find stars comforting or whatever, like . . . y'know, people wish on them and all." Kristen stared at the sky above her. The clouds had rolled back, and the inky dark was stippled with glimmering specks. "But that twinkle we see is, what? Thousands of years old? What if they all supernova-ed a decade ago and the universe is dead, and we just don't know it yet?"

They were outside, on a patch of unkempt, overgrown grass bisected by a concrete walkway to a parking lot. There were empty bottles and cans everywhere.

"Gee, that's cheerful." Tyler smiled. Kristen seemed back to her old morbid self.

She stopped stargazing and looked at him, seeming to read his thoughts. "Hey, sorry about before. I don't know if it was the crowds or the music or what, but I lost my cool. I was just feeling on edge and I didn't know what to do about it."

"I've got something that'll take the edge off," Barry said before he could comment, and Tyler rolled his eyes as he felt a tender moment slip away.

Kristen's head swiveled in Barry's direction. "Oh? Whatchu got?"

Barry reached beneath his shirt. There was something tied around his neck. He pulled at a cord and revealed a glass vial tied to a thin leather strap.

Kristen eyed the vial. "What is that?"

"Obsidian."

"What the hell is *obsidian*?" asked Tyler.

"It's like . . . the clarity of coke, but it'll open your mind up like acid. Totally smooth, but, like . . . fucking amazing."

"Yeah?" Kristen turned to Tyler with a devilish grin on her face.

"Kinda like molly," Barry went on. "Without the touchy-feely shit. It just . . . expands your senses."

Tyler felt hesitant. "I don't know, babe. I've never heard of this shit."

"Oh Christ, what's the harm?" she replied. Barry was unscrewing the top of the vial. A tiny spoon was attached to the underside of the lid. She stepped closer, staring down at the small utensil and the substance scooped from Barry's private stash. It looked like black glitter, and when the moonlight danced across it, Tyler saw a myriad of colors, like a powdered oil slick. Hunching over and closing a nostril with her finger, she brought her nose close to the small spoon. She inhaled, a quick, sharp sniff, then straightened, pinching her nostrils tight.

"Oof, this *stings!*" Her voice was distorted and nasal. She looked at Tyler and smiled, but the smile faltered. Already her eyes were glassy and distant. She winced, bringing her hands to her forehead. "Ow, fuck." For a moment she looked scared, then the pain crumpled her face and brought her to her knees. "Ahhh! *Ahhhhhhhhhh!*"

Tyler watched his girlfriend fall and the world was in slow motion. She gripped her head, heels drumming the ground, then a jolt ran through her frame and her limbs straightened. Her eyes were wide and full of pain or terror. Another jolt, her whole body jerking like she'd been poked with a cattle prod. When a third jolt came, she didn't stop moving. She convulsed and thrashed in the filthy grass, fingers flexing, grabbing at nothing.

"Jesus Christ," Tyler heard himself say. His voice sounded distant and alien. "Jesus fucking Christ dude, what the fuck is this? Hey! *Hey!*" His legs were finally moving, and before he realized it, he was straddling Kristen, cupping her head in his hands. "Hey, babe. Babe, it's okay. Kristen? Jesus Christ, Kristen!" Her eyes rolled up and her irises all but disappeared. There was a gurgle deep in her throat, and blood began to run from each nostril, painting red lines down her cheeks. "Oh fuck. Fuck! *Kristen!*"

"I . . . I don't think you're supposed to touch them, when they're . . ." It was Barry's voice, small, monotone. "When they're having a . . . a seizure."

And then Tyler was lunging at him, grabbing at his neck, shoving him against the concrete wall. "What the fuck is this shit, huh? *Huh?*" he spat, seizing the leather cord. He tugged hard and the cord broke with an audible snap.

"Wait. Wait a sec . . ." Barry mumbled. He wasn't looking at Tyler, but past him, over his shoulder. Tyler released him and turned, dreading what he might discover. The world swam beneath his feet when he saw Kristen lying in the grass, motionless. His heart hammered in his ears. A moment later he was kneeling at her side. He didn't remember moving. Somewhere, something in his head screamed and screamed.

"Kristen? You there, babe? Hello?" He stroked her hair, caressed her cheek, then leaned in so close his ear brushed her lips. "Fuck, I can't tell." He scrambled, grabbed her arm and pressed his thumb against her wrist. There was—perhaps—a limp pulse. It was hard to say.

He stood, head spinning. "Okay . . . *fuck*, I need to get her to a hospital. Now, Barry. *Hospital.*" He turned and saw Barry gawking at him, jaw slightly askew, eyes glassy and faraway. "Hey, *dipshit*, I need to get her to a *hospital.*"

Some semblance of life slowly came back to Barry's features. "Yeah. Yeah, there's one nearby." The words came painfully slow.

Tyler grabbed him by the shirt again. "You're gonna help her to my car, and then you're gonna tell me where the fuck this hospital is."

With some effort they pulled Kristen from the ground and managed to sling an arm over each of their shoulders. Behind them, a crowd pressed sweaty faces and hands against the glass, watching them leave with hungry grins.

Kristen's black sneakers dragged across the asphalt as they navigated the parking lot, weaving between cars and party-goers too inebriated to pay them mind. Tyler found his car on sheer instinct alone. It took a combined effort to get the door open without dropping Kristen, and when Tyler was finished propping her against the opposite door, Barry took the seat next to her.

"Now get me to there, but you make sure she's okay," Tyler told Barry. "Don't let her fall all over the fucking place." He opened the driver's door, flung himself into the car, and started the engine.

*   *   *

Barry's directions came a word or two at a time. "Right," he would say, or, "Left, here." Tyler obeyed, wheels squealing as he took each sudden, unexpected corner. The place was a labyrinth of ruin. He glanced in the review mirror. Kristen was still out cold.

"*Christ!* How much farther?"

"Not much."

Another few minutes lapsed, and then Barry shifted in his seat to lean forward.

"Here," he said quietly.

"Where?"

"On the left. Just pull in."

"Pull in *where?*"

"*Here!*"

There was an opening on the left, little more than a gap in a broken sidewalk, and the beam of the headlights caught an old, corroded aluminum sign by the entrance of what might've once been a parking lot:

St. Augustine Hospital.

Years of neglect had tarnished the surface and buckled the edges. It looked centuries old. Tyler cut the wheel and the car rolled into the vast empty space beyond. The headlights did little to penetrate the darkness. There were no lights anywhere. Tyler took his foot off the gas and the car rolled over the uneven pavement toward something emerging from the murk—a vast shape blacker than the night itself, all hard, unwelcoming angles. It was the ruin of a building, devoid of any signs of life. Not a speck of light dotted a window or door. The place looked long forgotten.

"What is this?" Tyler asked, softly, and then the absurdity struck home. "What the *fuck* is this, *huh*? Is this some kind of fucking *joke*?" He craned his neck and twisted in his seat to look Barry in the eyes. He had half a mind to leap into the back of the car and beat the shit out of him, regardless of Kristen or her condition.

But Barry's face was full of a bright-eyed wonder. "*Look*," he said with almost religious zeal, and something about his expression deeply troubled Tyler. A warm light spilled over Barry's features, and he laughed like a child. Tyler's rage wilted, replaced by confusion and an uneasiness bordering on terror. Barry shouldered the door open and exited the vehicle. "*C'mon!*" he said, already tugging at Kristen's body. Tyler slowly turned and saw the impossible: a wall made of filthy, discolored glass, lit from within. The amber light spilled across the cracked pavement and into the car. Above the glass doors and windows of the lobby, the sign should've been welcoming, but its garish red light seemed like a warning instead:

EMERGENCY

Staring at the sign, Tyler killed the engine. He pawed at the door handle and slowly got out of the car. "I don't . . ." he began, but couldn't finish the sentence. Trying to make sense of the situation made his head spin. Had someone been waiting for them within? Was this just another place like the factory, taken over by derelicts and turned into some drug den? "What is this?"

Barry had his hands looped under Kristen's arms and was pulling her from the car. He looked confused. "It's what you wanted."

*   *   *

The mechanism that opened the automatic doors seemed to be breaking down, the doors shaking as they slid apart. The smell hit Tyler as they entered: mildew mixed with smoke and dust.

The lobby was dingy, unkempt; perhaps decades had gone by since its last cleaning. A few of the track lights didn't work. The ones with power cast a dirty yellow glow on a worn tiled floor marred with scuffs and scratches. Carrying Kristen between them, they passed a waiting room to their left and saw dirty chairs arranged in haphazard, sloppy rows, all of them empty.

They were the only ones there.

To the right, a series of smudged and fly-specked windows led to a set of double doors. Above these windows, signs read Triage and Registration. A woman sat behind a sullied pane of glass. She looked to be in her forties, though it was hard to place an exact age to her nondescript, bland features. She wore no expression and offered no words of welcome. Behind her, sheet-draped machines lay scattered about the room, the occasional wire snaking its way out from the tattered cloth. A gurney had been pushed into a corner, concealing some crumpled form curled in on itself, covered by a white shroud. The receptionist continued to stare.

"Hey! *Hello?*" Tyler shouted. "We need some fucking *help* here!"

The woman's blank gaze didn't change. Eyes still locked, she reached down and slowly lifted a discolored, once-white plastic phone receiver from its cradle. She spoke into the mouthpiece, but he couldn't hear any words. The room crackled as an intercom system came to life, and after a few bursts of static a woman's voice issued a command in a language that sounded like Latin, distorted and monotonic. After a high-pitched squeal of feedback, the command was repeated. A moment later, the lights behind the desk flickered, and Tyler heard a noise from the hallway beyond. It was a rhythmic squeaking, the turning of a rusted wheel. The lights above and the ones in the hall sputtered out entirely. Darkness swallowed the room. The squealing grew louder as something was pulled into the waiting area. Tyler, disoriented and confused, instinctively tried to drag Kristen away, out the door behind them, but he felt hands on his shoulders, pinning him in place. Kristen's body slipped away.

"*Kristen!*" he shouted, and suddenly found himself wondering what Barry was doing, why he was being so quiet. He reached, felt nothing—and then the lights came back on, dim, red, like emergency lights. Barry wasn't there. Tyler whirled to face the windows, and there was nothing but a thick blackness beyond, like the world had vanished. He turned again. Even the receptionist had disappeared.

"What is this?" he asked himself quietly. "Hey! Barry!" There was a door to the restrooms across the way, and he rushed to it, calling out as he did. "Come on, man . . . *Barry!*" He pulled the door but it wouldn't budge. He pulled again. Locked. "You've gotta be kidding," he muttered. He spun around. "*Hey!* This isn't funny, asshole!"

The thought that this was some elaborate prank entered his head, some kind of performance art Kristen was somehow in on. He cracked a smile. "Okay . . . okay, you got me!" He assumed he was being watched from the shadows and raised his hands in mock surrender. "You guys can come out now!" Tyler walked back to the reception desk, then remembered Kristen's seizure, the blood running down the sides of her face. "Cut the *shit*, babe! This isn't funny!" He eyed the double doors, then pushed them open.

The hallway beyond was in even worse condition, tiled walls crumbling and smeared with grime. At least there seemed to be power in the main hospital, despite most of the overhead fixtures being in disrepair. Pale light sputtered in some of the fluorescent tubes fixed to the ceiling. Some had come loose and dangled precariously from wires. Tyler smelled the sharp, repugnant odors of formaldehyde and rotting meat.

"*Christ*," he muttered behind his hand as he clamped his nostrils shut. "What the hell *is* this?" He made his way down the hall to a large open room lined with semi-circles of stained, ragged sheets hanging limply from metal rings in the ceiling. His gaze moved from one dirty curtain to the next, knowing there was a bed behind each, hoping Kristen was here in one of the beds awaiting some kind of procedure. Some of the stains on the fabric were blood. Instinct told him to turn and run. He'd even begun to pivot when he heard a high, monotonous beeping coming from behind a tattered drape in the corner and froze.

A heart monitor.

He crossed the room, hoping the steady beat belonged to Barry or Kristen. The curtain was stiff to the touch, and the rings holding it up squealed as they slid on their rusty metal rod. In the dimly-lit space beyond, someone stirred in the bed and looked in his direction.

Barry's wasted face lit up, and he smiled a dreamy, sleepy smile when he saw his friend. Drops of sweat beaded his forehead, and his left arm looked strange and terrible. Swollen and discolored, it was longer than it should be. There was a thin tube in Barry's arm—an IV line—and Tyler couldn't help but follow its course to the bag hanging from the metal stand next to the bed. The pouch was filled with a rust-colored liquid, and floating in its contents was a dead, malformed fetus. A second vestigial head sprouted from its back.

Tyler took an involuntary step backward. Someone else was in the alcove, in the shadows, behind the curtain. There was a rush of movement and he glimpsed the figure as it stepped forward and pulled the curtain closed. The hand gripping the fabric was sheathed in a blood-stained latex glove.

Tyler turned and ran the other way, out of the room, carried by instinct and fear. He ran down the hall, following it as it turned right and then left. After another left turn, he realized this wasn't the way he'd come and slowed to a stop, heart hammering in his ears. The soiled tiles all looked the same. He turned and went back the way he'd come, wondering if he'd missed a turn. Somewhere— faintly—a woman began to scream, over and over. The corridor turned left.

"*Fuck . . .*" Tyler muttered, fighting off panic. The screams sounded like they could be Kristen's, but he wasn't sure. But he hadn't come from this way, either. There were signs on the walls that hadn't been there before:

Epidemiology

Paralogy

Thaumatology

Tyler didn't know what those meant, didn't know where he was or what was happening. He spun in place. The hallway behind him was dark now, though fluorescent lights had flickered overhead a moment ago. The screaming was louder and seemed to come from that direction.

"*Kristen!*"

He hoped the shrieking wasn't her, but the need for answers pulled him into the shadows. He risked a glance behind him. Down the hall a door opened—a door that hadn't been there before. Something was being wheeled out of a room. The figure in the long white coat guiding the wheelchair was surely a doctor, but there was something horribly wrong with its head, which was a pulpy, glistening mess of raw tissue. The thing in the chair twitched, enormous, fetal cranium rolling on frail shoulders, and gazed at Tyler.

Tyler turned and fled down the hall, which grew darker with each step. There was an open door to his right, a black rectangle in the gloom, and he ducked into the shadows around the door frame. Pressing his back flat against the clammy wall, he closed his eyes and held his breath.

There was a faint sound from across the room—fabric sliding against itself—and then Tyler heard a soft groan, like someone stirring in their sleep.

"Ty?" a familiar voice called out quietly. "Tyler, is that you?"

Tyler's heart leapt in his chest. "*Kris?* Oh my God, babe, I thought . . . I didn't . . ." Tears came, and he frantically groped at the wall. "Jesus, where the hell are the *lights?*"

"*Don't,*" Kristen said. "I'm still recovering." Her voice was syrupy and thick with sedation. "I don't want you to see."

Those last words dried out Tyler's mouth. "See *what?*"

There was a pause, and for a moment Tyler was afraid she'd fallen unconscious. "I went through a . . . procedure," she said finally.

Tyler reached out and stumbled toward the sound of her voice. "A *what?* Hey, what did they do to you?"

"It's okay . . ." Kristen sounded weak. "Babe, it's *okay.* They just took out the bad parts. You'll see . . ."

She sounded close. He took another couple of steps, feeling the air for obstacles. Something pressed against his legs and he realized he was at her bedside. He felt the cold metal rail lining the edge, patches of flaky rust rough under his touch. He reached beyond the barrier, trying to touch Kristen's shoulder, or where he guessed her shoulder should be, but there was nothing there. Again he heard the sliding of cloth, as something pulled away.

"*Don't,*" she said again, and she was *right there,* just out of reach.

"Babe, it's just me." Tyler leaned against the metal guard.

"We're getting outta here." His fingers grazed a tangle of wires and plastic tubing. He reached in and felt around, finally landing on the tattered cloth of a blanket. There was a sick smell in the makeshift cradle, an odor that reminded Tyler of Band-Aids. He felt farther, and when his hand grazed Kristen's cheek, she flinched and gasped. Her skin was hot to the touch. His fingers moved down her body but never found the soft curve of her shoulder or the arm attached to it. Instead, he discovered a disturbing *absence* of anatomy. Straining, he stretched his arm to capacity and touched a series of spongy lumps. Something squirmed under his palm and he jumped back.

He smelled the gloved hands before he felt them—the sudden scent of copper and iodine—and then they were gripping his head and face.

"Just let it happen," Kristen said, and there was a sudden sharp prick at his jawline. The world folded in on itself as he lost consciousness.

*   *   *

Coming to was like rising toward the surface of some deep, dark ocean. Tyler's senses came to life one by one, and the first thing he noticed was the pain—a dull ache between his temples, a fire at every joint. He was sitting down, but also moving. There were footsteps behind him, and screaming—men, women, things that were neither. His blurry vision began to clear and Tyler realized he was in a wheelchair, being pushed down a long corridor, tiled walls layered with years of accumulated filth. There were words and shapes smeared on the walls. He saw the same strange symbol he'd seen in the run-down warehouse, now seeming like a dream within a dream. Light the color of piss sputtered from the ceiling fixtures. The rooms lining the hall were little more than closets, each alcove containing some kind of anatomical nightmare, some malformed thing in a large glass tank or affixed to the back wall with buckles and straps. He couldn't move his head, so only caught glimpses of the half-dead deformities, but a glimpse was enough to turn his stomach. He closed his eyes.

Perhaps it was the dark that allowed him to remember: the warehouse, Barry, the frantic trip to a run-down hospital, Kristen. God, *Kristen*. She'd been in a dark room and she hadn't been herself, and she . . .

"Locked inside of every living thing there is a mystery."

It took Tyler a moment or two to realize the rasping, gravelly voice was *in his head.* He opened his eyes.

"That is a key." Tyler watched as a gloved hand pointed to a sigil on the wall, drawn in dripping blood. *"This is a key."* The hand now held a scalpel, its blade glistening.

Before Tyler could make sense of the words, the wheelchair was turned so he could look into one of the small spaces dotting the hall. Tyler couldn't see much beyond the hulking, swollen thing residing within. It was vaguely human in shape and had strangely colored skin—blueish-gray flesh glistening with a sheen of oily sweat. Tumors and large veiny sacs hung from its neck and drooped from its bloated, corpulent stomach. The immense form leaned forward as if to study Tyler, and when Tyler met its gaze he saw Barry's sublime smiling face, so small, all but lost in its vast, bulbous head. The giant with Barry's face gazed down at the thing cradled in its gargantuan arms, and Tyler was powerless to resist looking at what it held. By comparison it was tiny, a skinny malformed thing with limbs like sticks. For some reason, Tyler was reminded of an infant deer, perhaps born shockingly premature and feeble. Its oversized head rolled toward Tyler, and there, in the midst of its soft, misshapen skull, Kristen's perfect features smiled out at him.

Tyler wanted to scream, but couldn't. He lacked the anatomy. To scream. To fight back. To even lift himself from the chair. He was helpless, and could only writhe feebly against the straps holding him to the wheelchair. He was pushed into an alcove of his own, where he could do nothing but wait for further modification.

By the Living
Alan Marks

I'm not in her way, but still, she steers herself around me when she shuffles into the kitchen for breakfast. Not much of a detour, but hard to miss when all it takes is—at most—a couple of steps to cross from one side of the room to the other.

"Morning," I say.

No answer. Not that I really expected one.

Sometimes, the only sense I get my mother knows I'm here at all are the lengths she goes to in order to avoid me. The way she keeps her distance. How her eyes slide past wherever I might be, looking anywhere but my direction.

My whole existence is defined by negatives: Not touched. Not seen. Not heard.

Not really here.

Absence as presence.

She doesn't sit, just picks away at a slice of toast while leaning over the counter, letting crumbs spill wherever. She stares out the window at . . . not much of anything, really.

It's still early—the sun hasn't cleared the buildings across the street, yet—but, in the July heat, the room is already stifling. The kitchen's one window has been painted shut forever, so there's no way for the heat to get out or fresh air to get in. And there's nowhere you can go in the whole apartment where there isn't at least a faint whiff of dirty dishes left to soak too long and overflowing garbage. But maybe she doesn't notice that, either.

As weeks go, this has been a great one.

She didn't used to smoke. Now, she's already on her third of the morning. And her second cup of coffee. That lone slice of toast is something she chews more out of habit than hunger. Most days, she runs on caffeine and nicotine as much as food.

Her hair used to be black. And long. Now it's shot through with gray, and I can see her scalp in places, it's cut so short. She looks old. It bothers me that I can't remember when that happened.

In my memory, her face is fuller, the only lines the little crinkles she'd get in the corners of her eyes when she'd smile. Now, the light from the window behind her casts shadows into the hollows of her cheeks and the deep crevices around her eyes, around her mouth. I try to convince myself that it's the cigarettes. Or how thin she's gotten.

Not because of how long it's been since I died.

*   *   *

She reads to him. Every night.

It's a wonder she can stand it because he always wants the same story, even though they never manage to get very far before his eyes grow heavy and he nods off in her arms. Night after night at bedtime, he brings her the same tattered old book, always making her start over from the beginning. She should get sick of it. But she never does.

She only pretends.

Even at four—"Almost five," he insists—he can tell. He holds the book up to her, so worn the cover is all but coming off (eventually, it will), and she looks down her nose at him and grumbles, "Can't we read something else for a change?" Except the scowl on her face never quite reaches her eyes. There's always this little hint of a smile she tries to hide, though not very hard.

And if she pretends to look *upset, she never quite* sounds *it.*

So, he puts on his best pretend-worried face—which isn't very convincing, either—and pouts. "No, Peter and Wendy, Peter and Wendy." He holds it higher until she sighs and throws up her hands.

"Fine, but this is the last time. Tomorrow we're going to read something else."

He laughs, because that's just what she said last night, and the night before, and he knows it's the same thing she'll say when they play the game again tomorrow.

She sits, and he squirms up into her lap, her arms sliding under his to hug him tight to her. He keeps the book—she hardly even needs it anymore—and, hunching over, he turns the pages, following along with words he can't actually read yet. Her hair drapes down around him as she leans over to whisper in his ear.

"All children, except one, grow up. They soon know that they will grow up, and the way Wendy knew was this . . ."

* * *

Kitchen. Living room. Hallway.
Kitchen. Living room. Hallway.
I follow close behind while she paces. In the tiny apartment, it's the only thing I can do to keep out of her way. Out of her line of sight.
There was a time when I would *try* to make her see me. Make her touch me. Make her acknowledge me. One day, I stepped in front of her right when she came out of her bedroom. For a moment, as she stumbled through me and onto her knees in the hallway, weeping, we shared the exact same place at the exact same moment and . . .
I won't do that again. To either of us.
If I could leave this place, I would. I'm as stuck here as she is.
I could just go into my old room when she's like this, sit on the bed while she loops around and around the confines of the apartment, except she keeps that door open and, whenever she walks past, she peeks inside before turning into the kitchen across the hall.
I'm not sure she even knows she does it.
It's not like there's ever anything new to see. The same old stuff. The same in-between muddle of little kid and not-quite teenager. Batman sheets on the bed. Red Sox posters on the walls. Comic books mixed in with sports magazines. Action figures and video games.
Nothing from the past ten years.
And certainly nothing's changed from her last loop around the apartment. Still, it's down the hallway, a glance into my room so brief there's no way she really takes in anything—more like she's making sure the room itself hasn't somehow disappeared—then right turn into the kitchen and right again into the living room. Across to the opening into the hallway at the other end and—

careful not to trip on the bike leaning against the wall by the apartment door—back down the hallway. Like an animal at the zoo, circling and circling and circling the inside of its cage because, well, what the hell else is there to do?

She's stalling, and we both know it. Weekdays, she leaves me behind and goes off to work. Weekends, we're cooped up in here with each other. At least until she can't stand it anymore and has to get out.

Not that it helps all that much. She drags me along with her when she goes.

*   *   *

He looks so small on the bike, even though he's big for six. It's the smallest one she could find at Goodwill, though. The smallest that wasn't a girl's bike, and she'd never have gotten him onto the pink and white one that was more his size.

She'd stood in the store, fighting back tears. At not finding what she wanted. At not being able to afford a new one—he deserved more than someone else's castoffs. At her worry he might hurt himself on something this big.

A clerk took pity on her—she's not stupid, she's seen pity enough to know what it looks like—and offered to swap the training wheels from the girl's bike onto the bigger blue and black one.

"This is a good one," the woman told her while she worked. "My son had one just like it."

Maybe it hadn't been pity after all.

And he was so excited when she showed it to him, not noticing the scratches on the paint or the bits of rust on the wheels. And he loved how big it was. "It's huge," he said, an equally huge smile on his face. "It's waaay bigger than Tony's." He insisted they go out right away, even though it was well past time for dinner and already getting dark.

Something told her he wouldn't need the training wheels for long.

Still, there was a pang inside her that the bike wasn't new. But it was smaller now. Distant. Pushed away by his excitement. She found herself on the edge of tears again, except these felt different.

Only now, in the glow of the streetlights, he seems so small, *more so the farther away he gets, even though it's not really that far. He made her promise not to follow behind him, to let him go on his own. "I'm not a* baby, Mom," *he argued, and she said okay, she promised. She keeps it, standing in front of the little house they rent a couple of rooms in, watching him as he goes. But*

promises don't keep her from holding her breath every time he teeters on the edge
of losing his balance, even though that's what the training wheels are there for.

He pedals down the sidewalk as far as the end of the block, five houses
down the street. She promised not to follow but made him promise to stop before
he got to the corner and turn around.

He keeps his promise, too, and always comes back to her.

He has to get off the bike at the far end. There isn't enough room on the
sidewalk to ride it in a circle, and he hasn't quite mastered steering yet anyhow.
But he lets her help whenever he gets back to where she waits for him. She lifts
the front wheel up off the ground and walks it around while he holds tight to the
handlebars. By the third time, he's asking her to "Do a wheelie!" before he even
gets the bike stopped.

And then he's off again, leaving her behind. But he always comes back.

*   *   *

The stop right after we get on, a woman pulls herself up the
steps into the bus. Young and very, very pregnant, she carries a
grocery bag in each hand and, even though they look heavy, she
barely glances at the empty seat next to my mother—the seat where
I am—before crab-walking her burdens awkwardly toward the back
and sitting next to some kid in dreadlocks and headphones. They
ignore each other.

At the next stop, it's an older man—maybe on his way home,
maybe only going off to work. I'd have guessed retired at that age if
not for the smock from whatever store it is he's heading to or
from. The way he shifts his weight from one foot to the other, you
can tell they ache. Or maybe it's his knees. Or his hips. Still, he
doesn't so much as look in our direction, but stays near the front,
holding onto the overhead bar.

No one ever sits next to my mother on the bus. It makes them
uneasy, the way she stares out the window, never looking up as
other people get on and off, shuffling past her up the aisle. Some
days she sits there for hours, riding the route out to where the bus
turns around, back past our stop to the turnaround at the far end,
then around again. After a while, it feels like we aren't moving at
all, that it's everything else that does. We're stuck in here while the
world outside scrolls past us on a loop. She just watches it go by.

So do I.

Today, while we're stopped in traffic, waiting for the light to change, a little girl walks past holding the hand of a woman old enough to be her grandmother. I've never seen them before, but I can tell the girl is like me. Her knuckles are white from tightly gripping the woman's fingers, as if afraid she might get left behind. The woman doesn't grip back. Her hand hangs open and limp at her side. There's nothing special about the old woman, but the little girl is all dressed up. In her Sunday best, even though it's Saturday. Or maybe ready for a party in her fancy dress, blue with the bow in the back.

Neither of them seems to care—or even notice—that one of the girl's shoes is missing, giving her a lurch to her step as she struggles to keep pace.

And then the light changes and the bus is rolling again, and they're gone.

Farther along the route, a man in a suit stands in the middle of the sidewalk out in front of an apartment building. He's like me, too. Like the little girl.

His head is tipped back, facing toward the windows in one of the upper floors. Impossible to say which one.

He's always there.

He never moves.

Everyone else on the sidewalk, they part and flow around him. No one ever gets angry, or yells for him to get the hell out of their way. They jostle each other as they pass, but no one bumps into him.

Maybe it's me, and not my mother, the bus people shy away from.

*   *   *

"Did I ever tell you the game my dad liked to play on road trips?"

She's talking too loud. Smiling too much. He hasn't spoken to her since they got on the road that morning, and she doesn't know how to fix it. She's never known how to fix anything.

He sits up front with her, even though he's not supposed to. At eight, he's still too young for the front seat. She prays they don't get pulled over—a ticket's the last thing she needs. The last thing she can afford. But the rest of the car is packed so full it makes the back end sag and, even then, there was a lot they couldn't fit. They had to pull the wheels and handlebars off his bike to get it to get it in across the back seat. There was no way she was making him leave that behind, too.

"He'd have us make up these stories about people in other cars, or out on the street, or wherever. 'Look at them,' he'd say."

She points at the car in front of them on the highway. There's a man behind the wheel and a woman in the passenger seat. Every once in a while, a dog's head pops up in the back seat, then drops back out of sight.

"'No clue who those people are,' he'd say to me. And then he'd have us make up stuff about them. Who they were. Where they were going. What they would do when they got there. Best story won the game."

Only it had made her a little sad, that game, even if her father'd said her stories had been the best ones and declared her the winner, which he always did. All those people drove away, and she never saw them again. Never knew the truth of them. They were just gone. *All she had were memories, and not even real ones.*

Just the things she'd made up in her head.

"What do you think? You want to try that?"

He doesn't answer, and part of her thinks maybe that's for the best.

*   *   *

It's hard to tell what the building used to be. There was an empty field here, once upon a time. Then, whoever bought the place came in, paved it over, and plopped a building down on it. Some gray box that could have been a drugstore or a convenience store or some combination of the two before it went bankrupt and they boarded it up.

Office supplies, maybe.

Now it's a canvas for bad graffiti, closed in by a chain link fence that doesn't do a damned thing to keep people out.

We went inside once, her leading and me tagging along behind like always. There was a hole cut in the fence, and we crawled through to follow in the footsteps of all the would-be artists, the high school kids, the homeless, and the junkies who'd been here long before us. She had to watch out not to cut herself on the glass from broken bottles, or step on discarded needles.

None of that mattered to me.

Someone had dragged an old, stained mattress inside and into the office in the back of the store. Used condoms littered the floor around it like dead leaves.

We never went in again.

Now it's just where, when she's finally worked herself up to it, we get off the bus.

*   *   *

She's not following him. She keeps telling herself that and, if he sees her and gets mad, that's what she'll say. In a way, it's the truth. He went off in one direction, riding his bike down Sixth Street, baseball glove hooked over the handlebars. Once he was far enough away that she wasn't afraid he'd look back, she crossed over Sixth and onto Maple. Not a single tree on the whole thing, she noticed as she hurried along. Maybe once, but not any longer.

He'll meet a couple of friends on the corner of Elm—that one is lined with trees—and the three of them will go the rest of the way together. She'll wind through a maze of alleys and narrow side streets, a zigzagging route that cuts the distance almost in half. He'll still beat her there on his bike, but not by much.

So, she's not really following him. She only wants to watch him play.

She almost believes it.

There's just nine of them, so they can't have a real game. She doesn't know much about baseball, but even she can tell that. They never change sides and, if they keep score, she's not sure how.

One boy pitches and another catches. Neither of them hits, at least not while she's watching. There's three in the outfield, another boy and the only two girls, and three more in the infield, at least at the start. Plus the hitter.

He starts in the field, near third base—the bases, scraps of wood they scrounged from who knows where—and stays there until the first three have come up and all gotten out, two of them striking out and the other one hitting a good one but right to the girl playing left field. As each batter gets out, they grab their glove and swap places with someone in the field, working their way around in order of wherever they're playing.

It's kind of clever, she thinks.

Then it's his turn.

She's been hiding in the shadows of a building across the street, but the excitement rubs off on her. His attention's on the pitcher, though, so he doesn't see her move out to get a better view. Doesn't hear her little shout when he connects with the first pitch, sending the ball right through the gap between second and third. He's all the way to second base before they chase down the ball in the outfield and throw it back in.

Before he has a chance to notice her, she moves back into her hiding place. Then the game gets more complicated. The girl from left field comes in to hit and, with no one taking her place, everyone else has to shift to fill the holes. That makes the holes a lot bigger, and the pitcher looks nervous.

When the girl hits a little roller down the third baseline a few pitches later, there's no one there to stop it. He's running from second before the ball has hardly left the bat and is around third long before the boy who was left trying to cover half the outfield is able to get to it.

He's home safe. Home safe with room to spare, arms up in the air, friends all cheering him on.

She gives a last quiet cheer of her own, then turns and heads back the way she came, leaving him to make his own way home safe later.

*   *   *

There's no rhyme or reason to the route we take. There never is. Only where we start and where we end up. In-between, everything is . . . uncertain.

Which is kind of the whole problem.

Some places we move right along. From Elm down Third, past all the shops and all the restaurants and all the cafés. All the wide-open spaces where people are having lunch at tables out on the sidewalk in the sunshine.

We don't linger. Nothing to see here.

Other days we stick to the side streets, and we go slower on those. Elm, Oak, Aspen, Pine, Maple. Someone definitely had a thing for trees, once upon a time. The tree streets are narrow, the buildings closer together, the shadows deeper. I could have come this way.

Probably not. But you never know.

Today, though, we slow to a crawl as she winds a familiar, ragged path through the alleys that cut from street to street to street between the buildings. It looks random, but it isn't. She knows every street and every alley between our apartment and the abandoned building on the field where I used to hang out with my friends and, as crooked as it is, this is as close to a straight line between those two points as you can get.

Her eyes hunt for anything that might have been overlooked back then. Or that *she's* missed, the dozens (hundreds?) of times she's come this way since. A glimpse of a baseball glove poking out from underneath a dumpster, gray with bits of black here and there, woven into the pattern on the pocket, the beading along the seams.

Or in the shadows behind a garbage can, a worn old Red Sox cap. Too small, really, adjusted out to the very last snap. It was *lucky*, though, so it couldn't be replaced.

For anything. Anything at all.

It would be so much easier if she only knew. I stopped looking a long time ago.

One of us needs to be realistic.

*   *   *

"I'm sorry, I can't," she says, only halfway paying attention. She's late for work and can't find her keys. She could swear she left them on the little table in the hall, but they aren't there now. Some days, she swears she'd lose her head if it wasn't screwed on.

He stands in her way, like he can somehow block her from leaving, but she steps around him and goes into the living room. She might have left the keys in there. "Maybe this weekend. Payday's in a couple of days."

He says something to her, but now she's in the kitchen, a couple of rooms away—ah, there they are—and he's being pouty about the flat tire on his bike and about needing to meet his friends for baseball.

She can't deal with that right now.

"You'll just have to skip it today. Or walk. And could you please clean up this mess." She moves around him again, careful to keep away from his greasy hands and the pieces of the old bike spread out on the floor. The bike itself is right in front of door, flipped upside down with the back tire off. "Now, I need to go or I'll be late. Love you and see you tonight," she says, pulling the door open far enough to squeeze through, then closing it behind her.

If he answers her, she doesn't hear.

*   *   *

We sit, haunting each other.

On the same couch, her at one end, me at the other.

It was the middle of the afternoon by the time we got back, by the time we sat down, together but not. It's late now, though, and the only light is what little spills into the room from the hallway. In the dark, it's hard to tell how near or far she is. Or whether there is any separation between us at all. If I reached out, or if she did, would we feel each other there?

Neither of us does.

On the wall opposite, there's a picture of me. Me in fourth grade. Some version of me, anyway, one that never grew up. The details are as lost in the dark as she is, but I see them anyway. I'm wearing a shirt I don't like but that she insisted on. It makes me look older, she said. The same with my hair: neater than normal, parted and combed off to the side. I never looked like that except on picture day.

She stares out into the hallway at the bike leaning against the wall by the door. It's not new anymore, but it's never been ridden. Still has the tags hanging from the handlebars to prove it. Under the hall light it shines bright red, even through a layer of dust.

Look Before Backing
Jeffrey Thomas

I hesitate to reveal, even roughly, the location where I found the thing. However, over the years I've talked to family and others who still live in the town of Eastborough, Massachusetts, asking them either directly or in a roundabout way if they've ever heard anything about an LLV abandoned in the woods behind Lake Pometacomet. This question would often spark other stories about that supposedly haunted lake—named after Chief Pometacomet, also called King Phillip, who declared war on the white people's colonies. In this way I gathered a collection of strange personal experiences and urban legends, but never anything about an abandoned LLV. I'm left wondering if the truck I chanced upon was eventually reclaimed or whether the whole incident might only have been an especially impactful dream.

Then there's the possibility that little box truck is there still, even more overgrown. More than once, upon returning to Eastborough to visit my parents for this or that holiday—or wedding, or funeral—I've almost been tempted to make a side quest into those woods to see for myself. *Almost*.

I was fifteen, and skipping school that spring day, as I often did. In fact, I dropped out of high school when I turned sixteen, but at least I obtained my GED some years later. An angst-ridden teenager, but no more, really, than any other, despite me feeling like I was the very epitome of the misunderstood outsider. In my loneliness, I sought to wallow in greater loneliness—a physical loneliness—as if to pick at my inner wounds. And that was how I found myself in those woods that afternoon, killing time until I could return home as if from a regular day at school.

I had started out at Lake Pometacomet, skipping flat stones across its surface between puffs on a cigarette stolen from my dad before venturing into the trees massed darkly at its edge, where they were doubly massed in reflection. Wandering in my thoughts, listening to a cassette of Faith No More singing about a "Midlife Crisis" on my Walkman, I only realized after a fair amount of time had passed just how far into the woods I'd gone. When I finally stopped to look behind me, I could no longer even see the glint of the lake through the green clouds of leaf-bearing trees, the bristling arms of evergreens. Had I traveled only in a straight line? Would simply cutting a straight line back in the direction I faced return me to the water's edge?

I shut off the tape and turned in a little circle, still uncertain whether I'd deviated from a straight path in coming this far; not in a panic, but definitely feeling somewhat wary. It was while scanning the trees around me that I caught a glimpse of white through the new spring foliage, off to my left. Stepping as quietly as I could, in case what I was seeing was someone's house, I started in that direction to investigate. Perhaps what I found would restore my bearings.

What I discovered actually did nothing less than obliterate my bearings, at least for a time, in a metaphorical sense.

LLV is short for Grumman Long Life Vehicle, introduced in 1987 as the standard vehicle to deliver mail in the US. I only know these details now because a year ago my older brother Roy began driving a mail truck after being laid off from his biotech job at our hometown's East Coast Pharmaceuticals. He reported this news to me over the phone, since I'd been living in Texas for quite a while by then. But when I was fifteen, Roy was already away at college, so I'd never mentioned to him what I'd found in the woods until that particular phone conversation, prompted by him telling me about his new job. When I finally described my experience, Roy's only reaction had been to chuckle and say, "Wow, bud . . . Well, that's freaky."

This LLV—resting in the middle of the woods with trees crowded so closely around it I couldn't imagine how anyone could have driven it in this deeply—was typical of its kind. Boxy, white, with a trim of red and blue stripes and the stylized blue profile of an eagle stenciled on both flanks. For the safety of the carrier when filling mailboxes at the curb, its steering wheel and driver's door were on the right side. On that day in 1993, this one could only have been six years old at most, and yet here it stood like something derelict and discarded.

One thing I noticed right away was that despite the postal truck resting on four thoroughly deflated tires, there was no graffiti on all that white-painted metal, nor were any of its windows broken. They were simply opaque, or close to it, under a thick film of dust.

It was obvious that behind that obscuring dust, no letter carrier sat at the wheel taking a coffee break or stealing a nap. Plus, I heard no sounds of kids partying—or fornicating—inside. Still, I was timid about getting closer to the thing to peek through the windows, if that were even possible. What was it that made me so reluctant? Was it only the incongruousness of my discovery? What could possibly be inside to cause this trepidation I felt?

Shouldn't I be trying to find my way back to the lake? But then, who could subdue their curiosity in such a situation . . . particularly the curiosity of a fifteen-year-old boy? So, naturally, I crept up on the truck but maintained my stealthiness, as if there might be someone, or some wild animal, sleeping inside the vehicle after all.

I came up on the left side, and as it turned out the dust wasn't so thick that I couldn't see within. Nearing my face to the glass, my heart lurched in my chest when I saw a bulky black shape hunkered beside the driver's seat . . . a shape that was surely a person who had hunched down in hope of avoiding detection.

After that initial jolt, though, I realized what I was seeing: stuffed totes of flat mail, waiting beside the driver's seat for easy access when pulling up beside mailboxes.

Plastic totes stuffed full of undelivered mail? This struck me as even more anomalous, more shocking, than the presence of the LLV itself in these woods.

I went around to the back of the truck, to its rollup door, but when I tried the latch I found I couldn't lift it without unlocking it first with a key, which wasn't present. I wasn't afraid to rattle it in my attempt, seeing as how my glimpse of the truck's interior had proved there was no one inside. And why would there have been, my weird unease—which had felt almost like an intuition, or even premonition—aside?

I moved on to the right side of the vehicle. Here, a bush had grown flush against the driver's sliding door, as if to conceal a secret passageway. I parted the branches to reach for the door's latch, fully expecting to find that locked, too. If it was . . . well, it would be back to retracing my path to Lake Pometacomet. There was no way I'd be breaking any windows in a last attempt to gain access.

The latch turned, the door glided easily back under my hand, and the only thing hampering my entrance into the mail truck was that bush doing its best to hold me back. I got past it, though, hoping I acquired no deer ticks in the process, and clambered up into the postal truck's murky interior.

Settling into the driver's seat, I was confronted with the LLV's similarly dust-coated dashboard, mounted with a fan and with the words LOOK BEFORE BACKING stenciled in bold white letters above the steering wheel. And now there was no question about it: beside me rested totes so filled with bundled flat mail, and in one tote circulars and flyers, it seemed obvious this truck's carrier had not only failed to deliver all his mail, but *any* of his mail.

Trying not to inhale too deeply the moldy atmosphere long bottled up in the truck, I twisted around in the creaking seat to look into the back section. Packages rested on its floor: a variety of differently-sized boxes. Still, there weren't all that many; not enough that they had required stacking atop each other. You have to understand, this was decades before the advent of online shopping. Eastborough still had Caldor and Bradlees department stores back then, and even several bookstores. I miss those days.

Well, what would you have done in my shoes? In that driver's seat, that is, in a mail truck with flat tires abandoned for who knew how long in the middle of the woods? And again, staring at the young trees growing directly in the truck's path, I couldn't picture how it had ever been driven to this spot in the first place. I had seen no dirt path, even grown over, by which it might have come here. In any case . . . would you have been able to resist opening any of that mail?

I decided to start with some of the material up front, right beside me. Afterward, I'd work up my nerve to open some—or all—of those packages behind me. It might take a while—I might even have to come out here again—but it now seemed well worth such an expedition. Who could say what I might find of value here?

Then again, I knew the right thing to do would be to not open any of the mail—and wasn't that a federal offense, anyway? The right thing to do, I told myself, would be to go to the post office, or maybe even the Eastborough police, to report what I had stumbled upon.

Even as I thought this, I plucked a piece of mail from the tote at my left elbow, and before I could stop myself, I was slipping my thumb under the seal and tearing the top of the envelope open along its length.

I had already guessed, from the pale yellow envelope, that this was a greeting card of some type, and I was right. The card featured a cartoon father cat with kittens perched all over him, even on his head, and the words: *Happy Father's Day, From the Kids.* Inside, the card had been signed in blue ballpoint pen: *Suzy and Craig.* I flipped the card over, wondering if Suzy and Craig had dated the card, as we had always done in my family. Sure enough, in faded ink at the very bottom was written: *'92.*

Only a year before, and yet here the truck rested on deflated tires, new trees growing up all around it?

In my mind I muttered an apology to Suzy and Craig, and to the dad who had never received his Father's Day card. I carefully slid it back into its envelope, replaced it in the tote, and started flipping through other mail. I bypassed junk mail and bills— eternally boring and depressing, whatever the year—in search of more personal correspondence. This was in the time before email had all but replaced such a thing, so there was indeed personal correspondence to be found, and I opened one of these letters with a return address from Seattle, Washington.

I scanned the letter, handwritten in purple ink, so quickly that I took little of it in. After all, there was so much more to investigate in this treasure box I had climbed into. A few lines caught my eye and held me, however. The writer, who had addressed the letter to Geoff and signed it William, had said:

Every day it seems closer, and I dread it, but I sit here paralyzed by my own weakness, unable to escape the inevitable. The last thing I want is to worry you, dear friend, or worse yet have you pity me, but to hold in my anxiety is unbearable. I am lonely enough here as it, and reaching out to you across the miles brings me some measure of comfort. Even as my discomfort grows, and the blackness flows toward me . . .

Immediately I started refolding the letter, ashamed for having spied upon another human being's raw, exposed pain in such a way. I couldn't help but wonder, and worry, how William had fared; how he had dealt with whatever encroaching darkness had left him feeling so boxed in.

Just as I was about to tuck the sheet back into its envelope, I suddenly unfolded it again. I'd finally become conscious of the date I had skimmed over at the top of the page. There, in his somewhat flowery but still clearly decipherable script, this William person had written: *September 14th, 1988.*

A letter dated 1988 . . . in the same tote with a greeting card dated 1992?

I dove into the letters again, flipping through them with the intensity of a character in a movie searching through a file cabinet drawer before any villains can arrive. Rather than examining faded postal stamps for their dates, I tore a few pieces open more or less at random. One missive—its handwriting more ugly and scrawled than William's despite its pretty stationery—was dated from 1990, and read in part:

Why do you keep ignoring me, Greg? Do you think that if you do so long enough I'll simply cease to exist? That you can convince yourself I never existed at all?

This pained outburst was signed by a Susie. And the next letter . . . the next one was dated from 1978. Therein, someone named Ray had typed:

Sooner or later it will find us all, won't it? At least knowing that I share these feelings with everyone else on the planet makes me feel less targeted. What do you think, Will? Should that make me feel less alone with my burden? Blissfully fatalistic?

1978? Which so happened to be the year of my birth.

I was decades from that long, pleasant phone conversation with my brother, who would sound optimistic about his change of careers after the spiral of depression losing his years-long stint at East Coast Pharmaceuticals had brought on. Decades before he would describe to me—perhaps with exaggerated enthusiasm—the kind of vehicle he would be puttering around in every day. Still, even with my limited knowledge back then, I knew this particular piece of correspondence must predate the manufacture of the vehicle I presently found myself in.

I was coming to the conclusion that the person who had

hidden away this postal truck had been stashing mail within it for many years rather than delivering it. But to what end? I could at least understand, somewhat, if he or she had opened these letters and been moved by their contents as I was being moved, feeding some sort of inner emptiness by eavesdropping on the intimate connections of others. And yet, none of what I sifted through had been opened. Even the flyers looked undisturbed in their neat rows, the packages in the dark space behind me all resting there neatly sealed. Was secreting this mail here a disturbed act of maliciousness? A petty revenge against certain customers, or against innocent strangers in general?

I thought it was time I should open some of those packages, now more driven by a need to understand what I'd chanced upon here than in the hope of uncovering objects of value, and I had begun twisting around in my seat to reach back there for one when I heard the snap of a twig outside the driver's door, which I'd left gaping open. Jerking around again to look, I found my view mostly obstructed by that damned bush. I strained my ears, expecting it was only that I hadn't lost that weird sense of unease, and I was fretting over perfectly natural sounds of the woods . . . and then I heard a somewhat louder, somewhat nearer crack out there.

My first impulse was to take hold of the driver's door and slide it shut. Lock myself in and hunch down close to the floor. For a crazed, desperate split-second I even glanced toward the ignition to see if the keys hung from it (there were no keys there), as if I might drive this sad vehicle right on through the saplings that had grown up around it, flat tires be damned.

But no, I knew I mustn't trap myself inside, especially if the person apparently approaching was none other than the troubled soul who had been squirreling away all this mail for untold years. Instead, I slipped out of the driver's seat and pushed through the bush obscuring the door, hoping my own sounds wouldn't give me away.

A steady rustling advanced toward the truck through the trees, and I thought I saw the broken, indistinct form of a person back there through all the overlapping greenery. More a shadow, as yet, than a distinct figure. Hopefully they were unaware of me, and considered me nothing more than a shadow myself.

Then, someone called out, "Hey, bud."

The male voice sounded oddly farther away than the

approaching shadow, and it didn't seem particularly threatening, but nevertheless I spun on my heel and dove into the woods in the opposite direction from which the stranger came.

Tree branches raked my arms, lashed my cheeks and forehead in their cruel attempt to swipe across my eyes, and the air I gulped seemed to tear at my lungs, but on I plunged, on through the trees, until at last I burst out, gasping, onto the narrow, mucky strip of beach that bordered the allegedly haunted waters of Lake Pometacomet.

*   *   *

It was after my brother Roy's suicide, and upon my return to Texas following the funeral, that the first of the letters showed up in my mailbox.

Since my divorce, I'd been living in a somewhat shabby one-bedroom apartment in Corpus Christi. The units were all like miniature houses, single-story but with a duplex layout, and my wall-mount mailbox was affixed right outside my front door. That first letter lay hidden behind an electric bill (at forty-six I'm old school, and still prefer paper bills) and a weekly circular; a pale green envelope of the type containing a greeting card. I didn't recognize the scribbled return address in the corner, and was already tearing open the flap as I turned back into my apartment, the other mail tucked under my arm. Confused, I was trying to determine what occasion this could pertain to. Christmas wasn't far off, but then I realized: of course, it must be a sympathy card.

As I closed the screen door behind me, I glanced out and saw an LLV postal truck glide past in the road, so quietly I never would have known it was there had I not glimpsed it. Then it was gone, and I was drawing the letter from its sleeve. Not a greeting card, after all, but a piece of flowery green stationery in a matching envelope. Once again confused, I stood there over my kitchen table struggling to decipher the note's ragged scrawl.

Eventually, I worked out the opening of it, before the handwriting seemed to steadily deteriorate, and it read:

Well you got what you wanted, Greg. I'm totally alone now, all my old friends gone, cut off from my own family, and sometimes I don't even know who looks back at me in the mirror. Any day now I expect to see my reflection's abandoned me too. Does my emptiness fill you?

197

Perplexed, I checked the envelope again. Its single stamp caught my attention: a fifteen-cent miniature portrait of Dolley Madison. Fifteen cents, and yet this letter had been delivered? The cost of a single stamp in 2024 was sixty-eight cents.

And then, a long-forgotten unease began to seep into me, as if transmitted through the pale green paper into my hand, to spread throughout my bloodstream, and the next thing I knew I was in the living room sitting in front of my laptop to go online.

That fifteen-cent Dolley Madison stamp had been issued in 1980.

At last, into my mind's eye came that LLV, secreted in its dense nest of trees, hoarding its mysterious treasure. For a flash, I even irrationally thought of that vehicle as an entity in itself. As if no troubled person had hidden it away there, it having instead hidden itself . . . and all the human pain it held bottled up in its guts.

It wasn't possible that what I'd laid down on the desk beside my laptop was one of the pieces of correspondence from the totes within that truck. Yes, over the years I had asked a variety of people if they'd heard of it, and maybe someone had become curious enough to seek it out, but who would actually mail me one of the letters they'd found inside that truck, even as a joke? Again, there was only that single fifteen-cent stamp by which the letter had arrived here, and I finally noticed the letter wasn't even addressed to me. It was as if someone had come all the way out from Massachusetts to Texas to hand deliver it.

A shudder buzzed through me. I was tempted to tear the thing into shreds right there and then. I didn't, though. Almost reverently, as if I feared offending someone—whomever had written this message, whomever had delivered it—I folded it back into its envelope and slipped the letter into my desk's top drawer.

You may have noted I said this was the *first* of the letters I received.

*   *   *

Over the next few weeks there came a wistful love letter in a brown-stained envelope, dated 1944, from a sailor serving on the USS Princeton. I looked it up online, found that the Princeton had been an aircraft carrier, and a six-hundred-pound bomb dropped on her by a Japanese dive bomber had resulted in the loss of over a hundred crewmen. Without looking into it further I already knew the writer of the letter was one of them.

There was a birthday card from a daughter in Alaska to her mother in Tennessee, dated 1994—a year *after* my discovery of the LLV, showing it had somehow gone on collecting new correspondence. Or was it perhaps producing all that correspondence itself: clever approximations of human beings reaching out to each other longingly or bitterly? Human beings desperately crying out across aching distances both physical and emotional? If so, did the thing envy us those connections, or merely mock them?

There was a divorce decree dated from 2006. I knew what those looked like, having received my own only a few years earlier. I'd met Clarisa through an online dating service, had moved out to Texas to be with her and found work here, and it was because of my job that I now stayed on despite being so removed from my remaining family. I just couldn't rouse myself to seek new employment back home, my real home, in Massachusetts. Or was I lying to myself? Did I, even now, hope Clarisa would have a change of heart? I confess my own heart jumped when, in the midst of all this uncanny correspondence, I found in my mailbox a Christmas card from Clarisa . . . until I saw she had signed a man's name along with her own. A thoughtful gesture, or a petty act of cruelty? I put it in my desk's top drawer with all the other unexplained correspondence, half wondering if the LLV had created even this card.

I received an old, yellowed postcard with no date, and in fact no writing on it whatsoever. On its front was a hand-tinted photograph of a body of water, bordered by pretty clouds of spring trees, with a canoe in the foreground bearing a man and woman too far away for their faces to be anything but dark blotches. The caption read: *Lake Pometacomet, Eastborough, Mass.*

I wanted to speak to my mail carrier, to ask if they were delivering these pieces along with my regular mail. If not, I wondered if they arrived in my mailbox before or after the normal mail delivery, which occurred while I was away at work. Luckily, I finally dashed outside one Saturday afternoon and caught my carrier just as she was leaving, holding a collection of correspondence I had snatched from my desk. As I explained the situation, her face bunched in confusion, and she was wagging her head before I'd even finished. It was very odd, she agreed, but no—and of course it was no—she hadn't delivered any unusually old pieces of mail, particularly without sufficient postage. She said I could bring the mail into the office to ask the postal manager, to see what they thought, but it was better that I talk to the police if I thought someone was playing a prank or harassing me.

I didn't follow her advice. I knew all this was no prank. What I did, instead, was buy a security camera online that was delivered— and mounted outside my door, just like my mailbox—by Monday evening.

On Tuesday, during my lunch break at work, I ate in my car in the company's parking lot as I often did, to be free of the mindless chatter of my coworkers, even though they pretty much ignored me anyway. As I sat there with the window down, enjoying the fresh air along with the refreshing quiet, I opened the security camera's app on my phone to the live view outside my front door. Of course, there was no one conveniently loitering there, waiting for me to spot them. I knew the approximate time my weekday mail arrived, however—late morning, early afternoon—so I scrolled sideways through the timeline of recorded *motion events* to see if the carrier was the same woman I had spoken with on Saturday. As I got to around two o'clock, though, something caught my eye and I stopped scrolling. No person had been recorded within the camera's range of detection, despite the alert of movement, but a boxy white truck with the profile of an eagle's blue head passed by in the street beyond my short front walk. I played the brief recording again. Then again. The LLV was distant from the camera, and not all that clear in the bleached dazzle of afternoon sun, but I had the impression a clump of leaves was caught in its door, as if torn out from a bush.

I saw that about two minutes before the LLV had passed, another event had been recorded, so I scrolled to that one. I was greeted with the sight of a figure approaching my apartment door along the front walk. The recording seemed to glitch just before the person appeared, as if a few frames had been removed from a strip of film, because I didn't see them come along the sidewalk first or cross the street before turning into my walkway. At the start of the recording they weren't there, and then they were, walking silently toward the camera.

I stopped chewing my bologna sandwich, and I think my heart

stopped beating, too, as I brought my phone a little closer to my face.

With the sun positioned behind the figure they were merely a silhouette, but even accounting for the effect of the light they seemed altogether *too* dark, impossible to make out in detail from head to feet . . . even as they stepped right up to my door and pulled a single piece of mail from the sack slung against one hip. This close to the camera, in the shadow of the roof's overhang, the figure remained just as indistinct, more an outline of a human form than anything. I watched them reach for my mailbox, and heard the sound of its lid being opened on its hinge.

The lid was closed again with a little squeal, but instead of turning away the figure lingered a few moments there before my door, and I had the distinct impression—despite not being able to see their face, not even a glimmer of eyes—they were staring directly into my new camera. As if waiting for me to make eye contact with them somehow, regardless of the lapse of several hours. This had occurred at least an hour after my postal carrier had delivered the usual mail that defined my mundane existence. A special delivery.

A shiver flushed through me, and I watched the shadowy form turn from the camera at last and retrace its path down my front walk.

Another blip, again as if a second or two had been skipped, or had ceased to exist in the history of time's flow, and the figure was gone. The *motion event* ended . . . until the next one, recorded around two minutes later, when that Grumman Long Life Vehicle passed by from left to right. If it was the same truck I believed it was, it had a long way to go both in miles and in years.

*　　*　　*

I left work early, claiming to be sick. The way the eaten half of my bologna sandwich lay in my guts, it wasn't really a lie. I tried to maintain a reasonable speed on my drive home.

That special delivery awaited me.

In the box were a few other pieces of mail, which I tossed unopened onto the kitchen table. For a moment or two I stared at the letter I knew was the one I had seen the shadowy figure deliver. Unlike all the pieces I'd received up to now, this one was actually addressed to me, though there was no return address. The stamp was a current Forever Stamp. Was this just a conventional letter, after all?

Having absorbed all this, I was so quick to tear the envelope open that I won myself a paper cut on my thumb, but I was unmindful of the tiny beads of blood welling up as I began to read the single sheet within. What I read first, though, was the name signed at the bottom. I needn't have even read that, though, to know who the letter was from. I recognized the handwriting as that of my brother Roy.

The letter read:

Hey, bud.

Well, I gave it a shot. The Mr. Postman thing. No wonder those poor guys go postal. The stress is nuts. I found myself having to go well beyond the regular clock-out time to be sure I delivered everything in my load. Not to justify it, but I can see why you hear about carriers who just stash loads of mail at home or dump it somewhere or something. Yeah, I know, I would have gotten more used to it in time, found ways to speed things up, but the stress would always have been there. I just can't handle it anymore, man. It isn't just this job. It would be any job. Stress builds up to a breaking point. So do life's losses.

You're going to blame yourself for what happens, but do not. DO NOT. You were the best brother I could have asked for. It's selfish of me to hurt you and Mom and Dad like this, but you all have to focus on peace. You've all fretted about my peace long enough, too many years, and now ALL of us will be at peace. This is good. Really.

I was just about to write, "I'll miss our phone calls about movies and stuff." Ha. I hope you can appreciate that I chuckled over that, and I hope you even chuckled too.

I love you, bud. I hope you find your own path to peace and I pray that it's more constructive than mine. You really should move back to Massachusetts, man. We've all missed you since you left. But again, even if you'd been here you couldn't have changed this. You can't think that.

I love you, bud.

Roy.

*   *   *

That was the last of the strange letters I received at my apartment in Corpus Christi.

I haven't received any more since returning to Massachusetts, either.

And the Grumman Long Life Vehicle forsaken in the woods behind Lake Pometacomet? I haven't gone looking for it again since moving back to Eastborough. But I might, someday. I might.

About the Contributors

Artist **Aaron White** started drawing monsters when he was four years old. His life-long fixation with horror began as a child, with the help of his parents, who encouraged him to explore the creepy side of his imagination. A fledgling artist and avid reader, Aaron excelled at art and writing throughout school and into college, where he attended Massachusetts College of Art. Nowadays, he pursues various forms of art and writing. Over the years he's accumulated a few accomplishments under his belt, such as winning awards in juried shows, working with various publishing companies, curating art exhibits (including solo shows), and making it into one of Neil Gaiman's projects. He also dabbles in special-effect makeup and writes music under Order of the Black Pyramid. In 2020 Aaron released his first volume of work—a collection of illustrated short stories called *The Language of Shadows*, which can be found on Amazon and Barnes and Noble. Aaron lives in Hudson with his wife, Marjorie, and their cat, Teddy.

Alan P Marks fell in love with reading and (at least the idea of) writing early on, when someone gifted him his first Stephen King book, *The Dead* Zone—which *may* have been acquired by somewhat less-than-legitimate means. The first *adult* book he ever read; it's been followed by countless others (all legally purchased) in the decades since.

He eventually went on to receive his MA in creative writing from the University of Maine (Stephen King's alma mater, coincidentally) in 1998, and then just never left. For the last twenty-five-plus years, he has taught in the UMaine English Dept., with courses in composition, creative writing, and literature, including one on—you guessed it—Stephen King. Currently, he is entering his final semester of the Stonecoast MFA program in creative writing, through the University of Southern Maine.

Angi Shearstone is an award-winning professional artist with an MFA in sequential art (comics), a brother & sister pair of orange cats, unapologetic geek tendencies, and a great love of ska-core and punk rock. In addition to creating art, Angi is a published horror and science fiction author under the pseudonym Sidney Arcane. She sporadically blogs about creativity at www.creativityandcats.com.

Angi's work can be seen at www.angishearstone.com. She currently resides in New England. Favorite quote: "A painting is never finished; it simply stops in interesting places." ~Paul Gardner

Chad Anctil, a writer with a penchant for the eerie and mysterious, hails from Rhode Island—the very birthplace of H.P. Lovecraft's peculiar brand of fiction. His fascination with horror began at a young age—perhaps too young—but that's how Generation X rolled. After high school, Chad embarked on a military journey that took him from New England to the sun-soaked shores of California and the tropical landscapes of Hawaii. Along the way, he encountered strange underworlds—abandoned warehouses pulsating with electronic dance parties, vampire performance art in graveyards, and even frenzied robot combat beneath dark highway overpasses. These experiences fuel his imagination, leading him to create intricate landscapes where the supernatural intersect with the mundane.

By day, Chad works in cybersecurity, but when the candlelight flickers, he writes. His debut novel, *The Midnight Tree*, delves into middle school supernatural mystery. Additionally, his horror, crime, and weird fiction short stories have found homes in various anthologies, including *Christmas of the Dead: Yule Cat Codex*, *Flash of the Dead: Requiem*, *Masks of Sanity*, *Halloweenthology: Jack O' Lantern*, *Apocalyptales*, and *Femme Fatale Flashes* among others. Also keep an eye out for the debut novel in his upcoming urban fantasy crime series, set in Providence, Rhode Island, slated for publication in summer/fall 2024 by Perspective Publishing.

Christopher Kelly is a writer of weird fiction; obscure historical essays at his blog, *Synaptic Space*; various screenplays; and, increasingly, lists of things he has to remember to do. Christopher is also a filmmaker and musician who lives in southeastern Massachusetts with his wife, two children, and a handful of quadrupeds. There, he often wanders around looking at the beautiful scenery, wondering what sort of imaginary nightmares he can bring in to crash the party.

Cindy O'Quinn is a Bram Stoker Award-winning writer. Author of "Quondam," from *The Nightmare Never Ends*, "Lydia," from the Shirley Jackson Award-winning anthology, *The Twisted Book of Shadows*, "The Thing I Found Along a Dirt Patch Road," "A Gathering on the Mountain," and "One and Done." Her poetry has been nominated for the Elgin, Dwarf Star, and Rhysling Awards.

An Appalachian writer from the beautiful mountains of West Virginia, Cindy currently resides on the old Tessier Homestead in the woods of northern Maine, which is an ideal backdrop for writing scary stories and dark poetry.

Daniel G. Keohane is the Bram Stoker-nominated author of *Plague of Locusts, Margaret's Ark, Solomon's Grave, Plague of Darkness* and the devotional series *Stories from the Psalms*. His short fiction has appeared in *Cemetery Dance, On Spec, Abyss & Apex* (coming soon), *Borderlands 6, Fantastic Stories of the Imagination*, and dozens more. A founding member of the New England Horror Writers, Dan is an active member of the SFWA and occasional film reviewer. More information on his work, and life in general, can be found at dankeohane.com, at least whenever he can find the time to update it.

Elaine Labbee went to the University of Maine and received her masters from the University of New Hampshire. While not writing horrific tales, Elaine enjoys paint by numbers and trying to make round shapes on her vintage Etch-a-Sketch. She resides in the wilds of New England.

Jeffrey Thomas is the author of such novels as *Deadstock* (Solaris Books), *Blue War* (Solaris Books), and *The American* (JournalStone). His short story collections include *Punktown* (Prime Books), *The Unnamed Country* (Word Horde), and *Haunted Worlds* (Hippocampus Press). He has been a finalist for the Bram Stoker Award and the John W. Campbell Award, and his stories have been reprinted in *The Year's Best Horror Stories* XXII (editor, Karl Edward Wagner), *The Year's Best Fantasy and Horror* #14 (editors, Ellen Datlow and Terri Windling), and *Year's Best Weird Fiction* #1 (editors, Laird Barron and Michael Kelly). Thomas lives in Massachusetts.

Ghosties and ghoulies and long-leggedy beasties and things that go bump in the night: that's **Kristin Dearborn** in a nutshell. This life-long New Englander and horror writer was destined to write about anything that screams, squelches, or bleeds. Her first literary love was Michael Crichton (she was eleven), her second Stephen King, and she asserts *Jurassic Park*, one of her favorite movies, is a creature feature—her favorite type of horror flick.

At the University of Maine, Dearborn studied theater and English, and then went on to Seton Hill University where she earned her MFA in writing popular fiction (heavy on the monster horror). She's been on the horror scene since 2010 with her short stories and novellas, and has contributed to a number of anthologies. Dearborn is the author of *Faith of Dawn* (2024), *The Amazing Alligator Girl* (2022), *Sacrifice Island* (2018), *Woman in White* (2017), *Whispers* (2016), *Stolen Away* (2016), and *Trinity* (2012).

Kurt Newton's poetry has appeared in *Weird Tales*, *Strange Horizons*, *34 Orchard*, *Spectral Realms*, and in the anthologies *Epitaphs*, *Wicked Sick*, *Dangerous Waters*, and *Love Letters to Poe, Vol. 3*. His tenth poetry collection, *Songs of the Underland*, was published by Ravens Quoth Press in 2022.

Laura Cooney's work has appeared in various horror publications and in the anthologies *Bandersnatch* and *Dark Jesters*. She collaborated with her husband, L.L. Soares, on a joint short story collection entitled, *In Sickness: Stories From a Very Dark Place*. They also co-authored the apocalyptic novella, *Green Tsunami*. Laura lives in Massachusetts with her husband and their iguana, Osiris.

Mikio Murakami is a Japanese-Canadian graphic designer specializing in cover art, T-shirts, logos and drinking bad coffee. His design company, Silent Q Design, was founded in Montreal in 2006. Melding together the use of both realistic templates and surreal imagery, Silent Q Design's artistry proves, at first glance, that a professional for art is still alive, and that no musician, magazine, or venue should suffer from the same bland designs that have been re-hashed over and over. The evolution of artwork ranges both locally and internationally. Silent Q Design has commissioned work for Montreal and surrounding area bands such as Synastry, Endast and The Agonist. Likewise, Silent Q Design also boasts work for international musician Bob Katsionis (Toshiba-EMI / Lion Music / Century Media) as well as Montreal Radio station 90.3 FM's *Sounds of Steel* music program. Their works go beyond fantasy landscapes and surreal imagery, offering their customers personalized service. Silent Q Design prides itself on being a multi-faceted entity that can serve even the contemporary business world.

Morgan Sylvia is a metalhead, an Aquarius, a coffee addict, and a work in progress. A former obituarist, she is now a full-time freelance writer. Her fiction and poetry have appeared in several places, including *Pseudopod, Haunted House Short Stories, Endless Apocalypse, and* several of the New England Horror Writers anthologies. She is also the author of two novels, three poetry collections, and several novellas, and was one of the writers for the award-winning werewolf audio drama *Undertow: Blood Forest*. Her second poetry collection, *As The Seas Turn Red*, was nominated for an Elgin Award. Sylvia is a member of the HWA, the SFWA, the New England Horror Writers, Horror Writers of Maine, and Tuesday Mayhem Society. She lives in Maine with her boyfriend, two cats, a chubby goldfish, the cutest rescue dog ever, and an overgrown rose. You can follow her at morgansylvia.net

Poet Laureate of New Bedford, Massachusetts, from 2014 to 2021, author and playwright **Patricia Gomes** is published in numerous literary journals and anthologies. Gomes is the author of four poetry chapbooks. She is a Pushcart Prize nominee (2008, 2018, and 2021) as well as a five-time Rhysling Science Fiction Award nominee. Recent publications include: *Poem Alone, Horror Writers Poetry Showcase X,* and the soon to be published anthologies *The Lycanthropicon,* and *Potter's Field 8.*

Her last play, *Coffee, Eclairs, and the Conflict of Free Will,* was produced and performed by

Culture Park Theater in November of 2023.

Peter N. Dudar is the best thing to come out of Lisbon Falls, Maine, since Moxie was invented. With a writing career spanning over two decades, his fiction has earned critical acclaim and the adoration of fans of the horror genre. Peter is a proud member of the Horror Writers Association, the New England Horror Writers, and the Horror Writers of Maine. He lives with his wife, two daughters, and a dog named Princess Cupcake Zippety Dudar. He insists he didn't pick out that name.

R.C. Mulhare was born in Lowell, Massachusetts, and grew up in a nearby town in a hundred-year-old house up the street from an old cemetery. Her interest in the dark and mysterious started when she was quite young, when her mother read the faery tales of the Brothers Grimm and quoted the poetry of Edgar Allan Poe to her, while her Irish storyteller father infused her with a fondness for strange characters and quirky situations. Between writing projects, she moonlights in grocery retail. A two-time Amazon best-selling author and contributor to the Hugo Award winning Archive of Our Own, she has over one hundred twenty stories in print through dozens of independent publishers including Atlantean Publishing, Macabre Maine, DBND Publishing, Hellbound Books, Nocturnal Sirens Publishing, FunDead Publications, Deadman's Tome, Lovecraftiana Magazine, Tales of Wonder and Dread, and Weirdbook Magazine, with more stories in the works. She shares her home with her family, a vintage music-loving baby parakeet, about fifteen hundred books, and an unknown number of eldritch things that rattle in the walls while she's writing late in the night. She's happy to have visitors through her page at: https://linktr.ee/rcmulhare.

Salvantonio Clemente lives in Boston with his partner Darcie and their three daughters. In 2022, Sal retired after forty-five years in live performance and, encouraged and tolerated by his friends and family, reignited a lifelong passion for telling stories. He recently signed with Sara Crow, at Sara Crow Literary, who represents Sal's novel-length works, the first of which—*Eliza, Jack Spencer, and the Obelisk of Woe*—is on submission.

Steve Van Samson is the author of the novels *Mark of the Witchwyrm, The Bone Eater King* and *Marrow Dust*, the short story collections *Year of the Rattlesnake* and *Black Honey and Other Unsavory Things*, as well as numerous published short stories. A fierce proponent of character diversity & of avoiding cliché like the plague, his writing tends to be on the pulpy side—intermingling genres like horror and dystopian with dark fantasy and adventure.

When not tapping the keys on his Chromebook, Steve co-hosts the Retro Ridoctopus podcast and watches entirely too many black-and-white monster films.

Timothy P. Flynn is a dark poet from Massachusetts. His poetry resides in *Space and Time*, *Wicked Tales*, *Wicked Creatures*, *Wicked Sick*, the *HWA Poetry Showcase Vol 5*, *Vol 6*, and *Vol 9*, and online at Scifaikuest, Haikuniverse, and Haiku Journal. Flynn's first chapbook, *Embrace the Madness*, is available via eBook on Amazon. He is a member of the New England Horror Writers, an affiliate member of the HWA, and recipient of the 2021 HWA Dark Poetry Scholarship.

Follow him on Twitter, @TimothyPFlynn or Instagram, instagram.com/timothypflynnwriter

Trisha J. Wooldridge (child-friendly T.J. Wooldridge) is an award-winning pan-genre, pan-media chaos word witch. Find her in the Shirley Jackson Award-winning *The Twisted Book of Shadows*; some *HWA Poetry Showcase* volumes; all the NEHW anthologies (that she didn't edit); *Don't Turn Out the Lights: A Tribute to Alvin Schwartz's Scary Stories to Tell in the Dark*; *Pseudopod* podcast; and *34 Orchard* literary journal. She's currently releasing the five-book The Princess and the Dragon cycle, part of The 27 Kingdoms fantasy series from New Mythology Press. She recently released her first collection, *Where Monsters Pray, A Collection of Feminist Dark Speculative Writing* with Pink Narcissus Press. She also lovingly tortures consenting authors with her editing talents. She spends mystical *free time* with a very patient Husband-of-Awesome, a tiny witch and large witcher kitty pair, a rescued bay gelding, and a matronly calico mare. www.anovelfriend.com

About the Editors

In 2014, **Rob Smales** edited *Demonic Visions 5*, which took the year's Best Anthology award from the eFestival of Words, and in 2016 edited *My Mom, MS, and a Sixth-Grade Mess*, named Best YA Novel of the year by *Preditors and Editors*. Formerly one half of S&L Editing, he was co-editor for *Insanity Tales II* (2015) and *III* (2017) from The Storyside Press, and *A Sharp Stick in the Eye (and Other Funny Stories)* (2018) and the entire Terror Project trilogy from Books & Boos Press. He has worked on several private editing projects since S&L's dissolution in 2020.

On the writing side of things, as of the release of *Wicked Abandoned*, Rob has three novellas in print (*Friends in High Places* [2018, Bloodshot Books], *LaundryLegs* [2023, Weird House Press], and *Spearfinger* [2023, Bad Ideas Press]), and over four dozen short stories in various publications and anthologies.

You can find out more about his writing at RobSmales.com, and more about him in general—and his dog, Sage—on Facebook.

In photos of himself and Sage, he's the bald one.

By day **Scott Goudsward** is a slave to the corporate world; by night to the voices in his head. His preferred genre is horror, though he dabbles in both sci-fi and fantasy. Scott is one of the coordinators of the New England Horror Writers / Wicked Creative LLC. Current projects include a novella due in October 2024, a follow-up novella, and a YA novel that's currently in the wings waiting for some necessary attention. His most recent works are in the *Wicked* series and *Fright Train* from Haverhill House Press.

The New England Horror Writers (NEHW) provides peer support and networking for authors of horror and dark fantasy in the New England area. NEHW is primarily a writer's organization, focusing on authors of horror and dark fiction in all mediums (novels, short stories, screenplays, poetry, et cetera) in the New England area. We are also open to professional editors, artists and illustrators, agents and publishers of horror and dark fiction. NEHW activities include book signings, readings, panel discussions at conventions, online master classes, and social gatherings. With members ranging from Maine to Connecticut, NEHW events take place in various locations in an effort to provide support for our members throughout New England. Find us on Facebook at New England Horror Writers.

Acknowledgements

The editors of *Wicked Abandoned* would like to express their thanks to the following for their help and assistance.

KH Vaughan – Beta Reader and proofreader
Mary Hart - Beta Reader
Trisha Wooldridge – helping out with the poetry edits
Kristi Petersen Schoonover – helping with the back cover copy
Daniel G. Keohane – Layout.